THE BARTENDER'S BABY

A SINGLE DADS' CLUB NOVEL

SOPHIE ANDREWS

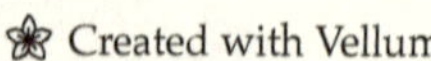 Created with Vellum

CONTENT NOTE

Nathan Kozlowski is a good man, Savannah. A GOOD MAN. And he loves with his whole heart. But the woman he turns from golden retriever to doberman for has been through some stuff including a mother who left and a father who has passed away. She has also experienced a late term miscarriage. All of this happens off the page, but it comes up in multiple discussions on the page. Please read with care.

To the woman who married the man who replied to a family member's Facebook comment about burning bridges, "There is no bridge I would not burn for my wife and daughter." Fuck, yes! Good for you.

And to all the women still looking for a man who will light a match in your honor, they are out there. I swear it. But until you do, enjoy Nate.

PROLOGUE

It was love at first sight.

I didn't know how else to explain it.

The small swath of brown hair. The pink cheeks. That tiny nose. Those blinking eyes and grasping fingers.

I was in love.

With an hour-old baby.

And his mother? That wasn't love at first sight, but it was love.

I had no idea when it started. Maybe the day I'd watched her lay out a customer who thought it was his right to grab a woman. I hadn't even been able to open my mouth before he'd hit the floor.

Maybe it had been that night when I'd heard her singing, a rare glimpse into an unguarded moment while she had cleaned up. I'd hidden in the corner, so she wouldn't notice how I'd watched her rocking side to side as her voice, lovely and melodic, carried to me. A surprise and yet not. After all, every new piece of information I learned about her was a revelation. A puzzle wrapped up in ripped jeans and a leather jacket, and signing Lady Gaga's "You and I."

Or maybe, very likely, it was the day she'd told me she was pregnant. That's when it had all become clear.
That I loved her.

ONE
NATE

I hit *send* on an email with the real estate agent, directing her to make the offer, hopefully closing the deal on what would be the space for a bistro and wine bar, and leaned back, stretching my arms up.

"Hey."

Startled, I nearly fell out of my chair in my effort not to be murdered, and I swung around, blood pulsing in my ears, only to find Tabitha. Slapping my palm to my chest, I folded over in relief. "Christ, Tabby cat. You scared the shit out of me."

She stayed silent, as usual.

"I swear to god, I'm gonna put a bell around your neck."

That earned me a stiff shake of her head. I'd never known anyone to make less noise than her. She mostly communicated with stern eyebrow arches and murderous glares.

"I hate when you call me that," she said finally, and I grinned.

"That's why I do it."

Those impossibly high cheekbones of hers pinked, and she straightened, plucking at her T-shirt, an unusual nervous tic. "I need to talk to you for a minute."

"Sure." I spun in my chair to fully face her. "What's up?"

Her long fingers, tipped with black nail polish, dragged over the side of her neck as she breathed deeply.

"Are you sick?" I asked, reaching for the trash can. I knew she hadn't been feeling well, even called out a few days ago, but I'd figured she'd gotten over it since she was back to her regular schedule and doing inventory today.

"No, I'm fine."

I didn't believe her and offered her my water bottle. She accepted it, took a sip, then played with the cap for a few seconds before twisting it back on. She cleared her throat and stood tall. "I wanted to let you know that I'm pregnant."

I froze, blinked, and blinked again. A long time passed before I finally spoke. "You're pregnant?"

She nodded. "That's why I haven't been feeling well lately."

"How are you feeling now?" I asked, hopping up out of my chair to push her into it. I didn't know much about pregnancy. In fact, I tried to actively avoid the topic as much as possible. But, fuck. Tabitha—*my Tabby*—was pregnant?

"I'm okay. I'm still a little nauseous now and then, but for the most part, it's passed."

"When did you find out?"

"A few weeks ago."

"A few weeks ago?" I nearly shrieked, annoyed that she'd been walking around here, working as if everything was fine. Everything was not fine. She was pregnant, and I was positive pregnant ladies shouldn't be serving beers to dumbass twentysomethings. I studied her, from the top of her head with dark, almost-black hair to the tips of her black boots. She appeared all right. But still. "Why didn't you tell me?"

"I didn't think it was important for you to know yet." She tipped her head back, lips pursed in a way I knew that was the best I'd get.

I took a breath, all kinds of questions forming in my mind, and picked the closest one. "How many months…?"

"I'm fourteen weeks, about three and a half months along," she said, with so much calm it made me nuts.

And everything else in my brain came rushing out. "Who's the dad? When are you due? I didn't know you wanted a baby."

Her right eyebrow arched so high, I bet she put a curse on me mentally. "Why would we have ever talked about children? All you say is you don't want them, so…"

"Yeah, but…" I pulled off my knit beanie and dragged my hand through my hair a few times. "This is different."

She laughed, low and reverberating, like a deck of cards being shuffled. An evil queen kind of laugh. "Why is it different?"

I tossed my arms out to my sides. "I don't know. It just is. Who's the dad? Don't tell me it's Henderson."

"Harrison." She folded her arms across her chest, briefly drawing my focus to her ample breasts. She was stacked. A true dime piece. And that simpering douchebag she was always on and off with wasn't worthy of spit shining her Doc Martens.

"Whatever." I waved away her correction, waiting for her answer. When she didn't give me any more, I had all the information I needed. I leaned against the wall, unexpectedly overcome with ire. Fucking Henderson.

"When did you tell him?"

"I didn't yet."

"Why the hell not?"

"Because I—" She halted, gaze slanting to the corner. The office at the back of Walt's was small, but it had never felt as small as when I noticed how her throat bobbed and her eyes blinked rapidly. Was she about to cry?

I sank to my haunches, curling my hands around the arms of the chair so I didn't touch her. "What can I do?"

"Nothing. I'm fine."

"It's a universally acknowledged rule that when women say they're fine, they are, indeed, not fine."

"Oh yeah?" She shot her gaze back to mine. "Where's it written?"

"The Feminine Mystique accords."

"Not a thing," she said, standing and forcing me away.

"Where are you going?"

"Back to work."

I jumped up, blocking the door. "I don't think so."

"*Excuse me?*"

"You can't work. You're pregnant."

She scoffed, and chills rolled down my spine. "Do you think pregnant people don't work?"

I shrugged. "I don't know, but how can you? Isn't it, like, against the law or something for you to work in a bar while you're pregnant?"

"No."

I looked down at her still-flat stomach. "What about your school? Didn't your semester just start?"

She rolled her eyes, shoving me out of the way. "Be a good boy and get back to your work, so that I can get back to mine."

Fat fucking chance of that happening. Now that Tabitha—my Tabby—was pregnant, I wouldn't be able to work another minute.

Not until I knew she was taken care of.

I followed her through the small kitchen, where Sydney fiddled with the knobs on the stove, readying for the day. Out in the bar area, another one of our bartenders, Mickey, appeared to be finishing up their station.

Tabitha had come in early to do inventory. Sunday mornings were the time when both of us prepared for the upcoming week. I completed reports and paperwork, while Tabby made orders of anything we needed. She also handled all the training of staff, and I hired and fired based on her recommendations. Hell, I didn't make any changes without running it by her first.

I trusted her implicitly with my bar—my baby.

And now, she was having a real-life human baby, and everything felt upside down.

I glared at her as she unlocked the front door, ignoring me. She didn't need me breathing down her back, but what the hell else was I supposed to do? My most important employee was pregnant.

I knew I'd lose her eventually since she had been slowly working toward her degree for the past few years, but I didn't think I'd lose her to someone else. A crying, wailing someone else.

A crying, wailing someone else spawned by a man who wore wrinkled khakis and had once brought a carnation into the bar for her. A goddamn carnation!

A fucking toolbag she'd once described to me as nice.

Nice.

Ha.

Tabitha didn't need nice.

She needed extraordinary. Because she was extraordinary, and I hadn't even been graced with the opportunity to see all of her puzzle pieces. I had the outline completed, most of the inside put together, but some of those unusual shapes hadn't quite fit yet.

And it pissed me off that I'd lost the chance to find how the edges connected. With a growl, I marched back into the office for my coat, keys, and water bottle then tapped out a message to my friends to find out where they were. Once a month, they all got together at this terrifying jungle-gym-type place so their kids could play, and when they confirmed that they were indeed there, I told them I was on my way.

I stomped back out to the bar, where our Sunday regulars lounged. I barely acknowledged their greetings, too intent on the unsmiling woman behind the bar who'd turned me inside out with only a few words. I slapped my water bottle on the bar top in front of her. "Drink this, and you're done at five."

"What? I—"

"I'm calling Juanita to cover for you. She needs the hours anyway." We closed early, at ten, on Sunday nights, and Tabitha usually worked twelve hours. She wouldn't be today.

Or any other day, in fact.

Winter was a slow time of year, especially January. Coming off the holidays, everyone tended to hunker down, and I wasn't about to have my all-star on her feet when she didn't need to be. She'd fight me tooth and nail.

Before she could bitch at me about it, I aimed my index finger at her. "If you're still here when I come back, so help me God, I'll hold your paycheck."

"Don't be an asshole."

"I will if you make me." Then I whirled around, Imagination Station and Play Center my destination.

I pulled into the lot about fifteen minutes later, parking haphazardly and tumbling out of my car like my legs didn't work anymore. Flinging open the door, I spotted my friends immediately. The three of them huddled in their usual spot, on a bench along the wall, in front of what was supposed to be a fake doctor's office. I charged at them. "Tabby's pregnant."

Jude, who I'd known since high school, squinted at me. "Are you drunk right now?"

"No, man. I'm completely sober, but I feel like I'm losing my mind."

Dylan, my future brother-in-law, eyed me from under his baseball cap. "Sit down. You're freaking the kids out."

I glanced over my shoulder at the dozen or so kids running around the place, playing dress-up and pretending to be cops or whatever. "Is that Finn?"

Liam nodded because, yes, it indeed was his four-year-old son blaring "Wee-oh! Wee-oh!" while waving his hand above his head as if riding on a bucking bronco.

"I can't sit down," I said, ripping off my coat and tossing it on the bench.

Jude held his hand up like I was a feral dog. "Slow down and explain."

I took a deep breath and set my hands on my hips. "Tabby's pregnant."

"Tabby, as in your bartender?" Liam asked, and I nodded.

Dylan set his to-go coffee cup on the floor. "Tabby, as in the girl constantly frowning?"

I tossed my hand out toward him. "That's rich, coming from you."

Dylan grunted, his mouth in a straight line, save for a tic in the corner. Grumpy motherfucker only started smiling when he'd begun sniffing around my sister.

Liam scratched at his jaw. "So, Tabby's pregnant? And *not* with your kid?"

"Not my kid," I affirmed, hating that fact but not super clear on why. "It's that real tall dickweed she's on and off with."

Jude grinned. "So that's why you're wild about this?"

"Of course I'm wild about this. She's my—" I stopped my pacing, Jude's words finally setting in. "What do you mean?"

"She's your what?" he insisted, biting into a cookie from a Tupperware on his lap like all of this was no big deal.

"She's my bartender, my manager," I said, snatching up one of the cookies before resuming my pacing.

"That's it? She's nothing else?"

"I guess she's my friend."

"Mm-hmm."

I wielded my cookie at him. "Don't look at me like that."

Dylan smirked, smug as shit. "You're so fucking dumb, bro."

"Why? And you know you're in the middle of this kiddie freakin' nightmare of a place, and you're cursing. You probably shouldn't be."

"Oh?" He cocked his head to the side. "You care about that now?"

I shoveled the rest of the cookie into my mouth, chewing vigorously. As if it would make me feel better. Make any sense of the burning in my chest and the spinning in my brain. I finally stopped pacing and chewing to stare at each of my friends in turn. They all watched me warily, as if I might tear off my face and reveal another one. But they'd all lost their shit before. I'd witnessed it, each and every time.

With Dylan, who went from commitment-phobe to borderline obsessed with my sister. I had clocked him when he'd lost it and broken her heart. Merited that shiner.

And Liam, he was the smartest person I'd ever met yet lost all sense of self when he'd met his son's nanny—and probably soon-to-be wife, with the way things were headed. But I recalled having to talk him off the ledge when things got a bit dicey.

Then there was Jude, the guy who deserved a good woman in his life, maybe more than any of us, and recently got together with his best friend after family drama with his kids. He'd spent weeks trying to balance everything and had the sleepless zombie eyes to prove it for a while.

So how they could sit there like a bunch of assholes, gaping at me as if I were a monkey banging cymbals together, I didn't know.

"I think you need to take a walk or something and cool off," Liam suggested. "Settle down."

I waved him off, jutting my chin to Jude instead. "Why are you smiling?"

"Because you're finally seeing it."

I glanced behind me. "Seeing what?"

"What's been right in front of you this whole time."

I rolled my eyes. "Don't talk in riddles, okay? Say whatever it is you want to say."

He shrugged. "You love her."

Again, I glanced over my shoulder. "Her who?"

"Tabby."

I choked out a laugh. "I do not."

Liam tipped his head side to side, that intelligent air about him baiting me. Like, *I know something you don't know.*

"I don't love her," I said, pounding my fist in my hand because I was serious.

Dylan mumbled a sarcastic, "Okay."

"I do *not* love her. I couldn't love her."

"Why not?" Jude asked, benignly curious.

"Because."

Liam sipped on his coffee. "Because why?"

"Because…" I spun my hands in the air. "She works for me. She's my best worker—*manager*. And she's scary in a probably knows witchcraft sort of way. Plus, she's…" I tunneled my hands through my hair. "She's… She's…"

"Special in a sort of indescribable way," Jude offered, and I nodded then immediately shook my head because that didn't help my cause at all.

"She's pregnant with another man's kid," I said, folding my arms.

Dylan grimaced. "Yeah, that one's a kick in the nuts, huh?"

"It doesn't matter because I don't care."

"No, you don't care at all," Jude agreed, while Dylan and Liam nodded along like my behavior made absolute sense for someone who didn't care.

I sighed. "I don't want to lose her. Strictly in the work sense."

Liam dipped his head in acknowledgment. "Right."

"She's gonna be done with her degree soon," I explained. "So she's going to be leaving anyway, and I already don't want to think about replacing her. But now she's baking a kid? What the hell am I gonna do about that?"

Dylan rubbed the backs of his fingers over his jaw. "Doesn't seem like there's much for you to do, is there?"

"Because you don't care," Jude added.

"Of course I care. I'm—" I didn't appreciate being trapped, and I wagged my finger at them. "Listen. I came here for advice, but since you want to act like immature assholes about this, I'm leaving."

Dylan flicked up the brim of his hat, his eyes practically glowing with amusement. "Say hi to Tabitha for us."

"Fuck off."

I grabbed my coat but only made it three steps before I swung back around with a warning. "This is cone of silence. Do not tell your girls about this."

None of them agreed, and I barely restrained from flipping them the bird.

"Uncle Nate!"

I stopped and bent down, catching Amelia—Jude's daughter, who'd recently turned six—when she jumped at me. "Hey, little Lu."

She played with the beanie on my head. "Where are you going?"

"Running some errands," I lied because she wouldn't understand what it meant for me to have to pick pieces of my brain up off the floor.

"Wanna play with us?"

"No thanks. Maybe another time, okay?"

"'Kay!"

The girl couldn't control the volume of her voice to save her life, but I loved her even more for it, and I hugged her to me, kissing the side of her head. That was when the rest of the rascals noticed me, the lot of them scurrying over. My grandfather, the one I named Walt's after, always joked I was like Saint Francis. Kids and animals flocked to me.

I handed out hugs and high fives to Finn, Scarlett, Tucker, and even Sebastian, Jude's eleven-year-old, who clearly did *not* want to be here anymore. Same, kid. Same.

"All right, you heathens. I need to get out of here." I shook off Finn from climbing on my back and patted Amelia's head before setting her down. When I looked back at their dads, they all waved cheerily at me like the bunch of assholes they were.

In my car, I slouched behind the wheel and pulled up the internet browser on my phone to search *pregnancy* then clicked on the first link. It was for an app that I immediately down-loaded because of the fetus growth chart. Tabitha hadn't told me anything about what she planned on doing with it, but...

Fuck.

I didn't want kids.

Nothing about being a father interested me, when my own relationship with my father didn't exactly set a great example.

And yet...

Fuck.

Why did the idea of Tabitha's baby have me clicking on the picture for fourteen weeks to find out it's the size of a lemon?

Why were they comparing fetuses to citrus fruit?

And did they all look like shrimp?

Did Tabitha know she was growing a shrimp in her belly?

Did she actually go home like I told her to? I'd sure as shit throw her over my shoulder and make her go home if I had to.

Because I loved her and wanted what was best for her...

I loved her.

I loved Tabitha Reynolds, my bartender.

Fuuuuuuck.

TWO
TABITHA

I didn't go home from Walt's because Nate told me to.

No. I went home because I was exhausted. My replacement showed up at five o'clock on the dot with a big smile, and I didn't fight it. I gathered my things from the office, and since Nate had yet to return, I left with a nod toward Juanita and Mickey, meeting my Lyft outside the back door.

Up until a few weeks ago, I'd been riding my Kawasaki as long as the weather permitted. But as soon as those pink lines showed up, I parked it in the garage, never to be ridden again. My bike had given me freedom when I'd needed to feel *something*. As much as I despised putting it away, it was an easy choice to make. I couldn't and wouldn't do anything that could cause any distress during this pregnancy.

To say the last few weeks had been a roller coaster would be an understatement, and I was *tired*.

The physical fatigue of the first trimester was mostly past, but the emotional and psychological stress overwhelmed me.

Though, if I was honest, finally telling someone felt like a weight lifted off my shoulders. As long as I ignored the fact that it was Nate whom I'd confided in first, as opposed to Harrison or any friends or family. Not that there were all that many I felt compelled to tell. Or there were any I felt attached to, whom I considered important enough to tell.

Except for Nate.

The one person who'd been a constant source of stability in my life. He'd hired me at a time when it didn't seem as though I'd be able to find my way, but he and his stupidly charming grin and endless sincerity had kept me returning. Day after day, I'd come back to life.

Because of him.

But if I ever told him that, he'd never let me live it down.

He was a jokester and teasing was his love language, so I could never confess that the day he'd sat me down in the office, I might have fallen a little bit in love with him. When he had listened as I'd admitted I'd recently moved to West Chester and didn't know a lot of people. Yet he'd never looked at me with pity in his eyes, like so many had done over those last few months. It's why I hadn't been able to stay. Why I'd needed a fresh start somewhere else, offered by someone who treated me like a whole person—and not as someone less-than like my step-family, or broken like Danny's family.

With Nate, I was simply me.

He saw me for my pride and strength and brains and probably all the dark stuff too.

All the things I'd wanted to hide from the world, the vulnerable and damaged pieces of myself that he'd protected. He'd never pushed me to be more or different, and he'd stood by me, been a steady anchor as I'd fought an internal battle he'd eventually calmed. He had never known that his confidence in me kept me afloat.

First, he was my boss—and then my friend.

My friend, whom I'd come to think of as an important person.

A very important person.

Maybe the most important person?

But I could never tell him. Because his ego was inflated enough, and he'd never stop giving me shit.

Better to keep those feelings to myself.

Like I'd done for a long time.

I'd been waffling about my pregnancy for the last month. About what to do and say. There had never been a question about terminating it—not after what I'd already been through—but the road forward seemed rife with uncertainty. Combating those questions, I did what I'd always done, took it one step at a time. And that first step was making a list of my most important tasks, like finding a different place to live, buying a car, selling my bike, and figuring out my job and financial situation.

I'd made no headway on my living situation and wouldn't be able to buy a car until I got the payment for my bike, but I was proud of myself for telling Nate. I deserved a treat and—as long as Nate was willing to pay for it—an early night.

I stepped out of my ride and made my way up the sidewalk to the small rental I shared with a friend of a friend. Even though I had turned thirty on January 2, I still hadn't reached the goals I'd set for myself, including finally graduating with my bachelor's. Without that degree, I couldn't get the kind of job I wanted, leading to the mortgage I needed to buy my own home. So, here I was, sharing a house with a twenty-five-year-old grad student.

As a suburb of Philadelphia, West Chester, Pennsylvania, was cute and quaint, if not inexpensive. The university was a major economic driver, not to mention the thriving downtown area, so I was no stranger to the difficulties of finding a place that didn't require emptying my bank account on the first of every month. Which was why I hadn't been looking forward to this conversation.

Tossing my keys in the bowl by the door, I hung my coat on the hook, along with my purse, then placed my boots on the shoe rack. Ming-Yue was a neat freak like me. She also stuck to herself, spending most of her time in the science lab at school or in her room when home. Now, I found her heating up leftovers in the microwave.

She turned over her shoulder when she heard me. "Hey, didn't expect to see you here."

"Got off early," I said, sliding into a chair at the small kitchen table. "Which is good because I need to talk to you."

Once she had her food plated up, she sat across from me at the table, waiting expectantly.

I swallowed down the lump in my throat to reveal my secret to the second person today. "I'm pregnant."

She froze with her fork halfway to her mouth. After a few beats, she stuck the piece of meat into her mouth, and I purposely stared at the off-white cabinets, breathing through my mouth. The smell of meats hadn't been settling well with me lately.

"Is this a congratulations thing or a you need help thing?" she asked, and I slanted my gaze back to her.

"Congratulations thing. I'm keeping it."

"Oh. Okay." She touched the thick purple frames of her glasses. "Congratulations, but…"

"But," I agreed with a nod. "I'll need to find another place to live, even though I know we've leased through June."

She let out a loose laugh, pressing her hand to her chest. "Good, and don't take this the wrong way, but if you were planning on bringing a baby here, we'd have a problem."

"I know. I understand. I wanted you to know so you had time to find another roommate."

"Won't be hard. People always need a place to stay around here." She forked another bite of food into her mouth, and I picked at my nail polish for a few seconds, grateful she was always straightforward. I didn't have to worry about stepping on her feelings.

Especially when my own seemed so unpredictable lately. Exactly why I squeezed my eyes shut at the burning in them. "Okay, well, I'm gonna head upstairs."

When I opened my lids again, my vision clear, I grabbed an apple and a water bottle, happy to have that conversation behind me. Inside my little bedroom with the radiator that didn't work, I changed into sweats and slipped a hoodie over my head before burrowing into the covers to eat my green apple, the slightly sour taste on my tongue negating my previous nausea.

Curling on my side, I reached for the black-and-white ultrasound picture on my nightstand and traced the blob, smiling through my tears. When I'd realized I was pregnant, I was terrified. And elated. Then alarmed. Until I finally settled on happy.

I was happy to have this second chance at what I'd lost. I often wondered about what could have been. What my life would be like now. How different it might be. What my child would look like, what they'd be learning in school. If I'd still be with Danny. Probably.

Maybe.

Placing my hand on my stomach, I closed my eyes and let myself remember, let the grief wash over me, then I let it go. That's what my support group had taught me all those years ago. To feel all the feelings and then let them go.

So that's what I did.

What I would continue to do.

After, I opened my laptop and played *Our Planet*. Though only a few minutes into the episode, my phone buzzed with a text alert.

NATE

I'm glad to see you can follow my directions.

I left because I felt like it.

NATE

What's that mean? Are you sick?

I'm fine.

NATE

Did you eat dinner?

Yes.

NATE

What was it?

I rolled my eyes. He never stopped micromanaging.

I'm not telling you what I had for dinner.

NATE

That means you didn't eat it.

NATE

You need to eat.

I do eat. I'm eating. I had an apple.

NATE

A fucking apple?!?!?!

NATE

An apple? Tabitha. A goddamn apple is not dinner.

Please stop texting me. I'm tired and want to go to sleep.

NATE

Not until after you have some real food.

NATE

Your dinner will be arriving in 25 minutes. I want proof it arrived and that you ate it, or I'll be knocking on your door later tonight.

I tossed my phone down with a huff. He was so fucking hardheaded. Stubborn and annoying as hell when he wanted something.

I'd hate it if I didn't respect it so much. As he'd said, the doorbell rang twenty-five minutes later with a delivery from my favorite Italian place containing my usual order—chicken parm with baked ziti, and oil and vinegar for the side salad. He even got me mozzarella sticks.

How irritating.

I sat on my bed with it all and snapped a picture to send to Nate.

> I won't be able to eat all this.

NATE

> I don't care. Eat as much as you can and then save the rest for tomorrow. Send me a picture of how much is left.

> You are out of your mind if you think I'm documenting what I eat.

NATE

> I know you, and I know you scrimp and save and would eat peanut butter sandwiches every day if you had to. So, no, I'm not out of my mind to make sure you're eating dinner.

NATE

> You need food. Good food.

NATE

> Eat it and say thank you.

I couldn't argue with him about being a pain in the ass because it all smelled so good, and I was pretty hungry now that I had time to relax. I ate the salad, about half of the chicken and ziti, and all but two of the mozzarella sticks. I sent him a picture of my leftovers, along with my middle finger.

His reply?

NATE

The nerve.

———

My weekly schedule remained mostly the same. Walt's was open every day, but I had Mondays off and preferred to close at the end of the night because it tended to be quieter. I'd always been a night owl, so it suited me, especially since my classes were all in the afternoon.

Though this was a college town, Walt's wasn't necessarily a college bar. It had more of a *Cheers* vibe, with regulars at certain times or days. We hosted trivia on Wednesday nights and occasional bands, including a standing gig for a group who called themselves the Anchormen on the third Thursday of every month. Which was when I worked another long shift. Because as much as Nate liked to micromanage, so did I.

It was why I usually found Nate behind the bar with me on those nights. Although I appreciated how he had no problem jumping in and getting his hands dirty, I did *not* appreciate how he glared at me all evening. Even as the guitarist announced he'd popped the question to his girlfriend, offering to buy the entire bar a round. Even as the sister of the bride—Kennedy, I think her name was—tugged on Nate's arm to go with her and talk to the band and his friend, Liam. Even as I handled all those freaking orders by myself. He glared at me.

Like I'd done something wrong.

I assumed he was pissed that I was pregnant. Guys were assholes like that. Yeah, I was his right hand, but I was also a woman. A capable woman, able to do multiple things at once, like manage his bar and grow a human.

I'd never taken him as one of those barefoot-in-the-kitchen types, but I might've been wrong about him this whole time. Especially because he snatched the rag out of my hand at the end of the night and pushed me to the office, ordering me to sit down.

I reeled on him. "If you're trying to get me to quit, it won't work. You want to fire me for being pregnant? Then do it."

He wrenched backward. "What?"

"I said you're gonna have to fire me." I was salaried, so he could cut my hours but would still need to pay me the same. If he wanted to get rid of me, he'd actually have to say the words. I held my hands out at my sides, daring him. "Do it."

"What the hell are you talking about?"

"You and your obvious hatred of my being pregnant."

He grumbled something I didn't understand then wrapped his hand around my bicep, ushering me to the office.

"Sit here. I can finish closing up. Then we're going to talk."

Closing never took long, mostly because I did my job well and made sure bathrooms were checked multiple times a day, and the bar was kept orderly and clean. The kitchen shut down three hours before close, so the only tasks that needed to be completed were counting the drawers and mopping the floor, which could all be accomplished in about twenty minutes.

Nate did them in about ten.

And then he was in my space, practically growling at me. "Let's talk."

I scooted away from him in the rolling chair, holding his gaze yet keeping my face devoid of emotion. "About what?"

He waved his hand at my stomach. "You and this baby."

I kept quiet.

"You drop a bomb on me and expect me to continue as if nothing has changed? When literally everything has changed."

I wiped my palm over my forehead. He could be so dramatic sometimes. "Nothing has changed for you."

He threw his arms up as if *I* was being the irrational one here. "Tab, you're having a *baby*, but you haven't talked to me about any of it."

"Why would I need to talk to you about it?"

"Because!"

I waited for him to explain, and when it became obvious he wasn't going to, I stood. "I don't want to deal with whatever male attitude adjustment you're going through. You—"

He sat me back in the chair and leaned over, his hands on either side of me, his face so close I would count the individual hairs in his short beard, the few random grays that from far away appeared blond until you got up close. And up close, they looked good. *He* looked good. With his gray-blue eyes and wide brow that often had a lock of golden-brown hair hanging over it, like it did now.

"You're not leaving here until you tell me what's going on," he said, more serious than I'd ever heard him. "I want to know everything because I...I care about you, and I know you're all tough-girl-doing-it-for-herself, but I won't be able to rest until I know you're taken care of. So, please..."

He gestured for me to fill in the blanks, but I didn't know how.

He was the talker. He had no problem expressing his emotions and wore his heart on his sleeve. It's what made him so successful as a bar owner; he could connect with people. I didn't have the same ability. I had a brain for numbers, a memory for taking orders, and lived my life one checklist at a time because if I ever stopped to look around, I might not be able to recover. I didn't have it in me.

"My life has nothing to do with you," I said eventually, and he merely shook his head.

Then he relaxed against the door, his arms across his chest, ankles crossed like he had all the time in the world. A silent threat to follow through. He really wouldn't let me out of here.

"I don't know what you want me to say."

He lifted one shoulder. "The truth."

THREE
NATE

Tabby's face drained of color at my suggestion that she tell me the truth. Whatever she'd been hiding must have been eating at her, and I wasn't a monster. I wouldn't force her to talk about anything she didn't want to, but she had to give me something.

"How about you tell me about your family? Do they know?" She rarely talked about her family, though I'd learned she'd never really known her mother and that her dad had passed from a stroke when she was in high school. She'd told me after I'd bugged her about why she always volunteered to work holidays. There had never been a Thanksgiving, New Year's, Father's Day, or anything in between she didn't work.

"Um, no," she said, shutting down any more conversation on that topic with a raised brow.

I tunneled my fingers through my hair, amazed I hadn't pulled out any clumps this past week for how often I'd been yanking on it. "What about your boyfriend? You told him yet?"

"Boyfriend is a gracious term."

"So, what? You're not together?" I asked because I couldn't pretend I didn't care anymore. Not when I could recall each and every thing she'd ever said about him, which hadn't been a whole hell of a lot. It was casual. They'd split up and get back together every few months, about when I'd happen to find some young thing to occupy my attention.

"You know it's more of a friends-with-benefits situationship."

That's right. I did know. "You don't want to tie him down."

She let out a humorless laugh. "I very much doubt he wants to be tied down."

"What about you?"

She shrugged. This girl. Maddening. Offered only enough to make me more curious.

"What do you even like about him?"

She answered that easily enough. "He's tall."

I slapped my hand to my chest. "I'm tall."

"He's six-five *tall*."

"I'm six-one."

"I know math's not your strong suit, but that's a four-inch difference."

I shot her a look. "So, his height? That's what you like about him?"

"And he's got blue eyes."

I pointed at my eyes, and as if she knew I'd argue the point, she said, "He's in finance."

"What's that got to do with anything?"

"He's got money and a secure future."

"I don't know if you've noticed." I circled my hand above my head to encompass the bar. "But we're doing pretty well here. I've made good investments, and I'm opening up another location."

Then I promptly shut the fuck up, realizing I was showing my hand. I had to stop talking, stop trying to prove I was the better choice.

Though, she didn't seem to notice anyway, too busy arguing with me. "You don't have security. This could all go up in smoke tomorrow."

I waved off the concern. "And if it did, I'd be fine."

When she didn't respond, I sighed. "So, that's it? His height, eyes, and his money all made you go, *Hm, I think I'd like his sperm.*"

She pursed her lips and clucked her tongue. Never a good sign. "Fuck you. Stop acting as if I would ever—" She stopped herself and blinked a few times, and shit.

"I'm sorry." I bent down to eye level. "I'm sorry. It's not my intention to make you feel bad about the situation. I'm sure Holden is perfectly nice."

"Harrison."

"Whatever."

I handed her a tissue, which she dabbed at the corners of her eyes, smudging the bit of makeup she wore. Her normally golden tanned skin was sallower, and I wouldn't bring it up now, but I planned on having groceries delivered to her house. Because this not-eating routine was going to stop *now*.

"Why haven't you told him yet?"

She hunched over, her knees pressed tight together, fingers worrying the tissue. "I'm not sure."

"Yeah, you are," I said because she was cool under pressure, always level-headed and even-keeled. No, she wasn't the type to laugh with strangers or make friends easily, but she was smart. And a planner. And so damn driven, there was no way she'd be avoiding this subject if not for a good reason.

Whatever that reason was, it killed me. Because it'd been visibly killing *her*.

She shook her head with a sniffle, and I lowered to my knees in front of her, placing my hands on either side of her legs. She didn't push me away, so I chanced a caress of her kneecaps with my fingertips and told her the truth. Or at least, some of it.

"I'm worried about you. If you want to have this baby, I'll back you one hundred percent. A thousand percent. But I need to know the truth from you."

Yeah, I grasped the irony.

But I couldn't tell her *my* actual truth *now*.

First, because she'd laugh in my face, and my ego couldn't handle that. And, secondly, I doubted she'd ever believe me.

I waited her out instead.

"I'm scared," she whispered eventually, and I took the tissue from her hands to wipe away the twin tears on her cheeks while attempting to rein in my temper. I was usually a pretty chill dude, but fuck with one of my people? My fuse wasn't just short; it was nonexistent.

I ground my molars. "Of *him*? Are you scared of him?"

"No. I'm scared of what could happen." She pulled the elastic band out of her hair, letting down the shoulder-length locks, combing her hands through it a few times, like she needed something to do now that I'd taken the tissue from her.

I wiped it under her nose, and she huffed a watery laugh with a soft apology.

I didn't like this. Tabitha didn't apologize for much, so if she felt the need to, this was *bad*.

"You don't need to be sorry."

She took a few deep breaths, and after I tucked her hair behind her ears, I reached for my almost empty water bottle on the desk. "Drink this."

She finished it off and then sat back in the chair, more clear-eyed, even as her nose remained pink at the tip. "Do you remember when you hired me?"

"Yes. Kinda. Why?"

"Do you remember what exactly happened?"

I furrowed my brow, not understanding what this had to do with anything, but I relayed what I recalled. "You were standing on the sidewalk when I walked by, and you asked if I worked here. I said I owned the place, and you asked me to hire you."

A ghost of a smile crept across her lips. "You said you didn't hire high schoolers."

"Did I say that?" I pulled a face, and her shadow of a smile became a full-on grin.

"I told you I'd just turned nineteen and that I had a lot of references. I had experience working in restaurants."

I snapped my fingers, remembering now. "And I said you could come back later so we could talk because you had on a Green Day shirt, and that meant you had good taste."

She nodded. "That shirt belonged to my husband."

I jerked my head back and then shook it. I must have heard her wrong. "What? Your *husband*?"

She lost the humor in her features, her mouth smoothing back into its typical line, her dark eyes no longer glittering.

"I got married right out of high school, and no, I'm not gonna talk about that, but..." She crossed her legs and arms, as if she could keep out my concern. Or maybe hold in her emotions.

Probably both.

After a deep breath that made her shoulders rise and fall, she went on. "I was pregnant and so happy. We were both really..." She sniffed, eyes unfocused somewhere behind me. "I had an appointment for the ultrasound to find out if it was a boy or a girl."

She paused again, and I dropped my chin to my chest. I didn't need her to go on, but I thought *she* needed to.

"There was some movement, gentle kicks and pushes, but I didn't think anything of it when I hadn't felt them for a few days. Until I went in to the office. There was no heartbeat."

I closed my eyes, the weight of her grief landing like a physical blow on me.

Her next words were remarkably calm, detached almost. "There was a knot in the umbilical cord. It's rare, happens in fewer than one percent of pregnancies."

I lifted my head to find her staring down at her hands, her fingers entwined, knuckles white. I wrapped my hands around hers, rubbing them, hoping to loosen their grip, and when she did, I placed her palms flat against each other, her fingers long and trapped between mine so she wouldn't bind them together again. I brought her hands up, kissed the very tips of her fingers, uncaring about giving myself away when she needed comfort.

"I'm sorry you had to go through that. I'm so sorry you had to experience it."

She brought her eyes to mine, and I could see straight through to her soul. This one tragedy did not define her, but it did help to form the woman in front of me. This incredibly strong and resilient woman who didn't take any shit and never asked for any help, yet never failed to show up. Never let anyone or anything keep her down.

I admired her, but I doubted she'd want to hear that. "Thank you for telling me, and you don't have to go through any of this alone. Whatever you want or need, you can have. I'll make sure of it."

She nodded, and I figured that was the best I'd get, so I stood up, towing her with me to hug her to my chest, my arms around her shoulders.

"What are you doing?" she mumbled against my pec.

"Shh." I petted the back of her head. "Let it happen."

She laughed, a short, breathy sound, and eventually wrapped her arms around my torso, skimming her hands along either side of my spine to settle in the middle of my back, her fingers fisting the material of my T-shirt. I held her tighter, hoping she didn't hear my heart hammering in my chest when she laid her ear against it.

"Give me a minute to lock up, and I'll walk you out," I told her once we finally released each other. She didn't argue or put up a fight about how she didn't need me to do that, and instead, she scrolled on her phone.

I locked the front door and met her at the back, happening to peek over her shoulder to see a rideshare app open. "What are you doing?"

"Getting a ride."

"No."

She whipped her head to me, but I covered her mouth with my hand before she could get one word out.

"You think I'm gonna let you get in a car with a stranger? Especially after you told me about your past and when I know you're not in the right frame of mind? And why are you taking a car in the first place?"

She couldn't answer with my palm over her mouth and rolled her eyes.

"You can't ride your bike anymore, huh?"

She mumbled something, but I only dropped my hand after I stole her cell phone to cancel the ride with a stab of my thumb.

"I'm selling my bike so I can buy a car," she told me.

"When are you doing that?"

She snatched her phone back and stomped out of the bar. "Tomorrow."

I followed her, pointing at my car. She didn't seem like she wanted to get in. Would rather take a frying pan to the head. Tempting.

I opened the passenger side door and all but tossed her inside. Even went so far as to buckle her seat belt myself.

She seethed silently as I took my seat behind the wheel, turning over the ignition.

"Who are you selling it to?" I asked, pumping the heat up and aiming the vents at Tabby.

"A guy I know through the motorcycle garage."

"Do you know him well? How do you know he's not a serial killer?"

"Because he's a retired middle school teacher who looks like Bob Ross."

"Not-so-happy accidents can happen with happy little trees."

She rubbed at her forehead. "You are insufferable."

"Where are you buying your car from? Do you have one picked out already? Have you test-driven—"

"Nate, I don't need you up in my business. I'm taking care of it."

"You know you don't have to, though, right? I'm all for you doing what you want, but you don't *have* to."

"I do, though," she murmured, so I leaned over, leading with my ear to make sure I heard her correctly.

"You do, though?"

"I don't have anyone else to do it for me, so…"

I tightened my grip on the steering wheel because I was sitting right here next to her. I volunteered as tribute. But of course, she didn't see it. She'd been on her own for so long, she'd probably lost the ability to ask for help or even recognize when she needed it.

"I've made my decision. I'm keeping the baby, and I can figure everything out on my own. No matter what."

"No matter what," I repeated in a grumble, stewing in my own frustration.

We spent the rest of the ride in silence, save for the nearly muted volume of Tracy Chapman's "Fast Car." Until I stopped in front of the little house I knew she shared with some grad student. I'd never been inside, but I could guess it was a piece of shit, like some of these college rentals were. Most likely full of busted tile and peeling paint.

"You know when this house was built?" I asked, and she shook her head.

"Seventies, I think."

I hummed. They were still manufacturing lead paint in the 1970s. "You don't have any weird symptoms? Vomiting, fatigue, joint pain…?"

"You're basically describing pregnancy."

I made a mental note to find out more information about this house, and I waited until she was safely ensconced inside before driving the few minutes to my place. Though, it was a few more hours until I finally finished my research on lead poisoning.

And yeah, she had to get the hell out of that house.

FOUR
TABBY

I bid farewell to my bike the next morning without any tears but didn't have the patience to go to the car lot like I'd planned, so I stayed in bed, getting a jump start on my weekend homework. Good thing, too, because a delivery showed up on my stoop. Bags of groceries.

I didn't need to guess who they were from.

And they included all my favorites: double stuffed Oreos, Ruffles, and multiple bags of snack-size Skittles. Plus, some healthy options like apples, clementines, eggs, Greek yogurt in three different flavors, and whole grain bread with all the fixings for sandwiches. I texted Nate.

Thank you.

NATE

You better start eating more. You're supposed
to be eating at least 2200 calories a day.

I didn't know how exactly to define the feeling in my chest at the idea of him researching pregnancy tips, but I pressed my phone to my heart and helped myself to three of the little Halos.

NATE

How'd it go this morning?

Fine.

NATE

One of my favorite things about you is just how expressive you are.

NATE

You get a car?

No.

While I had more physical energy than during my first trimester, it felt like I'd been losing more and more control of my emotions. I'd been so used to stuffing everything down, but this pregnancy pushed it all back up. It was terrifying to be so out of control.

Of myself.

Of my future.

Of whether I could bring this person into the world or not.

NATE

So that means you need a ride to work?

NATE

You're on for eight tonight so I'll pick you up at 7:45.

Before I could finish typing out my answer—that no, I didn't need him to pick me up—he sent another message.

NATE

Don't fight me on this. Or I'll be there even earlier.

Fine.

It was no use arguing. When he set his mind to something, that was it. His dogged persistence was one of his most admirable qualities. Also one of the most exasperating when directed at *me*.

After lunch, courtesy of Nate, I walked to campus for my two afternoon classes, Auditing and Forensic Accounting. I'd been taking classes for years, a few credits a semester. Unlike other undergrads, I had to balance a full-time job and bills with academics, but I was so close to graduating. After this semester, I only needed to complete one more 400-level accounting class and my capstone project. Although, I had no idea what I would do once the baby was here.

If...

Shaking that terrible thought from my head, I refocused on my professor's slides, while trying to ignore the idiot frat dude next to me. I'd chosen accounting as a major because I could graduate into a steady job. Every company needed an accountant, and lots of people used them for their personal taxes as well. With this degree, I'd never have to worry about unpredictability.

But a lot of these children—that's what they were—didn't give a shit. About anything. Besides maybe their next party or lay. Too bad I was stuck with two of them for a group project.

The professor finished explaining how each group would be given a hypothetical case scenario involving suspected fraud or unethical accounting practices at a fictional company. It would include background information, financial statements, accounting records, emails, and other documentation hinting at potential irregularities. Each group needed to analyze the materials as forensic accountants, identify any red flags or suspicious transactions, and determine what additional information or evidence they would want to obtain in an investigation. We would also conduct our own forensic accounting procedures, such as data mining, ratio analysis, risk assessments, and interviewing techniques to uncover and quantify the extent of the fraudulent activities. Each group would then prepare a report detailing their findings, calculating the financial impact, recommending internal control improvements, and potentially suggesting legal actions based on the evidence gathered during their simulated forensic investigation and present it to the class.

My assigned group was Kevin, the reincarnation of John Belushi from *Animal House*, and Maureen, the girl failing the class, which I knew because she'd asked me if she could borrow my notes since she'd missed a bunch of classes and tanked the first exam. So, this was going to be great.

Fucking great.

I took charge, because *of course*, and outlined what I wanted each of them to do, giving them different dates and times to meet up to discuss it. I didn't trust either one of them to get anything done on their own.

Back at home, I warmed up under the blankets and relaxed a bit before I made myself dinner and dressed for work in my usual dark denim and Walt's T-shirt. Although, I slid a flannel on over it, partially to ward away the cold and partially to cover up the slight bump of my belly.

I stood in front of the mirror for a long while holding up my shirt, turning this way and that, rubbing my hands over my stomach, hope and fear blossoming inside me with every new day. I hadn't been raised with religion, but I had taken to talking to whatever deity was up there to get me and this baby through it. Miscarriages were common, but that word didn't seem big enough for my situation, or others like mine. To deliver a baby girl who never even took her first breath. To hold the tiny bundle, only to have to decide if or where I wanted to bury her. I was grateful for the kindness of the hospital staff and to live in a state that didn't force me to do anything. Rather, the decisions were left up to Danny and me. When we were practically babies ourselves.

We made the choice to cremate her, but neither one of us had the heart to name her. That made it feel too real. After everything

I'd been through, I hadn't thought I'd be able to handle that. Danny had ordered special urn jewelry so we would be able to carry the last pieces of her with us every day. A braided leather bracelet with a thick bead in the center for him, and a gold necklace with a starburst pendant for me. I remembered how he'd put it on me and kissed my cheek, saying, "We're all made out of star stuff anyway. You'll have the entire galaxy with you every day."

It was the best thing he could've said.

One of the last things he'd said about it.

A few months later, we were divorced, neither one of us capable of working through it together.

Once again, I allowed myself to feel those feelings and then set them aside to put on my coat and meet Nate outside. After I buckled in, he gently tossed something into my lap. I held up the thirty-two-ounce stainless-steel water bottle and bit the inside of my cheeks to keep from laughing at the customization of Maleficent with the words *Mistress of Evil's water*. A running joke of how he insisted I had the cartoon villain's vibes. I didn't mind.

Could be worse comparisons than a witch snubbed by a baby. Appropriate, really.

"Thank you," I said, opening it up to take a drink as he pulled away from the curb.

"You need to drink two of those a day," he told me, making a left at the stop sign. "How are you feeling?"

"Good."

He kept his eyes on the road but leaned toward me, evidently wanting more.

I sighed. "I'm fine."

He turned down the volume of the radio so I couldn't even listen to it. My punishment.

I tucked the water bottle in my bag and stared out of the window. "I feel better now than I did a few weeks ago. I have more energy, feel more clearheaded."

"Good. What'd you have for dinner?"

I angled my head to glower at him. "What did *you* have for dinner?"

"A bacon cheeseburger with sweet potato fries, thanks for asking. It was delicious. Now, you go."

I made a sort of gagging noise.

"What?"

"The idea of eating meat has been making me..." I stuck out my tongue.

"Baby's a vegetarian, eh? Good to know. So what'd you eat?"

"Yogurt with granola and a banana."

"That's it? That's a *snack*, Tabitha."

"It was my dinner, *Nathan*. That's all I was hungry for."

"Did you pack food?" When I stayed quiet, he huffed a disappointed sound. But this was my body and my baby, and I didn't need him looking over my shoulder to make sure I was taking my vitamins or whatever. I didn't even know why he was so interested.

Then again, he had an ear for listening and a penchant for problem-solving. A meddlesome mother hen stuck inside the body of a CrossFit meathead.

"Listen, I never had a big appetite before, okay? I usually eat one bigger meal per day and then graze."

"Yeah." He threw his hand up. "Exactly. You should've brought snacks to graze on."

"Stop micromanaging me."

"Stop being so stubborn, and maybe I will."

"Pot calling the kettle black," I grumbled and flicked the volume back up to drown out any more of his bothersome questions. That were only a little bit sweet. Like, the tiniest. Mostly annoying.

The drive to Walt's was about ten minutes, and he parked in the back. I set my things in the office and relieved Mickey. For a Friday at the beginning of February, the crowd wasn't too bad. The closer to Valentine's Day, the more people tended to brave the cold weather, and I noticed Nate's sister, Genevieve, in a corner booth with her fiancé and one of Nate's best friends, Dylan. The guy was *hot*. Also, completely and utterly smitten.

Gen waved when she spotted me, offering me one of her bright smiles, her blue eyes shining even in the dim light of the bar. She and her brother were similar in that way, both of them full of sunshine like they were born into a children's cartoon. She was one of the few people whom I would call a friend. Even though we didn't hang out, I had her number in my phone, and I always responded whenever she texted me a photo or link to something she thought reminded her of me. Endearing, really. These two siblings.

Nate clapped me on the shoulder as he checked in with me, once again reminding me to drink from my water bottle, before sitting with Gen and Dylan. I served up drinks, opened and closed tabs, emptied the dishwasher and refilled it, all while keeping an eye on that corner booth, sometimes curious as to what story Nate told with his hands moving all over, earning giggles from his sister and smirks from Dylan.

I'd been so preoccupied, I didn't hear someone calling my name until he stood right in front of me.

"Tabby. You avoiding me or what?"

I blinked up to Harrison, frozen in place. Because, yes, I had been avoiding him.

We'd been texting on and off the last few weeks, as per usual. Our pattern had always been the same. On through the spring and summer, off before the big holidays hit. Which was okay for me. I could do my annual hiding away. I didn't like making them into a big deal, not when I didn't have anyone to spend them with.

Though, hopefully, I would soon.

I instinctively placed one hand on my belly. "Hi. How—hi."

"Hey, beautiful." Harrison smiled easily, his nice-guy dimples carving both of his cheeks, his blond hair styled to messy perfection. He had a Zack Morris thing about him. Comforting in that I always knew what to expect.

Which was why I'd been avoiding him. I knew what he would say when I told him I was pregnant, and if I were honest with myself, it wasn't what I wanted to hear.

I wanted a family. A whole family. I always had. And no matter how I'd planned for it, I hadn't been ready to face the inevitable yet.

But I guess the time had come.

"How are you doing?" he asked, and I swallowed hard.

"Good. You want a drink? I'd like to talk to you, but it'll be a bit before I can take a break."

"Yeah. Do you have that porter I like?"

"From Deschutes? Yeah." I tapped him his beer on the house, and he pointed to an open two-top in front of the windows.

I worked for a few more minutes, formulating how I'd give him the news, until Nate sidled up next to me. "What's Howard doing here?"

I didn't even bother correcting him. "Came to see me."

Nate held on to my wrist, stopping me from passing him to get to a customer, and assessed me with his steady gaze. "You okay?"

"Mm-hmm."

"You don't look okay."

If I weren't so tied up in knots, maybe I'd cry at his observation. But it was all I could do to keep myself together for what was about to happen. "Can I go talk to him for a few minutes?"

"Are you telling him?" When I nodded, Nate's gaze flicked over my shoulder to where Harrison sat. "Take all the time you need." Before I could step away from him, he pushed my water bottle into my hands with a stern eyebrow raise and a quiet, "You'll be all right."

I made my way over to the table, slipping onto the seat. Harrison grinned at me. "Missed you. We haven't talked in a while. You won't text me back."

"Been busy."

"With what?"

I wouldn't categorize what we had as a real relationship, but it was close enough to one where we knew the basics about each other. At least, I knew the basics about him. He either always forgot or didn't care enough about mine.

"School started," I said, and he tapped his knuckles on the table, next to his glass.

"Right. Right. Well, I thought I'd come see what you're up to. Thought maybe I could take you home."

I attempted to clear the golf ball stuck in my throat. "Maybe not tonight."

He reached out for me, tracing his thumb over the shell of my ear. Normally, I liked that. I didn't tonight. Not when Nate glared daggers at us from his place behind the bar. I scooted my chair over, so I didn't have a full view of him as I made this confession.

"We have to talk," I started, lacing my fingers together.

Harrison waited with his usual ease, as if nothing in his life could go wrong. For him, probably not. He came from an affluent family with All-American white guy good looks. Life was a breeze.

Welp…

"Harrison, I'm pregnant."

The smile melted from his face like a landslide pulling a house into the Pacific Ocean. He gaped at me. Blinked. And gaped some more.

"It's yours," I said, and that snapped him out of it.

"Are you sure?"

I huffed in irritation. "Yes."

He didn't appear to believe me, tap, tap, tapping his knuckles on the table. Had he always tapped like that? I couldn't recall.

"How do you know it's mine?"

My jaw dropped. "Are you serious?"

"Yeah. How do I know? You could've been out here fucking all kinds of people." He shrugged, his gaze coasting around as if I'd fucked everybody in the bar. "I have no idea."

"Harrison." Offended, yet unable to come up with an appropriate comeback, I had trouble finding my words. I hadn't practiced enough for this. "You know I haven't been with anyone else."

He stared at me, the wheels turning behind his angry eyes, obviously searching for a way out. "You're not keeping it, are you?"

"Yes, I am."

I didn't think he'd be happy about this revelation, but I also never would have guessed how disgusted he'd be. His lip curled. "Why?"

"Because I want to. I want this baby."

"Aren't you all my body, my choice? What about now? Why aren't you getting an abortion?"

I exhaled a stunned sound. "I don't want one. *That* is my choice."

"I'll pay for it," he said, pulling his phone out of his pocket.

Goose bumps dotted my skin, tears pricking at the corners of my eyes from anger. "What? Are you going to Venmo me?"

He raised his gaze to mine. Every bit of attraction I'd ever felt for him was gone. Evaporated with the utter revulsion in his stare. "I'm certainly not paying for this baby. I want nothing to do with it." He stood, stepping closer to me, into my space, so I had to tilt my head back. I refused to back down, though all my martial arts training had drained from my brain. I doubted I could even land a strike with how my hands trembled. "This was *never* part of the plan."

"I know. I—"

He leered over me. "Did you do this on purpose? Are you trying to trap me?"

I shook my head, struggling to see with my blurry vision. "Don't accuse me of forcing you to do anything you don't want. I just wanted to let you know."

"Oh. You wanted to let me know," he mocked. "Well, thanks for nothing."

He practically spat the words at me, and from the way he aimed his pointer finger at me, I assumed there was more to come, but he didn't get it out. Because a body suddenly careened into him.

"Son of a bitch!" Nate roared, grabbing Harrison by the collar of his shirt to pin him against the window.

I was so shocked, I didn't know what to do or think. Could only watch this scene play out in front of me.

"You don't fucking talk to her that way," Nate gritted out, his jaw so tight I worried he'd crack a molar.

Harrison struggled with his footing. While he had the height advantage, I doubted the guy had ever done an ounce of manual labor in his life. He would have no idea how to fend off someone, let alone Nate in this wild state.

I touched Nate's shoulder. "Let him go."

Nate ignored me, pushing Harrison up to force him out the back door. Patrons gawked at them, but I had no idea how to fix the situation. Thankfully, Genevieve jumped behind the bar, directing everyone's attention to her as Dylan appeared at my side, both of us following Nate as he wrestled Harrison outside.

"You don't even fucking look at her anymore." Nate tossed Harrison away and finally turned over his shoulder to me. "What did he say to you?"

I shook my head, refusing to answer, but that dumbass didn't have the same reluctance. Harrison flung his hand in my direction. "She's pregnant and is accusing me of being the dad."

"*Accusing*?" Nate repeated. "You are the dad, you jackass."

"Then she can get an abortion."

In the blink of an eye, Nate was on Harrison again, landing a brutal blow to his face, shouting curses about how he never deserved me. He landed a right hook to Harrison's side, audibly knocking the breath out of him and taking his feet out from under him.

I rushed toward them. "Nate! Stop!"

Dylan caught me around the waist. "Stay here," he directed, pulling me back a few steps. "I'll take care of it."

Nate got in one more punch before Dylan hauled him off Harrison, one arm around his shoulders, the other around his torso, immobilizing his arms at his sides. "Enough."

Harrison struggled to get up, slipping on a patch of ice, his breath forming clouds in front of his bloody mouth. "You crazy motherfucker. What the hell do you think you're doing?"

"What am I doing?" Nate fought to get away, but Dylan held him tight, leaving Nate to thrash against his hold. "I'm taking out the trash."

Harrison wiped at his face and patted down his coat, as if that would make a difference, and then waved at the bar. "Say goodbye to this piece-of-shit place because this will all be mine once I press charges and sue you."

That's when I leaped forward, standing in front of Nate and Dylan. "You do that, and I'll take you to court for child support."

Harrison weighed his options and decided his ego wasn't worth his child's life. With a flippant wave that he was *done*, he stalked away from the bar. And me.

Even through my shock and hurt, I recognized the quiet rustling behind me, a few murmured words from Dylan about him not being worth it, and then, "Take care of your girl."

The back door opened and closed with a thud, and a moment later, Nate's arm banded around me, his familiar smell a comfort, his heat a balm to my soul. I turned into him and released all the tears I'd been holding back.

"I got you," he rasped against my ear, tucking my head against his chest. "I got you."

No one had ever stood up for me like that. Defended me so vehemently.

And I couldn't help but appreciate it. More than that, *love* it.

FIVE
NATE

brushed my hand over Tabitha's hair again and again, my lips against her temple, whispering words of how I had her, it was okay, I'd take care of her. She sniffled and shivered, and I hadn't even realized we were outside on a thirty-degree night. I'd watched that asshole get in her face, and I'd lost it.

"You're freezing," I noted, running my hands over her arms, and she nodded, but when I tried to pull her back to the door, she shook her head.

"I need another minute."

So, I held her hand, laced our fingers together, and tugged her to me, keeping her warm as best I could. When she finally met my gaze, her eyes pink and watery, she whispered a quiet apology, and I couldn't stand it. "You have nothing to be sorry for," I told her. "This is on him."

"I know, but… I don't know. I don't know why I'm apologizing. I don't know what I'm doing." Her breath stuttered, and she wiped the backs of her hands over her cheeks. "He obviously doesn't want anything to do with me or the baby."

I couldn't even feel bad about that. "He doesn't deserve to be involved. Not if that was his reaction."

She sniffed. "He said he'd pay for the abortion."

Hearing it for the second time tonight made my blood boil.

I was all for everyone living their lives and making their own choices, but telling someone else what they should do or not do with their body was wrong. Worse, telling Tabby to terminate a pregnancy after the loss she'd suffered was despicable. I didn't give a shit if he knew about her past or not, it wasn't his place. And I stared off in the direction that son of bitch had walked. Maybe I could catch up to him. Finish what I'd started.

"Please don't," she said, like she could read my thoughts. "I assumed he wouldn't want anything to do with it."

"But he shouldn't have treated you like that." I caught her chin between my thumb and forefinger, lifting her face up to mine. "I protect…" *Mine*, I didn't say. "I protect my people. You are one of my people."

She sniffed once again and eked out an impression of a smile.

I tried for a real one. "I mean… I appreciate you letting me take him down, but I really would've liked to see you land a kick or two."

That earned me a husky laugh. "Yeah, it's been a while since I got to dust off my skills."

I stretched my neck in a search around us. "You want me to find a board or something to break?"

"No. I'm good."

"Yeah." He slung his arm around me. "You are."

We stepped back into Walt's to find Evie manning the bar with Bran, a college drop-out Tabby had convinced me to hire. At the time, I hadn't thought anything of it, but maybe she saw something in him that she saw in herself. The need to work, the drive to do his best, even if it was slinging beers at a neighborhood dive. A lot of patrons appeared to have exited in the last few minutes, and I only had myself to blame for that.

The regulars knew me. The generous customers who kept this place running knew I wouldn't fly off the handle half-cocked for no reason. And those who didn't? Well… *Hope you enjoyed the show.*

I shouldn't have lost my temper. But I didn't regret it. Wouldn't take it back even if I could.

"Handed out a bunch of shots," Evie explained, meeting me at the open lip of the bar. Her attention coasted over my face and down the length of me, as if checking for injuries, and then her gaze panned to Tabby. "You okay?"

Tabitha nodded, though not very believably, and my sister extended her arms, a silent offering. Surprisingly, Tabby took her up on it, embracing Evie. I jutted my chin toward Dylan, now seated at the corner of the bar. "Thanks, man."

"You've really got a hard-on for punching people at your workplace, huh?"

I checked out my knuckles. Just a little red. "I rule my kingdom with an iron fist."

"That's what you call it? Ruling?"

"I am the king."

He grunted a sound of amusement. "How's your girl over there?"

I glanced over my shoulder. She was still shaken up. There was no way I would make her work after that. "Come on," I told them all. "Let's go to the office."

The four of us were a tight fit, but I sat Tabby down in the chair, and Genevieve hopped up on the desk. She had worked here for a few months while recovering from a dance injury before hitting the stage again, and I'd enjoyed having her home and working with me. I was glad she'd decided to come back and settle down with Dylan. Sure, I gave them a lot of shit, but I couldn't be happier for them.

"So, is anyone going to explain what happened?" she asked, and I glanced at Dylan. When I'd told my friends not to tell their girls about my meltdown a few weeks ago, I had fully expected them to anyway. From my sister's confusion, I guessed they hadn't.

Dylan shrugged at me and leaned back against the wall, staying silent, as usual.

I looked to Tabitha for direction, what she wanted to do or say about this. I tried to imply with my eyes that I'd follow her lead.

She breathed deeply and set her shoulders before letting it out. "I'm pregnant."

Evie's jaw dropped. "Oh my god! Are you okay? How are you feeling? How far along are you? Wait—" She threw up her hands, connecting the dots. "Wait, that was Harrison, wasn't it? Is he the father?"

Tabby nodded. "I wouldn't use the term father to describe him after tonight."

I grumbled. "I should've fucked him up more."

Dylan cut in then. "You did some pretty good damage."

Evie wagged her finger at me. "Did you know?"

"Did I know what? That she's pregnant? Yes."

"I told him last month. But I only told Harrison tonight," Tabby said, and my sister's eyes went wide, if not a little giddy. Whatever idea she had in her head, I didn't like it, and I motioned to Dylan to control her. He rolled his eyes.

"I take it Harrison is out of the picture?" she deduced, not waiting on an answer because it was obvious. "And my big brother defended your honor?"

Tabby refused to meet my gaze. Though, she did nod.

And, fuck yes, I did.

I would defend her honor again and again and again.

I could see the wheels in my sister's head turning, so I collected Tabitha's things from the hook and handed them to her. "I want you to go home."

"What? No. I still—"

Ignoring her protests, I told Dylan, "She needs a ride."

Tabby stood up, her fists at her sides. "You can't send me home."

"Last I checked, I was still in charge here, so yeah, I can send you home." Over her head, Dylan and I nodded at each other. And when she still refused to move, I placed her coat around her shoulders and slipped my beanie over her head. Then I looped her bag over her shoulder and pushed her water bottle into her hands. Like a little grumpy Barbie.

"And I'm taking you off the schedule for the next week."

She roared. "*What?*"

"You need to rest, and I want to see what Bran is made of."

"You—"

"Are so thankful, I know." I grinned, my hands on her shoulders, and spun her around to face the door. "Have a good night."

She still tried to argue with me even as Dylan herded her over the threshold. My sister threw herself at me, snaking her arms around my neck, squeezing me tightly. "I'm so proud of you."

"For what?" I accepted the hug, still hearing Tabitha's dissertation on why she needed to stay here. She had loyalty, that was for sure. When her voice faded, I imagined Dylan bodily picking her up and putting her in his car. He was gallant like that.

"For being you." She slapped my back a few times then stepped away. "For standing up for Tabby. For stepping up for her. That takes a lot of bravery."

"I'm not…" I tugged at my hair, reading between the lines. "I haven't done anything."

"You will, and we'll help you as best we can. You deserve it. So does she."

I walked with her out to the floor. Dylan and Tabby were nowhere in sight. "Text me when she's home. Since she's pissed at me, she won't respond to my texts now."

She smiled. "Of course. We'll take care of her for you."

"Thanks."

After a stop at the booth they had been sitting at to pick up her coat, Genevieve was out of the door, and I was behind the bar.

Bran greeted me while hanging glasses on the rack above our heads. "'Sup, boss?"

"What would you think about taking on more responsibilities around here?"

"Yeah?" He brightened. "I could handle that."

I patted his back, passing him on my way to help a patron. "Yeah. I was hoping you'd say that."

SIX
NATE

t didn't long for my "best friends" to start up their bullshit.

JUDE

So.

JUDE

We gonna talk about it or…………?

DYLAN

hes ignoring us

LIAM

We can also go back to our own thread and talk about it.

You talk about me in another thread?

LIAM

Yes.

JUDE

Obviously.

JUDE

Especially when you beat the shit out of
Tabby's baby daddy.

I should have killed him.

DYLAN

u gave him a split lip black eye and some
kidney shots

Like I said.

Not enough.

JUDE

What happened? Because I got it from Brooke.

LIAM

Who got it from Kennedy.

DYLAN

Gen told her

Lot of fucking gossips you are.

LIAM

Remind me of the definition of irony.

JUDE

You can literally never keep your mouth shut
about anything.

But this isn't MY thing.

DYLAN

your acting like it is

LIAM

Correct.

JUDE

Because you want it to be your thing.

———

Two hours later…

LIAM

He's ignoring us again.

I'm working.

JUDE

Since when can't you text and work?

Since you assholes are bugging me about this.

DYLAN

u shud have seen him. An animal.

I ignored Dylan's dyslexia, even though it was the one thing I could shove in his face right now to make him shut up about last night.

Listen.

The shit he said to Tab was disrespectful.

Fucking horseshit.

Utter bullshit.

And he made her cry.

DYLAN

im not saying he didnt deserve it

LIAM

Yeah. I might have done the same thing.

JUDE

At least you weren't arrested.

Because of Tabby.

JUDE

How? What did she do?

Said if he pressed charges, she was going to take him to court. He doesn't want anything to do with her and the baby.

JUDE

How do you feel about that?

————

Thirty minutes later...

LIAM

Do you notice it's always when he has to answer straight-up questions about how he feels about her, he doesn't respond?

JUDE

Remember when he showed up at Imagination tearing his hair out because she was pregnant WITH ANOTHER MAN'S BABY?

DYLAN

remember when he beat the shit out of that guy?

JUDE

That's the story we'll tell each other around the fire when we're old and wrinkly.

Fuck off.

All of you.

And the story we're going to tell is how I clocked Matthews.

I'll make sure your children know.

DYLAN

when there hanging out with your kids

JUDE

Think we should allow him in the club?

Fuck you.

What club?

———

Next day…

WHAT CLUB?

SEVEN
TABBY

The morning sun filtered through the thin curtains, rousing me from sleep. I stretched languidly, my muscles pleasantly warm. I hated to admit it, but Nate had been right. I did need to rest. That night at Walt's two weeks ago had crippled me. As much as I'd like to say it didn't hurt to sit across from a man I'd had a relationship with, it did. No, it hadn't been love, but it had been *something*. At the very least, I should have been respected.

But he couldn't even give me that. So, I took the days off that Nate had offered me and focused on school and making plans. I'd returned to work this week refreshed and with a *new* plan.

One that didn't rely on anyone else. I was the one to decide to have this baby, so I needed to put all my energy into building the best life I possibly could for us. First step, purchasing a car. I couldn't depend on Nate to pick me up and drop me off every night like he'd been doing this past week. But I had to admit, it was nice not having to worry about transportation, especially as my energy levels seemed to fluctuate with the changing weeks of this pregnancy.

And sure, Nate's charming yet irritating tendencies didn't

hurt. I'd been looking after myself for so long, it was nice to have someone else do it.

Plus, the baby apparently liked it too. I'd felt it move a few days ago, while I'd been working. I'd frozen mid-pour, the beer spilling over the glass, and Juanita sent me back to the office. Of course, Nate was there, mother-henning me until I told him I'd felt it. Then he stared at my torso for a good minute. Our work T-shirts were unisex and loose, and I'd always found ways to make them more formfitting, but ever since I'd found out I was pregnant, I'd been wearing them baggy, hanging over the waistband of my pants.

I'd snapped my fingers in his face to bring him back to earth, and then he had handed me a sleeve of Oreos he'd been keeping in one of the desk drawers, cleared out of anything except snacks for me. He'd even labeled the drawer. *For Tabitha. Any other hands in here will be cut off.*

So, the two of us had stood there in the office while I nibbled on the cookies, waiting, and when the baby moved again, I'd let Nate place his hand on the side of my stomach to feel it. He'd gotten that faraway stare again, but I hadn't minded. I'd understood.

Ever since, the baby seemed to know when he was around, poking me as if it wanted attention. Not much different from Nate.

As long as I'd known him, he'd always been against having kids of his own, yet he had been pouring himself into this kid's life. It didn't make sense to me, but I appreciated it anyway. He wasn't only my boss; he was my friend. He had my back.

Standing up in front of the mirror, I smoothed my hands over my bump. It had popped overnight. Not very big, but noticeably *there*. I wouldn't be able to hide it anymore.

And a wave of awe and trepidation crushed me. Happy to have been given another opportunity like this but afraid I would suffer the same loss as my first pregnancy. Although, before I could get too into my feelings, a knock sounded on my bedroom door.

Ming-Yue stood on the other side, coffee cup in hand, glasses in place, appearing to be headed off to the lab. "Some guy's here."

That guy was Nate, and he was way early.

When we'd talked about my car situation last night, I'd told him I was going to purchase one today, and he'd somehow weaseled his way into the task. "How're you gonna get there without me?" he'd asked, and then, "Don't you want a second opinion to make sure you're not buying a lemon?"

I hadn't been able to argue. While I'd had my driver's license since sixteen and my motorcycle license since twenty, I had never owned my own car. To say nothing of purchasing one. Even with all the research I'd done over the last few weeks, it would be nice to have someone there with me, so I'd agreed.

But now, he was here, and I was in my pajamas.

"I'll be down in a few minutes," I told Ming-Yue.

"I have to go, but can he stay here alone with you? He's not going murder you, is he?"

"I heard that!" he hollered from downstairs. These walls were paper-thin. "And she *could* murder *me* if she really wanted."

"It's true," I said, to which Ming-Yue shrugged.

"Okay. I'm going. Bye."

I rushed off to the bathroom, hearing Nate downstairs offering Ming-Yue a cinnamon roll and promising he was not a murderer. I laughed as I brushed my teeth, taking that light, fluttery feeling into the shower with me, where I shaved and exfoliated, making up for the extra scrub by not washing my hair.

I figured I'd take a few of my new maternity purchases for a spin and dressed in super-comfy leggings and a long-sleeved mint-green shirt that displayed the bump proudly. Downstairs, I found Nate in the kitchen, exploring.

"What are you looking for?"

He answered with his back to me, a cabinet open in front of him. "Mouse poop."

"*What*?"

"Yeah," he said conversationally. "I noticed a crawl space on the side of the house."

"Why were you looking at the side of the house?"

He went right on, ignoring my question, opening and closing each cabinet. "So then I took a walk to the back and found a distressing hole right where the gate meets the corner of the house. I checked it out, and it looked like there was a nest in there." He circled around. "You got a basement?" He stopped his mouse rant and stepped toward me, smiling. "Good morning."

"We have mice?"

He slid a small pink cardboard box my way. "I brought cinnamon rolls from the bakery on Aster. It's right across from where the new place is gonna be, and—"

I snatched the box from him. "Mice!"

"Hey, hey, hey," he cooed, shuffling around the small kitchen island to seat me at the table. "It's okay. You can give the landlord a call and get somebody down here to take care of it."

My landlord managed a bunch of properties around the college. Didn't care much for upkeep during the academic calendar since most college kids didn't care.

Nate swirled his finger at my face. "What's the face for?"

"Nothing."

He eyed me dubiously and pulled his cell phone from his pocket, tapping something into it, all the while I imagined mice crawling over me. I shuddered, and Nate held on to my shoulder. "All right?"

"Thinking about the mice…" I gagged.

"Yeah. I'm taking care of it."

"How?" I opened the bakery box, momentarily forgetting about miniature pests and inhaling the delicious cinnamon and sugar scents of the warm and still gooey buns. I dove right in, peeling one of the rolls off the paper. When the first delicious bite hit my tongue, I closed my eyes, the flavor pure bliss.

Nate made a kind of tortured grunt, and I fluttered my lids back open to find him glowering at me. I licked my fingers, talking around the pastry. "What?"

He merely shook his head, full attention on my mouth.

"What?" I repeated, completely garbled.

"I know a guy," he said after a moment when he dragged his gaze up to mine. "Stop making those sex sounds while you eat."

I didn't often blush, but I was happy he spun around to face the cabinets because I felt myself go beet red.

Nate picked up a glass and thoroughly examined it, as if still searching for traces of mice. But our house was clean. Ming-Yue and I were both neat freaks. He finally opened the refrigerator for the jug of orange juice he'd had delivered a few days ago and poured me some before setting it in front of me.

"Why?"

He sat back down. "Why should you stop making sex sounds? Because it's distracting, and I keep forgetting what we're talking about." He slapped two napkins on my sticky fingers. "Now, please, use a napkin to wipe your mouth before I forget where the hell I am."

I rolled my eyes, hoping I wasn't blushing again, and wiped off my mouth and my hands. "I meant why are you doing all of this for me?"

He propped his elbows on the table and fisted his right hand in his left, tipping his head side to side, thinking about his answer more than I assumed he'd need to.

In the meantime, I studied him—and the wild lock of hair that drooped over his forehead. I'd always thought he was handsome. If you liked that brown-haired, blue-eyed, bearded-jaw thing. But having him sit here in front of me with sunshine streaming in through the window, he was beautiful. Or maybe it was because of all the ways he'd been taking care of me lately.

I couldn't ignore him or how I'd always thought he was the

ideal guy. Funny and caring, reliable yet layered. The problem was he'd always gone from woman to woman, and I'd been nursing a broken heart for a long time. By the time I'd recovered, I'd found Har—He Who Shall Not Be Named.

But at this particular moment, I couldn't ignore how the tips of my fingers tingled with the need to touch Nate's trimmed beard, tease him about those few grays coming in, trace my thumb over his lips.

And of course, I couldn't ignore the soft patting at my belly.

When I scooted back from the table to rub over the spot, Nate's eyes expanded. "How's the tadpole doing? Jumping around a lot?"

"I think it's the juice. Likes citrus."

"Like Mama."

The support group I had joined for grieving mothers espoused we were mothers, no matter where our babies lived, but without that weight in our arms, it was a hard concept to accept. How could I be a mother without a child?

But this time…

My nose stung, and I stood up for something to do. That was when Nate threw his arms out. "Whoa! Look at you." He hopped up from his chair, stopping me from throwing my trash away. He always waited for permission to touch my stomach, and when I nodded, he gently cradled the bump. "Look at this."

"Sort of appeared overnight."

He rubbed here and there, and the thunderstruck look on his face never ceased to amuse me. Gone from thinking babies were gross to pure astonishment. "You're seventeen weeks, right?"

When I nodded, he muttered something that sounded like "pomegranate."

"What did you say?"

"Oh, uh…" His face flushed pink. "Reminding myself about an article that listed fruits you should be eating."

I didn't believe him. Well, actually, I believed that he read the article because he was an overbearing ogre hidden under a *Sam Malone, but make it millennial* costume.

I had a hunch something else had made him turn pink. Something the honest-to-a-fault guy didn't want to admit out loud, and I'd never been more curious.

As he backed away, his gaze journeyed over me, from the messy bun at the nape of my neck to my socked feet and back. "You're glowing."

The unexpected compliment warmed me from the inside out. "Don't be ridiculous."

"I'm not," he insisted, tucking an errant strand of hair behind my ear. His fingers lingered a moment, gently caressing my jawline before dropping away. "You're beautiful."

We stared at each other, tension crackling between us. Part of me wanted to lean into him, to let myself be swept up in the moment that had been simmering between us for longer than I cared to acknowledge.

But the wiser part of me knew that was a bad idea. He didn't do permanent, let alone babies.

Clearing my throat, I brushed past him to throw away my trash and put my cup in the dishwasher, making sure to leave no crumbs for the evident mouse empire that had taken up residence here.

Nate followed me down the hall to the front door, where I stepped into my boots. "So, what's up with you and babies?"

His grin was positively delighted. "*You* are asking *me* a personal question. I am honored."

I ignored him, tying the laces. "Don't make me regret it."

"There's not much of a story. I don't mind babies. I love my buddies' kids. They're all basically my nieces and nephews." He shrugged, hands in his coat pockets. "Just never wanted any of my own. Don't think I'd be a good dad."

I straightened and slipped on my coat, considering him. Then I gave in to a quiet laugh as he plucked his black beanie that had recently become mine from the hook and tugged it on my head, making sure my ears were covered.

I thought he'd be a wonderful dad.

Before I could ask him a follow-up question, he changed the subject. "So, you know what you're looking for today?"

"Yeah, I've got a couple in mind, depending on the price."

"Okay." His trademark smile settled on his face. "Let's see what we can do."

I locked up behind us. "I don't like the gleam in your eyes."

"Oh baby, you'll be thanking me later."

I didn't understand what exactly he meant until he opened the glass door to the sales office and slung his arm around my waist, his hand over my hip in a grip that could only be described as possessive.

"What are you doing?" I elbowed him away, but he pulled me tighter to his side.

"Play along," he whispered, head ducked down, beard scraping along my jaw in a way that sent shivers down my spine and settled between my legs. I momentarily lost my place in space and time, only to be hauled back by the salesman.

"Hi, my name is Matt. How're you doing today?"

"Great, thanks," Nate said, shaking his hand.

Matt, who appeared to be in his late forties, propped his hands on his hips, hopeful. "You here to buy a car today?"

"I hope so." Nate's thumb skated over my hip bone. It didn't matter that I had on at least three layers of fabric. He might as well have been caressing my naked skin.

Matt nodded between us. "Excellent. You're in the right spot. Why don't you tell me your names and a little bit about what you're looking for?"

"I'm Nate," he said, moving me in front of him, settling a proprietary arm across my collarbone, "and this is my wife, Tabby."

I was stunned into silence.

He kept right on going, cupping his hand over the side of my bump. "And this is the reason we're here."

Matt's face lit up. "Congratulations. I've got three at home myself, so I know what it's like. Is this your first?"

"It is." Nate bent, lowering his face to mine. "And we're so excited, right, honeybabe?"

I had the urge to mush his face with my hand and burst out in laughter at the same time. A mixture of a groan and giggle left my throat as I nodded along with this silly game.

Nate kissed my cheek. "I need something safe for my gorgeous wife and our little tadpole here, but we need it to be affordable." He stood up to his full height, the weight of his arm too much, forcing me to lean against him. He supported me, his chest to my back, his fingers burrowing under my open coat to rest on my shoulder. "I'm sure you can understand what it's like trying to manage everything, especially with your brood at home."

Ugh. Nate was just so goddamn likable.

Matt motioned for us to follow him to his desk, where he showed us the framed photos of his kids and promised he'd get our "little family" settled into something nice.

"See?" Nate laced our fingers together as we walked out to the lot, Matt aiming us toward a Subaru that could "grow" with us.

"See what? How we're suddenly married?" I hissed, holding on tighter to him in the cold.

"Yeah. People love a good love story. So, buckle up, buttercup. Hey, yeah, I really like this one," he said to Matt as he kept me physically connected to him at all times while he and Matt discussed four-wheel drive, tires, and miles on the car. I was more interested in where the baby seat might go and how I would feel driving it.

"What do you think of this one, honeybunch?" Nate asked, and I *barely* held back from rolling my eyes.

"I want something a little smaller. I've been looking online, and I know you have a few compact SUVs."

"Sure, sure. I've got a RAV4 here." He led us a few rows over to the silver automobile, and Nate nodded.

"Oh yeah. All the moms drive this."

I tilted my head up to him. "How would you know?"

"You jealous?"

I didn't know how or why, but yeah.

He snickered, pulling me into him, my back to his front again. I fit perfectly underneath his chin. Nate and Matt exchanged some questions and answers about the car, but once again, I'd been rendered mute. Pretending to be husband and wife with a baby on the way, it was a game. But the way he held me didn't feel fake. It felt very real.

Like I belonged at his side, his palm against mine, talking about everyday things like gas mileage.

By the time Nate brought me back to reality with a push to sit in the driver's seat, Matt had retrieved the keys. The three of us took it for a short spin, and I liked it. It had been a while since I'd driven a car because I'd been riding my bike everywhere, but I didn't have much issue, save for getting used to the height difference.

"I can see everything up here," I mused, and Nate reached his hand over, squeezing my thigh with a pleased smile.

"You look good, sweetie pie."

From the back seat, Matt pointed out different buttons on the dash, though I didn't pay much mind, attempting to ignore the five-finger imprint Nate had left on my leg.

As I pulled back into the lot, Matt asked how I liked it, and I told him I thought it was great. But before we could go on, so I could get into the budget, Nate pointed at a blue van. "Ooh, honey cakes. We gotta take that beauty out for a drive."

I frowned at him. "I don't want…"

He gave me an almost imperceptible shake of his head before

turning to Matt. "Prince Charming had a few different ladies try on the glass slipper before it finally fit, right?"

"Right." Matt chuckled. "Bet you'll love this one."

As Matt preceded us to the van, I poked Nate's side. "What the hell are you doing?"

"You can't take the first offer. If he knows you don't need any convincing, we won't have any wiggle room on the price. I know what I'm doing, hm?"

I heaved a sigh and let the two of them chat about the minivan with three rows of seats and in-floor storage as I attempted to stay warm. While Matt skedaddled back to the office for the key so we could test-drive it, Nate held my cold hands between his, blowing on them, rubbing the backs as if starting a fire. "How are you feeling?"

"Good."

"Don't lie."

"I'm cold. It's windier than I thought it was going to be."

He nodded and folded me up, rotating us so he blocked all the wind.

Damn chivalry.

"We're almost done. I'll take you out for lunch."

"You don't—"

"I'm hungry for a burrito. You can get a veggie one. What do you think?"

Seeing as how he remembered I wasn't currently eating meat, and he kept me so warm, I couldn't deny him. "You know, you're very good at this."

"At what?"

At all of it. Being my friend. Being there for me. Being my pretend husband and baby daddy. But I didn't tell him any of that. Saved by Matt. "Okay, who wants to take the wheel this time?"

Nate snatched the key faster than a dog stealing a treat. "Called it!"

I snorted and hopped into the passenger seat, enjoying the heat from all the vents he pointed at me. This time, I was allowed to watch him drive, his fingers curved around the wheel, arms relaxed, smiling as he spoke to Matt in the rearview mirror. So at ease with himself and with our game, it was easy to believe it.

To want it to be real.

"You look good," I murmured to him, earning a gigantic grin.

Matt agreed. "This is a real *dad* vehicle right here. Imagine how good you'll look pulling up to soccer practice in this."

"Yeah, imagine," I teased, but instead of the laugh I thought I'd get in return, Nate's eyes filled with something I couldn't read, though it sent goose bumps down my arms.

He hummed thoughtfully and reached for my hand, lacing his fingers with mine. He brought them to his mouth, his lips brushing along the back of my hand when he said, "I can."

I didn't dare to hope.

After these last few weeks when everything felt so precarious, I couldn't hope.

Every choice I made from here on out would affect the rest of my life and the life of the person growing inside me. I couldn't bear to make the wrong decision. Or, worse, hang my hat on something that wasn't real.

When Nate parked the van back in its spot, I excused myself to use the restroom. I needed a few minutes to remember who I was and what I was doing before going back out, determined to buy the car I wanted without getting lost in the scheme Nate had invented.

Except, by the time I met them, Nate and Matt were shaking hands. As if the deal was done.

What the fuck?

I stormed up to them, intent on tearing into Nate, but he caught me around the waist. "You'll be happy."

Matt motioned to the two of us. "I know how hard it is starting a family."

"And he offered us a very generous deal," Nate finished.

"I knocked two thousand off the sticker price and took care of the taxes and tags. We'll also be putting new tires on the RAV as well."

For the third time today, I couldn't speak. He'd done it. Nate's dumb plan worked. "Wow. Thank you," I choked out. "Thank you so much."

"Your husband tells me this will be your car? We can sit down and get all the paperwork taken care of. Do you need a snack or anything?"

"No, I'm—"

"I see a little table of snacks over there. Is that for customers?" Nate asked, steering me toward Matt's desk.

Matt nodded. "Help yourself."

Once I was seated, Nate peeled off and returned a few moments later with a pack of Goldfish. And that's how I signed on the dotted line, with Nate smiling down at me, opening a packet of kids snacks.

Son of a bitch.

I had a problem.

Because hope had taken root deep in my chest, already threatening to bloom through every part of me.

EIGHT
TABBY

February sailed into March with a new pattern for my life. I'd go to school, eat my food still being delivered via Nate's grocery order that I'd pretend didn't please me exceedingly, then I would ignore how his gaze constantly tracked me at work. How he had me take more and longer breaks and was *always* present. He hadn't been like that before. He owned Walt's and often showed up, but he let me run the bar. Now, he *never* let me work alone.

Never let me feel alone.

And that dangerous hope grew like wild flowers.

Especially when he had "his guy" come to take care of the mice situation. Unfortunately, I'd spotted some of the traps he'd set out—their job done well—and I'd spent a few nights tossing and turning. The evidence of my fatigue had shown, and Nate had known something was wrong. He'd, of course, bugged me about it all night until I confessed that I'd felt tiny little claws creeping over my arms and legs the previous few nights.

That was when the links to rentals started appearing, along with daily morning check-in texts.

The last time I'd felt so cared for was when my dad was still alive. When I'd had someone to take on the world for me.

So, it was Nate I called when I couldn't calm down now. I'd woken up in a cold sweat this morning, knowing what I faced today, and hoped a shower would help. When it didn't, I tried some ginger ale and crackers, but my hands trembled so bad, I could barely hold on to the drink.

I was due for my second ultrasound in an hour, and while I was technically a high-risk pregnancy because of my past history, there had been no reason to worry or need extra tests. My doctor had repeatedly assured me that what happened before was a complete fluke. A very unlucky and tragic accident.

But that didn't help me.

Nausea churned in my stomach as memories bombarded me. Of this same appointment when my world had shattered. Danny hadn't been able to attend the ultrasound, so I'd gone on my own.

Faced with the technician's strained expression as she called for the doctors. The deafening silence when they turned off the monitor, unable to find a heartbeat. That cold dread settling into my bones as I realized my baby was gone.

And I'd been alone.

Curling into a ball on my bed, my entire body shaking with the force of my grief, I knew I couldn't do that again. I couldn't go through this appointment alone. I couldn't face that same traumatic situation alone. If there was no heartbeat…I wouldn't survive it.

I found my phone and called the person who had been the one constant in my life for years. If only I'd recognized that earlier.

"Tabby cat," he answered cheerfully. "Didn't expect you to be calling me so early. I figured you and the tadpole were still getting your beauty sleep."

"Nate." My voice broke on his name, and I thought I could hear a screech in the background, like chair legs scraping on the floor.

"What? Tabby? What's wrong?"

His concerned tone made my breath catch in my throat as I tried to explain. "I c-can't… The ultrasound…"

"Where are you? I'll come to you. Where are you?"

"Home," I managed, and he told me he'd be here in ten minutes.

"I'm going to hang up now so I can drive, but I'm coming. Hold tight, and I'll be there soon."

Not even eight minutes later, Nate was pounding on my front door. I flung it open and launched myself into his arms, burying my face in his solid chest as harsh sobs racked my body.

"Shh, I've got you, Tabby cat," he murmured, cradling me close. "Just breathe. I'm here."

He held me, gently rocking me back and forth, until I calmed. When I finally pulled back, he cupped my face in his hands, swiping away the tears with the pads of his thumbs.

"What's going on? You're scaring me. And not in the will-put-on-curse-on-your-kingdom kind of way."

I managed a watery laugh despite myself and drew in a shuddering breath. "It's my second ultrasound today. That's when…"

I could tell he understood from his single nod and the way his grasp on me tightened ever so slightly.

"I can't go through that alone. I can't."

"You're not alone. I'm right here." He kissed my forehead, tangling his fingers in my still-damp hair. "I'm not going anywhere, all right?"

He pulled me in for another embrace, my face against his throat, his pulse pounding where my lips brushed it. He combed his hand into the hair at the back of my head, holding me in place, murmuring gentle nothings, quite literally keeping me from breaking.

And when I was finally ready to go, he filled up my water, grumbling something about "this goddamn house" and stuck a banana in my bag before bundling me in my coat.

It was a gray day, looked like rain, appropriate for my mood, and Nate kept his hand on my thigh as we drove. With him next to me, I felt safe in a way I couldn't fully comprehend but was what I'd always dreamed of.

He held my hand as we were ushered back to the sterile ultrasound room and stayed quiet as I answered a few questions. He helped me up onto the table and held my gaze as the tech grinned like we were a happy couple.

This time, it didn't feel like it did when we'd pretended at the dealership. This time, it didn't feel like pretending at all. It felt necessary.

I lifted my shirt, displaying my rounded belly, halfway through this journey, and Nate's blue eyes shifted down before flicking back up to mine as if he'd been caught doing something wrong. I shook my head. "It's okay."

And then his focus was there again, staring in wonder. His fingertips brushed over the curve below my belly button once before the technician squirted warm gel there. I held Nate's hand in a viselike grip, but he merely offered me a smile and stroked his thumb over my knuckles.

The tech smiled at me. "Let's take a look at your baby."

I couldn't watch the screen light up. Nate didn't look either, his gaze locked with mine, nodding, reminding me he wasn't going anywhere.

I'd been feeling the tadpole move—even on the car ride over here, I had a foot or elbow jam into my side—but I'd been holding my breath until that strong heartbeat filled the room. I gasped in relief, tears stinging my eyes and flowing down my temples, into my hairline.

"Oh," I cried. "Oh my god."

Nate stood over me, his face so close to mine. "The most beautiful thing I've ever heard."

He wiped at my face, both of us laughing a little deliriously —because he seemed relieved too—as he finally turned to view the screen, the technician busy tapping and typing and moving the wand around on my stomach.

"Look at that." He rubbed his free hand over my arm. "Not much of a tadpole anymore, huh?"

"No."

"Is that the heart?" he asked, and the technician zoomed in on the screen, to the flickering organ.

"Yes, and it looks great." She moved the picture a tiny bit. "And these are the lungs. Nice and healthy."

"Healthy," I repeated, barely able to see through my tears.

"We have the kidneys…and spine." Tap, tap, tap. "The top of the vertebra and skull."

"Got a big brain in there," Nate joked, glancing at me to run his knuckles over my temple. "Like its mama."

The tech repositioned the wand. "Here's the good stuff. You see that? The face."

Nate inhaled audibly and stepped closer to the screen, mouth slack.

"Cute, right?" The technician smiled over her shoulder at us. "You think this baby takes after mom or dad more?"

Neither one of us corrected her. That Nate wasn't the dad. But he did slant a glassy gaze at me, the corner of his mouth quirked up, his single lock of hair hanging over his brow. The rest a mess from his hands and how he'd been tugging at it on the drive over. He appeared perfectly rumpled and amazed.

Maybe even grateful.

And my heart burst wide open as he released the full strength of his smile. "This little frogger is the most perfect thing I've ever seen. Like its mother."

The tech snapped a few pictures of the face, of the teeny tiny nose, the little mouth, and the waving hand that had all three of us chuckling.

We looked at the arms and legs, the bones Nate deemed sturdy, and then it came time.

"Would you like to know the sex?"

Nate raised his brow, obviously waiting for me to answer, but

I didn't know. Almost as if it was bad luck to find out. But that was silly, and I didn't want to admit it.

"Could you put it in an envelope? Maybe we can look later," Nate suggested, and I nodded, pleased with his idea.

"Yes, I can definitely do that for you." She tapped and snapped and moved the wand around for a few more minutes before shutting everything down and wiping off my stomach with a towel. She left us with pictures and a manila envelope then wished us a good day and an easy rest of the pregnancy.

As soon as I had my shirt down, Nate gathered me into his arms right there in the exam room, letting me bury my face in the crook of his neck as I cried—this time from sheer, unbridled happiness.

"Frogger's okay," I whispered raggedly. "My baby's okay."

He pressed a lingering kiss to my temple. "More than okay. Perfect. Your baby is perfect."

For so long, I had resigned myself to going through this journey alone, convincing myself it was better that way. I could avoid further heartbreak. But having Nate here, sharing my fear and joy, was the best thing that could have happened to me. Or Frogger.

And then this over-the-top, overprotective, outrageously idiotic man went and ruined it all when he said, "Move in with me."

NINE
NATE

Tabby glowered at me, her eyebrows in a slash, mouth turned down in evident outrage at the idea of living with me. "What did you just say to me, *fool*?"

The *fool* was implied.

I took her hand to help her off the table, absently skimming my hand over her stomach. She wore leggings and an oversized button-down shirt. Likely an ex-boyfriend's. I'd like to burn it.

Undeterred, I repeated myself. "Move in with me."

She didn't seem any more amenable the second time around as she gathered up her hair to tie it on the top of her head with a few twists of her hands, loose strands by her temples and ears. With her nose still pink from all the crying she'd done today, she looked like she needed a hug. But with her spine straight and chin proud, she might take me to the mats instead.

That was what I loved, her dichotomy. At once, both quiet and confident, strong yet wounded. I'd always understood these different facets of her, appreciated each part of her, but it hadn't been until the day she'd told me she was pregnant that I really realized I couldn't lose her.

I couldn't ignore the strange fascination and odd possessiveness I'd always had with her.

I couldn't stand the thought of her being with anyone else. Of having someone else's baby.

And I didn't even want a kid!

At least, I hadn't until it was Tabby's. As if now that I'd been shown a vision for a future I hated, I chose a different one.

And after seeing Frogger with my own eyes? Hearing the steady *ba-dump, ba-dump, ba-dump*? I was toast.

I had no goddamn idea how to be a dad, but I'd figure it out. I'd prove to her that she wasn't alone. I'd show this kid they never had to fear anything. I was here now.

"I'm taking you out to eat." I handed her the envelope with the index card revealing the sex of the baby, along with the printed photos from the scan. With her attention diverted to the picture of the baby's face, she didn't fight me.

Step one, hit her over the head and drag her back to my cave.

Step two, love her.

I opened the passenger side door of my reliable Honda that appeared to be able to fit a car seat, but I didn't really know how big those things were. In my head, they were like a bucket. Babies were little, so I assumed the things you carried them in couldn't be much bigger either. But after I closed the door and rounded the trunk, suddenly I considered space and safety and how truly excellent that minivan seemed now.

As I buckled in, I glanced over at Tabby to find her going through all the photos, her barely there smile so timid, as if she was afraid to be happy, and my heart attempted to karate kick out of my chest to get to her. I smoothed my hand up and down her thigh, and it only occurred to me at that very moment how touchy-feely Tabby and I had been these last few weeks. Sure, she'd push my shoulder when I annoyed her or finally give me a high five after I stood in front of her with my hand up for five minutes, but we'd never been like *this*.

These natural embraces and fingers laced together and thigh rubs.

Almost like she didn't mind.

Almost like she *wanted* it.

I hit the road with a smile on my face, cueing up my Spotify, and Tabby didn't mention anything when Hall & Oates floated through the speakers. Didn't even blink an eye when I used the steering wheel like a drum kit. I might've even caught her lips pursing, fighting a smile as I sang along to the chorus, about a girl making my dreams come true.

"Don't quit your day job," she muttered when the song ended and another one started. A favorite from my childhood, "Chasing Cars" had been perfect for me as an emo teenager, struggling with my parents' divorce, desperate for the attention of Katie Pritchard.

I had thought I'd grown up from that kid, but maybe I never really had. Maybe I'd never been able to fully let go of all I'd been holding on to. Until now.

Until I stopped chasing women I'd hoped would heal that bruised part of me, leftover feelings of inadequacy from my father and being used as a weapon by my mother. I wanted something I couldn't quite grasp.

Until I opened my eyes and recognized what had been in front of me all along.

I didn't need Tabby to soothe me or fix whatever broken bits I had inside me. Hell, she was broken too. I couldn't know how many bits and bobs had been rearranged in her over the years—and wouldn't until she allowed me to know the full story—but what I did need was for her to say yes to me. So we could take all our broken and bruised fragments and build something new and lasting, all our own.

"We're gonna sit down, have some lunch, and then negoti-ate," I told her, making a right turn toward Tony's, her favorite.

"Unless it's for another raise, I'm not interested."

I shot her my best grin, which she responded to with a bored expression.

Tough nut, my little mama was, but I'd get her. I'd pull out every trick in my book if I had to.

Seated at the corner pizzeria, I ordered a couple of slices for me and the usual for her, chicken parm with baked ziti. Over the years, it had been easy to spot her patterns, identify how she scrimped and saved. On more than one occasion, we'd talked about spending habits and loans. Since she helped me make almost all my business decisions, we were pretty open with each other in that respect. When she'd decided to go to school, she'd wanted to keep her expenses down and come out with the least amount of debt possible. That was why I'd given her any and every opportunity to make more money.

I'd been fortunate to have been gifted a nice nest egg from my grandfather. Walter Kozlowski had survived World War II on his family's farm in Poland and immigrated to America shortly after with his brother. They'd found work as furniture salesmen, which eventually parlayed into their own furniture manufacturing company. Walt had married a nice girl named Doris, and they'd had three kids, including my father. When Walt died, he had left each of his grandkids a good sum of money to make our dreams come true since he had been able to do that himself. I remembered when they read the will, I had thought that line was so sappy about how his dreams were having a family and providing for them.

But boy did I get it now.

After college, I'd put Grandpa Walt's money to use, along with my marketing degree and the same enthusiasm I'd had for playing football, to pivot toward opening my own business. Like Walt.

"I got the permits for the new place," I said once we started eating, and Tabby nodded.

The idea for the wine bar and bistro had come from her. Of course.

She'd mentioned she would like a place to drink a nice glass of wine and eat a good dinner in a quiet atmosphere. Basically, the opposite of Walt's, which was more of a corner neighborhood bar, and not exactly highbrow.

Not quite Tabby's "scene."

"Tell me about your dad," I said, and she froze with her fork halfway to her mouth.

"Why? What do you want to know?"

I shrugged. "I know you were close to him and he's the one who taught you karate, but besides that… Was it like a Mr. Miyagi situation?"

She fought a smile. "No. We didn't wax on and wax off, and he didn't teach me. We learned it together."

I gestured to her with my pizza crust. "Was it always just you two?"

She carefully chewed and swallowed her food, staring off into the distance over my shoulder. "Yeah. I never knew my mother. My dad was in the navy, and from the little he told me, he wasn't with my mom very long before she got pregnant. They married, had me, and I guess they tried to make it work, but she left before I was a year old. My dad once told me he thought she was suffering from postpartum depression, although he wouldn't have known because she was on the base with me while he was out on the ship. He came home, and she was gone the next day."

"Oh man, I'm sorry."

She lifted her shoulder, outwardly not too put out about it as she scooped more food into her mouth. "I never had a chance to miss her, so it never really bothered me until I was older. Until I would've rather talked with my mom about stuff than my dad."

"Makes sense," I said. "Did you keep living on base?"

She wiped her mouth and took a sip from her personalized water bottle, which satisfied me immensely. "Yeah. He asked for a transfer to Norfolk. I was just a baby, so the base was really all I knew growing up. My dad took a job working in logistics, making sure the ships had all their supplies loaded properly before deployments. It meant long hours, but we lived in military housing. I was never far from him and sort of raised by everyone there. So, I don't know. In that respect, I guess I was lucky. I had a lot of people around who loved me."

I pictured Tabby running around among all the men in uniform, all of them treating her like their own daughter. I guessed that was why she was so regimented. It was literally in her blood. "Where did the karate come in?"

She smiled wistfully. "Dad started taking me to martial arts classes when I was six. Said it was important I learn self-defense, but I think he wanted something for us to bond over. By the time I was ten, my dad and I practiced side by side every night."

"How'd you end up here?"

That was when her smile faded. "Uh, my dad met somebody, he retired, and moved us here."

I inclined my head. "And…?"

"And that's all you're getting out of me today."

I accepted her boundary with a nod and offered her something of myself. "I'd always had a crush on my dad's secretary. She was super hot and the first real-life girl to give me a boner."

Tabby huffed, shaking her head at me like I was a bad puppy.

"She'd always be like, 'Hey, handsome,' and run her hand over my head and neck. Literally sent chills down my spine."

Tabby's eyes narrowed, and I smiled. Because I was positive it was jealousy. Even over this story about me as a horndog kid.

"And then my dad married her."

Her eyebrows rose into severe arches. "So you had wet dreams about your stepmom?"

"Basically," I admitted, earning an amused snort. "Makes family dinners real awkward."

"But you talk to your mom a lot," she noted, accidentally giving herself away. She knew more about me than she probably wanted to concede.

"Yeah, but only because I don't really know how to say no to her. My sister used her job as an excuse to avoid everybody, but I don't have that same willpower. I mean… It's my mom."

Tabby studied me, her head ticked to the side. "You're a mama's boy, huh?"

"I wouldn't say no to her wanting to take care of me. She can be a little overbearing, but…" I shrugged.

"So, that's where you get it from."

"Get what from?"

"You being so overbearing."

"I'm not overbearing. I'm…protective."

"You're more than protective. You're—" She wagged her fork at me, a bit of chicken on it, so I caught her wrist and shoved the bite into my mouth. "Hey!"

It was a perfect bite, of chicken, cheese, and sauce, and as I swallowed it down, I took the fork from her to scoop up another perfect bite. Holding it out to her, I said, "I might be overprotective and occasionally overbearing, but I don't know how else to be. I'm not close to very many people."

"You have a lot of friends."

I moved the food up to her mouth, urging her to take the bite. She closed her lips around the tines, her fingers on my wrist, as she ate it. I watched her lips purse, her throat swallow, and her tongue glide along the corner of her mouth to lick away the dot of sauce there, stealing away my opportunity to do it.

"I have a lot of friends, but not a lot of people I trust," I explained. "I only really care about a handful of people, and I would do whatever I had to if they were hurting or needed something. Because when they hurt, I hurt. When they're happy, I'm happy."

She didn't need me to tell her she was one of those people. She had to know it already. She had to feel it. Because she offered me a slight nod, her eyes going watery again.

So, I went for it. "I want you to move in with me."

But her answer was immediate. "No."

"Why not?"

"Because."

"Not a reason."

She flapped her hand around, appearing to struggle to name one. "Because you don't need to fix this for me. This is my life, and I'm not going to intrude on yours when I know you don't even want kids."

I stopped her there. "Things change. Wants change. People change."

"So, how do you know what I want? How do I know what you want?"

I set my elbows on the table, heaving a sigh. This was bull-shit. Because she knew. *I* knew *she* knew everything. She just didn't want to admit it. She didn't want to trust me.

"Besides," she went on, "my life has nothing to do with yours."

And, yep. She wanted to poke the bear? She'd get the bear.

"Please, Tabitha. We've known each other for a decade. I knew you before you were even able to buy a drink legally. I hired you when you still had light brown hair and sad eyes. I watched you level a frat guy when he got handsy with a girl and then go right back to slinging beers without breaking a sweat, and I promoted you to my manager the next day. I know you study on your breaks for a degree you've been working on for years. I know what you look like when you don't want to talk about something you love, and I let it go because I know you'll eventually tell me one day, and I know that you've been dealing with this life-changing thing for months on your own. *And* I think it's about goddamn time you start accepting some help from people because your life has everything to do with me, you understand? I don't want to see you hurt or, god forbid, some-thing worse happen. I wouldn't be anywhere without you, so don't give me any of your bullshit. Now, please say yes to me with a smile on your face before I lose it."

She sat across from me, no smile to be found. "I'd say you already lost it."

Yeah. Yeah, I had.

I'd lost my head, my heart, my whole fucking cool for this girl.

And clearly, I'd have to call in backup, but for now, I texted my friends an update.

Went to the ultrasound today.

Saw the baby.

I'm going to convince her to move in with me.

I don't want to hear any of your I told you so bullshit.

TEN
TABBY

t had been one week since Nate had come to my rescue for the ultrasound appointment and completely ambushed me with his demand that I move in with him. One week of him hovering over me until I finally snapped at him, yelling at him, "I'm pregnant, not an invalid!" One week of waking up to texts from him, ranging from the standard "good morning" to random, ridiculous ideas, like a picture of a T-shirt he wanted to buy me that read "Pregosaurus" or the matching frog Halloween costumes for Frogger and me. When I reminded him that October was more than six months away, he sent another photo of a family dressed as breakfast foods. Couldn't help but notice, it was a family with a man, woman, and couple of children included.

Subtlety? Never heard of it.

And whenever he tried to bring up the topic of my moving in with him, I usually used the "gotta pee" excuse. Pregnancy was handy like that sometimes.

But I knew I had to come to a decision soon. Especially since Ming-Yue had informed me last night that she had someone interested in moving in. "No rush, though," she'd said, staring at my baby bump like it was contagious.

The future loomed ahead, a huge unknown I didn't know how to prepare for. *If* I was even really prepared and capable of raising a child alone. Yes, I had Nate's support, but he had made it clear for years that kids were not in his life plan. What if I moved in, and he suddenly realized this was all too much?

Not to mention the fear of how moving in to his house would change everything. I would have nowhere to run or hide, and I'd have to face this *thing* that had always been between us. The thing that had started ten years ago with a handshake and had steadily grown, with patience and understanding on his part and my desire to be in his orbit.

Sometimes it felt like déjà vu. When I'd catch him looking at me or when he'd offer a light pat to my shoulder or when I'd crack a smile at one of his dumb jokes and he'd pump his fist like he *got me*, it felt like we'd done it all before.

And his plan to *get me* this time involved his sister. Because she had texted me last night to see if I would meet her for manicures and pedicures then lunch. Before I could even answer thanks but no thanks, she replied that her brother was treating us, and he was always one goddamn step ahead.

That was why I found myself perusing the hundreds of nail polishes to choose from while Genevieve tried to decide between two reds that appeared exactly the same to me. "I like how this one sparkles a little more, right?" When I shrugged, she nodded to herself. "What are you getting? I like that glittery one." She pointed to the iridescent one in front of me that was black, green, or purple, depending on the angle. "Reminds me of space."

I turned to her. "That's what I thought too."

She flipped the bottle upside down and read the name. "Stardust."

Well, hell. I guess I had to get it now. Absently touching my necklace, I accepted the bottle back from her as we were escorted back to pedicure chairs next to each other and already filled with bubbly water.

"You didn't have to go to any trouble for me," I told her once we were settled, and she waved a dismissive hand.

"You're growing a tiny human. The least I could do is pamper you a bit. Plus, I wanted to spend some time with you and have a chat."

"Because your brother asked you to?"

"Yes and no. Even if he didn't want me to convince you of all his wonderful qualities, I would've texted you anyway."

"You wanted to hang out?"

She snorted a little laugh. "We are friends, aren't we? I hope you weren't faking it this whole time."

I'd met Genevieve a handful of times in the ten or so years I'd worked at Walt's, but when she'd moved back to West Chester about two years ago, that was when I'd really gotten to know her as she'd bartended with me. Gen was exactly as easygoing and approachable as Nate but without the aggressively pushy attitude, so it was easy to be around her. She was just so *nice* all the time.

I used to be nice. Until life got hard, and then I didn't have the patience for it. To smile and have conversations. I didn't have any fucks left to give. But I gave a fuck about Gen. Gave even more about her brother.

Didn't have enough hands to carry all the fucks I gave about him.

Fuck.

"Sorry. I'm not used to…any of this," I said by way of explanation, hoping I didn't sound like a total loser. It had been a long time since someone had taken care of me the way Nate—and, by extension, his sister—had. I'd been alone for a long time, shutting people out to keep what was left of my heart intact, but being here with Gen was wonderful. And yeah, I guess I could use more of it. "But I'm happy you invited me."

She grinned, and we talked about things like the dance classes she taught and how she'd been getting a funny pain in her hip lately. I told her I did too, but that it was a round ligament pain from Frogger growing. That had her very interested and led into some questions about my pregnancy, her chin in her hands as she listened intently to the tidbits of information I offered.

"But you're feeling good?" she asked as we were led out of our pedicure chairs to tables for our manicures.

"Yeah. I'm feeling really good. Aside from the emotional stress, physically, I feel really great."

She eyed me, and I could see her wheels turning at my admission of emotional stress, but she didn't offer me her pitch yet. Instead, she jutted her chin for me to sit and enjoy my manicure, which I did. And when we were both finished, she talked me into taking a selfie with our new nails. "Proof of life," she said, sending it off to Dylan and then to Nate with, "He wants to make sure his money is being well spent."

"And that you're convincing me to move in with him in a timely manner?"

She laughed. "Yeah, that too."

We made our way outside with the intent of grabbing lunch at the Panera at the other end of the strip mall, but I'd only taken two steps when Gen tugged on my arm. "Hey, I actually need to tell you something."

I pivoted and tipped my head up since she had a few inches on me, waiting as she seemed to gather her words. "No one knows besides Dylan, but I'm pregnant."

I stared at her with my mouth slightly agape. "You...*what*? Really?"

"Yeah." Her giggle sounded relieved, her smile practically radiant. "It was a complete surprise. Well, not a surprise *surprise*," she said in a stage whisper I assumed was because those two were doing it like rabbits. At least, that's what Nate always made it sound like. I thought they were merely two people very much in love.

"When did you find out?"

"I took a test two weeks ago, so I'm only about eight weeks

along now, but I'm excited and kinda feeling like I could jump out of my skin."

I understood that feeling. "You didn't even tell Nate yet?"

She shook her head. "We wanted to keep it to ourselves until the second trimester, but since you're…" She motioned to my stomach then to her own. "I thought we could, like, go through this all together. You know? I don't have any pregnant friends, and I don't want you to feel like you can't talk to anyone and—"

I stopped her rambling with a hug, throwing my arms around her without thinking. "Yeah," I breathed, nose stinging with the unrealized longing to have people around me. She was offering me what I'd always wanted; I only had to be brave enough to accept this new family. "Yeah, I want that. You and me going through it together."

She laughed, all watery, and so did I. When we broke apart, we held hands, smiling through elated tears.

"Frogger is making me so emotional," I said, wiping my cheeks.

Gen pulled tissues from her purse, handing one to me and using the other one herself. "Frogger. That's adorable."

"Your brother."

She nodded, needing no further explanation. Once we pulled ourselves together, we walked to Panera, ordered our meals, and found a table by the window.

Gen picked at her salad. "Okay. So. Ready to hear it now?"

I swallowed down a spoonful of the French onion soup, pulling on a string of melted cheese. "Sure."

"I know you know Nate in ways I never could. You probably know things about him that I wouldn't *want* to know. I also don't think you really need any convincing about moving in with him because, like I told Nate a long time ago, he's *right there*. And I feel like you already knew but have been waiting for him to catch up."

"I don't know what you're talking about." I shook my head,

but I couldn't pretend. According to her wry smile, she didn't buy it either.

"You two complement each other. You're both smart, driven, and stubborn, but you also even each other out." She waved her fork around with a cucumber stuck on the tines. "He's all outward emotion and brash acts, while you're more thoughtful and… I wouldn't call you gentle—" I snickered at that "—but maybe tender…in a way you don't let many people see."

I hated that she was right and stuffed a piece of bread in my mouth to keep from telling her I didn't appreciate being read this way.

She ate her bite of food and sipped on her water. "Nate's mostly a big golden retriever, but when it comes to the people he loves, he turns into a Doberman pretty quick. Right?"

"Yeah." And I didn't need to ask who she meant by "people he loves." The implications there, about me and this baby, were clear.

"I know he's been an overbearing dick," Genevieve went on. "But when Nate chooses someone, that's it. They're his for life. They're his family, and I'm sorry to say he's chosen you."

My first instinct was to admire the man for how big and loud he loved. My second was to feel unworthy. How could anyone be deserving of such a gift? His unwavering support, his endless generosity, but mostly, his all-encompassing love.

It was too easy to feel like it was too much, too fast, too big, too soon, too everything.

I'd survived so long on barely enough. It was incredible to imagine that I could have everything. I could be a glutton. With Nate basically hand-feeding me.

"Did he ever tell you about our parents' divorce?" Gen asked, pulling me from my daydream of giving in. Of saying yes.

"Not much. Only that he was fourteen and it was rough."

"I really struggled, but he…" She winced. "He was crushed. I don't want to speak for him, but I know he always wanted a closer relationship with our dad. I guess he saw how other boys were with their dads, and he wanted the same thing. Then when our parents split, there was no chance for that to happen, and it all sort of unraveled from there. You don't need a psych degree to see the connection. He'd always said he didn't want to be a dad because he didn't know how to be one. He didn't know how to fix his relationship with our dad, so how could he have a relationship with his own kid?"

She met my eyes, tucking her hair behind her ears, smiling a secretive smile that made me feel like we had our own sorority. One with only two members who understood the inner workings of Nate Kozlowski. "But you and I both know he just needed the opportunity to show up. The chance to step up and be the guy he'd always wanted growing up. Be the man who loves with all his heart. And he's got so much to give, it's like he doesn't know what to do with it all. Maybe it would calm him down a bit." She laughed at herself. "Besides, don't you think *you* deserve it? To be loved like that?"

I blinked and blinked some more, swallowing down the lump in my throat, placing my hand on the fluttering in my belly. *Yeah, Frogger. I get it. We're talking about your favorite person.*

"Honestly." I sniffed. "I've never cried more in my life than with this pregnancy."

"That's all right. I'm sure Nate's already bought the economy-size tissues from Costco."

I had a feeling tissues were the least of his purchases, and accepting that fact felt both thrilling and terrifying. To know he would give everything he had to Frogger and me.

But if we committed to this, everything would change. The careful boundaries we'd maintained for years would crumble. There would be no going back, no more hiding from the complicated thing that had lingered beneath the surface.

Was I ready for that? Was I ready to let him all the way in after keeping everyone else out for so long? I didn't know, but before I could slip too far down the rabbit hole of anxiety, Gen distracted me with a picture Dylan had sent her of him and his kids. In it, he scowled while his kids played with what seemed to be Easter egg dye all over the table.

"He doesn't look happy."

Gen flipped her phone back to stare all gooey-eyed at it. "He's got no patience for that kind of stuff. I told them to wait until I got home, but he's a total sucker for them. Can never say no."

I huffed, recalling what I knew of Nate's friends. All of them dads, and all of them useless under the control of toothy smiles and a few pleading words. Nate wasn't much better.

And his sister plucked the words straight from my mind. "You better get ready. Because Nate will be the worst of all."

I didn't know if I could ever be truly ready, but I was willing to be open to all the possibilities and ridiculous Halloween costumes it would bring. I found my phone to type out a message.

> You think you can borrow someone's truck?

NATE

> Yeah. What do you need?

> To move some boxes.

Instead of a text back, my phone buzzed in my hand. Genevieve lifted her attention to me as I held it at my ear, Nate's voice loud enough that even she could hear. "You could have held out longer, you know. Evie was only level two."

"How many levels did you have planned out?"

"Five."

I bit the insides of my cheeks, fearing they might crack if I gave in to the threatening grin.

"So, I'll see you tonight?" he asked, and I didn't think twice about my answer.

"Yes."

ELEVEN
TABBY

Between making arrangements for Ming-Yue's new roommate, finding time to borrow a truck from Brooke, Jude's girlfriend, and packing up all of my belongings —though I traveled awfully light—it had taken a few days to get everything sorted. But here I was, in Nate's house.

A part of me still couldn't quite believe I'd agreed to live with him. That I'd willingly disrupted the relatively stable life I'd built for myself these past few years. But his persistence had worn me down, and if I was honest with myself, some deeper part of me craved that connection, that sense of belonging.

I didn't want to be alone anymore.

Especially when my other option insisted on making me dinner while his dog, Lucy, sat at my feet, begging for attention. When I had shown up at the door, she'd peed all over the floor. Of course, I'd known about the wiener dog's anxiety issues, had heard the horror stories of how she'd chewed clear through a chair during a thunderstorm, and had already met her multiple times, but I hadn't expected pee-level excitement.

"You have to get used to me," I whispered to her, still inspecting the surroundings of my new abode, a brick town-house built in 1890 on a corner lot with a small, fenced-in backyard and beautifully updated interior. Located downtown, it wasn't too far from Walt's but closer to Nate's new bar location, which he had yet to offer much information about.

The first thing Nate had told me when I walked inside was, "Heating works, and there's no mice. Sit down and put your feet up. Drink some water."

He and Jude had moved all my possessions inside and upstairs in two trips with the truck, while all I had to do was drive my RAV4 over with a few bags of my personal items. Now, I lounged on the couch like some princess waiting to be served.

"Come on, Luce. Let's see what he's doing." The dachshund followed me, her nails click-clacking on the wooden floor from the navy-blue living room, through the pale-green dining room, to the white-and-gray kitchen, wide and open.

Lucy plopped down on the mat in front of her food and water bowls, helping herself to dinner as I made my way over to Nate. He stood with his back to me, something sizzling on the stove, and remained unmoving as I approached, his head bent down. I peered around him, noting his phone in his hand, as he obviously read some kind of pregnancy website. His thumb scrolled over the screen on what appeared to be a tracking chart. My baby was as big as a papaya.

Nate murmured something to himself, and that was when I understood the pomegranate comment from two weeks ago. He'd been tracking Frogger's growth all along.

I breathed out a shocked yet delighted laugh, finally snagging Nate's attention. He jumped. "Tabby cat!" He gasped, hand over his chest. "For fuck's sake. I'm doing it. I'm getting you a bell. I'm not living here with you silently skulking all around like some kinda ghost." He swiped his hand down his face. "Holy Jesus. I can't—are you crying?"

"No."

He set his phone down to cup my jaw, swiping his thumb over my cheek. "Must be imagining this tear, then."

I nodded and picked his cell up from the counter. "What were you reading?"

"Nothing." After a few moments of my staring at him, he gave in with a sigh. "Did you know there is differing information about how to compare fetus sizes? Some apps and websites will give you food comparisons, some will give you item comparisons. I personally prefer the fruit analogies. Easier to understand than saying, like, a cassette tape. Because, first of all, who still uses cassette tapes? And, second, I'd rather imagine my baby as a coconut. You know what I mean?"

I did and I didn't, too overwhelmed by that *my baby* comment to comprehend his endearing babbling. Instead, I threw my arms around his neck and kissed him.

I kissed him for taking a chance on me when I'd most needed it years ago, for bugging the shit out of me until he made me laugh, and for understanding me when it sometimes felt like no one else did.

I kissed him because I needed to find out if his lips were as supple as his smile made them out to be and to learn what his hair felt like when I combed my fingers through it.

I kissed him like I'd wanted to for a long damn time.

He froze, stunned at my sudden attack, and pulled back, his hands on my waist, eyes flying back and forth between mine, mouth open and breathing hard. He quirked his brow. "Tab?"

"I needed to know."

His gaze filled with so much tenderness my chest ached, even as he backed me up against the refrigerator. "Well, now you know."

Then his lips were on mine again, all his surprise replaced by confident strokes of his tongue, searching for mine, and advancing touches of his hands, up my sides to my face and hair, holding me in place. As impulsive as my first kiss was, his responding one felt calculated. He touched me like he'd done it before, gripping my hair by the scalp, using it to angle my head, and licked into my mouth like he'd been imagining it. Many times.

Maybe as many times as I had.

I curled my hands into fists, gripping his T-shirt at his chest, as if I could keep him here, with me, all the time. But I knew he wasn't going anywhere. If the past few weeks weren't evidence enough, the steel pipe in his jeans grinding against my hip certainly was.

And like Gen had told me, didn't I deserve this?

Yes.

Yes, I fucking did.

I pushed my hips out, giving in to the need to relieve the pressure building between my legs, and covered his hand with mine, guiding it from my neck to my chest, groaning in relief as he gripped my breast, my nipples contracting almost painfully inside my bra. With my energy up and my sex drive at what felt like an all-time high, I'd recently taken to masturbating every morning. I'd been too busy to do it today, and my body practically screamed for an orgasm now.

I grasped at his shoulders, urging him on, lifting my leg to his waist, but he stopped me, holding me at arm's length, a half smile on his face. "Gimme a sec."

He flipped around to shut off the burner and pointed a stern finger at the dog. "Luce, cover your eyes." Then he faced me again, serious. "Here or on the couch or—"

"Here. Now. I can't stand it." My heartbeat pounded in my ears and between my thighs. "I need to come. Now."

He stood there grinning like an idiot, his gaze lazily roving over me as if he had all the time in the world, while I was here sweating and panting and losing my goddamn mind.

I gripped the hem of his shirt and yanked, glowering up at him. "Be a good boy and give me an orgasm before I tear apart your gorgeous kitchen."

"*Our* gorgeous kitchen," he corrected, curling his fingers over the waistband of my leggings. He pulled them down just enough to slip his hand inside my underwear, his other hand up my shirt, teeth tugging at my earlobe. "I'll be a good boy for you, and when you come, I want to hear you scream my name."

I tilted my head, needing his lips on mine, releasing my first moan into his mouth as he teased his fingers up and down the seam of my pussy. He moaned right back at the wetness he found there.

Already, I was close, and he'd barely touched me, but that was pregnancy hormones for you.

Finally being allowed to touch Nate didn't help either.

His fingertip circled my clit as he bent, licking at my nipple after he pulled the cup of my bra down. "Shit," he murmured against my skin. "Do you know how long I've had to look at these tits and pretend they didn't do anything for me?"

"About as long as—" I sucked in a breath when he plunged his finger inside me "—as long as I've had to put up with you rubbing my back when I solved some problem for you." I licked my lips. "Or when you'd pat my hip when you passed behind me."

He stopped his ministrations and raised his head to meet my gaze, eyes curious. "I didn't even think about that. Do I do that with other people?"

I shook my head. "I think you might've seen my black belt come out more often if you did that to more people."

"Huh." He went back to teasing the overly sensitive bud of my sex, his eyes narrowed on my lips when I licked them again, my breathing fast, my heart rate spiked. "So, that's what gets you going? Some friendly pats on the back?"

I rolled my hips, letting my head thump back against the refrigerator. "I liked that we were comfortable enough with each other that you could treat me like that. It was second nature. And I liked feeling special. You treated me special."

"Mm-hmm." He kissed me again. "Because you are special. I've always known it." He twisted my nipple between his fingers as he rubbed my clit, and I was so close, shaking in his hold. "Yeah," he murmured. "Yeah, I feel it. You wanna come?"

"Yes. Fuck, yes. Make me come."

"You know what to do."

I did. I knew what to do to make this thing between us real.

I stared at him, my eyes on his, unblinking even as I fought to keep them steady. "*Nate.* I need you to make me come."

He smiled into a kiss then he curled his fingers into me, finding that swollen spot inside me. With only a few strokes, I careened headfirst into an orgasm. The first one in months that I hadn't given myself.

"God, that feels good," I mumbled, arching my back as he licked down my throat, scratched his beard along my collarbone, and scraped his teeth on my nipple. "*Ooh*, Nate, yes."

"Want another?"

I wouldn't mind another, but not at the moment. "I'm hungry," I told him. "And tired of standing here with shaking legs."

He chuckled and straightened up, dragging his wet fingers out of my underwear. Then he righted my clothes, careful not to smear my slickness on anything as he did it. "Go sit," he instructed, turning toward the sink to wash his hands. "I made rice and veggie stir-fry. Are you still no meat?"

"I don't know. Somebody walked by me with a cheeseburger at school the other day, and it smelled really good to me."

He nodded as he dried his hands. "We can try tomorrow."

"You going to cook for me again?"

"Every day," he said, plating up the food to set it in front of me along with another personalized water bottle, this one clear with purple writing on it. *Drink water and mind your business.* He added some slices of fresh lemons and limes to it because this man paid attention.

Once he sat down, I asked him about the new bar. He told me he'd spoken with Liam's brother, Collin, a chef who seemed interested in Nate's plans. They'd made arrangements for him to visit for a few days, which seemed really positive. He also asked about school and my group project, which was going terrible. Surprise, surprise. But I was concerned about more important matters.

"We have to talk," I said, and he nodded, pulling his phone out of his pocket.

"Good. Because I have a list."

I bit back a smile. "I love a good list."

"I know you do. I have a list of things the baby needs and—"

I coiled my fingers around his wrist, jerking on it so I could view his screen. "You have a list of things for the baby?"

He furrowed his brow at me like *yeah, obviously.*

While that made me so happy my heart danced beneath my ribs, other discussions had to come first. "We need to talk about *us.*"

He set his phone down, and with his full attention on me, those soft blue eyes taking in every inch of my face as he patiently waited, I almost didn't want to ruin the moment. In case the other shoe dropped. Like it always did.

I forced my question out. "With me here, what does that mean for us?"

"I don't understand."

"Are we…? Dating? Together? Still boss and employee?"

He shrugged, totally unfazed. "Well, you won't be my employee much longer, so I don't think you have to worry about that. Plus, I am human resources, and if you have any complaints about your boss, you can direct them to me."

I rolled my eyes.

"Besides, do you really want to be working at Walt's that much longer? You can't tell me you like being on your feet all those hours."

"People have done more under worse conditions."

"That doesn't mean you have to. If you want to work for the next couple of weeks, fine, but I can already tell how you're slowing down. The further along you get, the harder it'll be."

"I know," I agreed eventually, hating to give up that part of me.

"I get it, though." His hand found my knee under the table. "You're independent and want to have your own money and your own thing. I'm sure it's hard making these decisions, but I want you to know that you have more than one option of working until you're in labor, okay?"

I nodded. If we weren't eating dinner together after I'd spent the day moving all my stuff here, maybe I would be more worried. But I was here, at the kitchen table with Nate, and I didn't *have* to worry. I knew that much.

"Now, as for your question about us." He slid his hand up to my stomach, to the spot Frogger liked to kick. They weren't currently moving right now, so Nate smoothed his palm to my hip bone, his fingertips dipping under the elastic band of my leggings. "I want to be with you. Not for fun and not for a certain period of time or until the baby comes. I'm committed to you, to *us*, and I'm sorry it's taken me so long to tell you. To *see* you."

"It's not like I did anything about it either."

"No. I should've…" He closed his eyes for a moment, jamming his thumb and index finger into them as if attempting to rid himself of a memory. "He'd come into the bar or I'd see you texting him, and I'd… I'd go out and find the closest woman to take my mind off of it. Of you with him."

"Yeah." I winced. "I remember when you'd started dating Denise. She came to the bar and…"

"Jesus," he groaned, tossing his hands in the air. "She even looked like you! And I convinced myself that I wanted her, that I loved her. I was just so fucking desperate." He reluctantly slanted his gaze to me. "I'm such an asshole."

"So am I."

"No, you aren't." He booped my nose. "You're perfect."

I thought back to Denise, the woman he'd dated for a few months about two years ago, when Nate had inadvertently become the other man since he hadn't found out until the end that she was married. "I can't believe you were so obsessed with her."

He grimaced. "I know. But it should make you feel better that you drove me to her. Like some Shakespearean tragedy."

"What would the name of that one be?"

He shrugged. "Ye olde pub and cuckold. I don't know."

I giggled, and his eyes lit up. "I love when you laugh."

"You're the only one who makes me laugh."

He leaned in, slipping his hand around my neck. "You better get used to it. I got a lot more where that comes from." He kissed my forehead before standing to clear the table. "What do you want to do?"

"I'm kinda tired, actually."

"We could watch one of your shows," he offered. One of my shows, meaning the science docuseries I enjoyed.

With my water bottle in hand, I waited until he finished loading the dishwasher to run it, admiring how the man cleaned up after himself. Honestly, how didn't we see it? How well matched we were.

I'd been to his house before, for a handful of parties he'd thrown. I'd known he'd done a lot of the renovation work himself, with some help from the guitarist of the Anchormen, the band that played monthly at Walt's. I'd been informed of the new AC and heat pump he had installed last summer, which he'd been awfully proud to get a good price on. "Those negotiation skills," he'd said with an eyebrow waggle.

The house was colorful yet understated. The rooms displayed no stereotypical bachelor décor, and he'd clearly put some thought into the personal items he'd set out. A few pictures hung on the walls of him and his friends, his sister, one of him and Lucy at a campsite. This man had a full life, and he'd invited me into it.

Now, he was inviting me upstairs, where I'd never been. He held my hand as Lucy plodded up ahead of us. "I didn't know where to put your stuff because I didn't want to be presumptu-ous." We stood at the top of the steps, the boxes stacked along the hall. He pointed to the different rooms. "I finished the attic upstairs, which you could use as an office or something. I've been using it as a catchall. There's a bathroom, bedroom, smaller bedroom—" he caught my eye "—that might make a good nurs-ery. And here's the primary. I took down a wall, so it's got an en-suite bathroom now. You have your pick of places to sleep. Up to you."

I didn't hesitate, squeezing his hand. "With you. I want to sleep with you in your bed."

He grinned, eyes shining. "*Our* bed."

"Our bed," I agreed, and I helped myself to running in and jumping on the mattress. Nate followed immediately, leaping on top of me, his head near my belly.

"Hear that, Frogger? You're sleeping with me."

TWELVE
NATE

Tabby and I had been living together for three days. Three glorious days.

And yeah, they'd all been right, Evie and my friends. I was competitive and hated losing, but in this instance, let 'em have it. Because nothing had been easier in my life than settling in with her at my side.

After that first night, when we'd snuggled together watching a show about how the human brain works…or something—I hadn't paid all that much attention—we'd woken up our first morning together, facing each other, our hands almost touching on the mattress. I'd blinked awake a moment before her eyelids had fluttered open, her dark eyes widening ever so slightly in surprise and then going soft when she'd remembered.

Remembered where she was.

Remembered she was with me.

I'd kissed her softly, stroked my hand along her stomach, then tucked the blankets back up under her chin so she could go back to sleep while I went to the gym.

I was up early every morning, no matter how late I'd worked the night before. I had to get my workout in early or else I'd never get it done. Plus, activity in the morning got blood flowing to my brain so I could function better. Which was good because I'd been moving double time the last few weeks between Walt's and putting my plans in motion for the bistro. And since Tabby had moved in with me, I'd taken her off closing shifts. It had been an argument, but I eventually convinced her I needed to get Bran, her replacement, comfortable with everything. She'd bitched and moaned at me about not letting her train him, but I won that one too because Bran was going to be *my* manager, not hers.

This morning, I stopped at the grocery store on my way home from CrossFit to buy a few things to make my apology breakfast and a small plant. Tab never struck me as a flower type of girl, but when I spotted the cute little squirrel pot with the tiny succulent in it, I grabbed that too. I parked behind the house and let myself in the back door, where Lucy waited. Although she'd been cool about Tabby moving in, she was still attached to my hip, and anytime I left the house, she lingered by the door for my return. At first, it was adorable. Now, it was annoying as shit. Especially when she got overanxious and tore something up.

"Luce, come on. Tab is upstairs. You should be up there with her," I told my dog, who danced around my feet. I wiggled my foot to get her off. "Come on. Stop. Go lie down." I nudged her away with my toe. "Go."

After a minute of pawing at me, she lay back down, and I put the groceries away except for what I needed to make the pancakes. With the batter cooking in the pan, I tossed in a few blueberries. I also liked to add some sliced almonds to mine, but nuts were the one food I didn't know if Tabby could eat or not. I scooted upstairs in my socked feet and opened the door to the bedroom, assuming I'd have to wake her up to ask if she liked or could even eat almonds.

But she was definitely *not* asleep.

I froze, one hand on the doorjamb, the other hanging limply at my side, totally and completely useless, while I gawked at Tabby—*my Tabby*—getting herself off with her hand.

That was my job!

But could I move from this spot?

No, I absolutely could not, too entranced at how her neck arched, her eyes squeezed tight. Enthralled at the way her feet slipped on the fitted sheet, failing to find purchase. And fucking engrossed in the pretty pink skin of her pussy. She held herself open, the index and middle fingers of her left hand in a V, revealing her clit, her right hand moving, fingers working in tight circles.

Fuck, it was the hottest thing I'd ever seen in my life.

I was so hard, wanted my fingers there, my face, my cock, but I didn't want to move one goddamn inch either. I couldn't ruin this beautiful sight in front of me. I was bewitched.

If I wasn't before, I certainly was now.

She was mostly naked, her underwear thrown on the floor, and her skin flushed, spreading from her throat down to her chest. But she still wore a tank top, so I didn't get even a glimpse of her tits. A shame. Because they were the prettiest ones I'd ever seen. Full with big nipples, like a bull's-eye she hadn't let me suck on nearly long enough in the kitchen. We'd still been getting used to each other these last few days, and I didn't want to make any plays for her physically. Didn't want to rush her.

But now? Fuck that.

I absently stroked my dick over my athletic shorts, breathing hard, though not as hard as she was. She moaned a quiet "Yes," although I wanted to be the one drawing out those sounds.

Heat crawled up my spine the longer I stood here. Witnessing how close she was to orgasming, I felt my own skin break out in goose bumps, and I reflexively leaned closer to her, waiting so fucking patiently.

I'd never been more patient as I watched my girl touch and touch and touch herself, until *finally*.

I exhaled harshly and took one step forward.

Floorboards creaked, and she whipped her head up from the

pillow, her eyes huge, her mouth open in an embarrassed yet silent "oh."

I glowered at her, my fingers twitching at my sides. "What the fuck do you think you're doing?"

She squirmed, jerking her legs together, her knees meeting with an audible smack. "I… I was… You…"

I stalked closer to the bed, taking in every inch of her body, from the sparkly black nail polish on her toes to the birthmark on her upper thigh, to the star necklace she never took off, to her plump lower lip. "How dare you touch what's mine."

She shook her head, eyebrows furrowed. "You can't—"

"You need to get off, you tell me," I snapped, shooting my hand out to grab her wrist. She gasped, her pupils blown wide as I brought her still-wet fingers to my mouth and tasted her for the first time.

Tangy like an IPA on a sweltering summer day. Sweet like my favorite memory. Like déjà vu. "Fuck, you taste good." I even licked the webbing between her fingers, and when she was good and clean, I tugged on her hand, towing her upright, enjoying the sleepy yet stunned expression on her face. "You do this all the time?"

She nodded slowly, and I tsked. "Why?"

She shrugged, her voice still rough with sleep when she said, "Hormones are high when I wake up."

"From now on, I'm going to take care of that first thing." I wrapped my fingers around the hem of her tank top, silently directing her arms up with a jut of my chin. When she raised them, I pulled it up and off her. "I was going to make us breakfast, but apparently I get to eat first."

"What are you—"

I flopped on the bed, not caring that my T-shirt was still damp with sweat, and pulled her toward me. "Come on up here." When she understood what I meant, her grin grew positively evil. "Yeah, you like that, huh?"

She carefully crawled up my chest, her gloriously naked

body settling over me, her knees on either side of my head. I wrapped my arms around her thighs and inhaled deeply, her scent burrowing so deeply in my brain, it would be the last thing I thought of as I took my final breath. I skated my palms over the bottom of her round belly and stared up at her, watching her breasts sway with each of her breaths. "God, you're gorgeous."

"You're only saying that because I could choke you out right now."

I closed my eyes. "Lord, if it's your will, so be it."

She sniffed a laugh, and I opened my eyes, grinning for a moment, enjoying the lightness in her features, the looseness of her smile. And maybe I liked this morning version of her the best, before she put on her armor to face the day. Here, she was soft and relaxed, and I was grateful to have this part of her. Although, I was really fucking fond of the sharp-tongued evil queen side of her too.

"Hold on to the headboard," I instructed, then gripped two handfuls of her ass, pushing her forward and down, onto my mouth. I wasted no time, spearing my tongue into her, lapping up every bit of my new favorite breakfast treat. She cried out, her hands slapping against the headboard, head thrown back, and it wouldn't take long for her to explode with the way she rode my face.

I barely had to do anything, simply allow her to grind on me, suck at her clit, and enjoy the show. The bouncing of her tits, her keening pleas, and, best of all, the wet rush of her orgasm when she finally came, muttering my name and calling out to God over and over. That was cool. I liked thinking of myself as a god.

She swiped her hands over her forehead and hair, rolling her hips one last time against my mouth before bending to put her hands on the mattress, pushing herself up and off me. I licked my lips, making sure I didn't miss one last—

"Is something burning?" Tabby tilted her head, nose in the air.

"Oh fuck!" I carefully nudged her aside and sprinted out of

the bedroom, down to the kitchen to shut off the stove. I flung open the back door and all the windows to get rid of the smoke, hoping the fire alarm wouldn't go off. Lucy would literally shit all over the place.

"Everything okay?" Tabby called.

"Yeah!"

"I'm getting dressed. I'll be down in a minute."

I grumbled a few curses and tossed the burned rubber pancake into the trash. I shook my head, annoyed with myself for being so careless, and waved my hands a few times, not really helping the smoke situation but needing to do *something* anyway.

This was my fault. I hadn't turned off the stove because I'd only meant to be upstairs a minute, tops. But then I got distracted and…

Tabby's hands skated up my back, her chin against my spine. "You made breakfast?"

"I was making you pancakes, but I walked in on you and forgot where I was."

She kissed my shoulder blade. "It's okay."

"It's not." I turned, folding my arms around her. "I could've burned the house down. I could've—"

"But you didn't. And I hate to tell you, but I'm not a great cook. I burn stuff all the time, so you better get used to it."

I knew she was trying to make me feel better, but in that moment, thinking about the what-ifs of how I could have possibly hurt her or the baby clouded my brain.

"Hey." She dug her index finger into my pec. "I'm fine. Frogger's fine. No big deal."

After a few moments, I curled my hands around her jaw. "Yeah. Sorry. Minor meltdown."

"Down, boy," she teased, offering me a flirtatious smile, and I took in her pink cheeks and bright eyes. Orgasms did her body good. Like a shot of vitamins.

I grinned, taking credit even if she didn't offer it, and kissed her. "I'll cook up another batch. You like almonds?"

"Yeah." She helped herself to digging out plates and utensils for us, along with maple syrup and some OJ. A few minutes later, I had our breakfast plated up, and we took out our cell phones, checking our combined schedules.

As far as I was concerned, a synced Google calendar was as good as an engagement ring. We were practically married.

"You're meeting with contractors today?" she asked, testing my sanity once again when she licked a dot of syrup off her fork.

"Yeah. With Collin coming, I want to show him some tentative plans."

"You really think he's in? Because didn't I hear you talking to Liam about how he travels a lot?"

"Yeah, but he's apparently tired of that life, and he likes the idea of going in on ownership with me, so he has some stake in it as opposed to being hired to work under somebody."

She chewed, her eyes taking on that same sort of faraway glassiness whenever she was in thought. Eventually, she tipped her chin up to me. "If you like him, I'm excited to meet him."

Then, to my utter despair, she dragged the tip of her index finger along the rim of her plate, collecting more of the maple syrup, and sticking it in her mouth. If my burned pancake hadn't so rudely interrupted us, I wouldn't have the problem currently camped out in my shorts right now.

Tabby, completely unaware of how she had my heart and cock wrapped around her little finger, drank down her orange juice and then stood, taking our plates to the sink, where she rinsed them off before sliding them into the dishwasher. She even stacked the plates the right way.

I mean, honestly. Was there anything this girl didn't do perfectly?

"I'm heading out early to meet with my group before the presentation," she said, making her way back over to me.

"Good luck," I told her, tugging her down for a kiss.

"We'll need it." Pivoting away from me, she wrapped herself up in her coat and looped her bag over her shoulder. With a pet to Lucy's head, she plucked her keys from the basket and waved goodbye to me.

"Hey."

She stopped, glancing over her shoulder, brow arched in question.

"I'll see you later at work."

She nodded and smiled before heading to the door.

And *that* was what she didn't do perfectly.

That smile she tossed my way. The guarded one that barely tilted the right side of her mouth. The one that let me know she still wasn't all in.

Sure, I knew she had feelings for me. I couldn't deny that. She had placed her trust in me years ago, but especially these last few months. It hadn't been easy on her to come to rely on me, yet a piece of her still waited.

I didn't know what exactly she was waiting for, but she hadn't closed the door all the way. As if she needed a quick getaway. Just in case.

THIRTEEN
TABBY

By the time I pulled into Walt's parking lot, I was fuming, having had enough time to properly stew. The group project went terrible. Even though Kevin had completed his portion, when it came time for him to explain his portion of the slide deck, it was as if he'd never seen them before, so I could only assume he'd found someone else to do his work. And Maureen. Poor Maureen. After working with her these last few weeks, I found it obvious she had some kind of anxiety disorder. In-person classes were probably not the best option available for her, to say nothing of being required to give an oral presentation to a classroom of about thirty-five people. The girl couldn't make it through one paragraph.

I ended up taking over for her and pretty much carried both Maureen and Kevin on my back, but I couldn't get us anything past a C. When I spoke to the professor after class, he was understanding of my plea that I deserved a better grade but reiterated that this was a *group* project, and he actually would have given us a lower grade if not for me. So, I had to accept this less-than-stellar grade and swallow it, bringing my average down for the semester.

I wasn't one of those people who argued for every point, but

I was an A student. I wouldn't waste my time or money on taking classes to earn anything less.

So this shit really fucking pissed me off.

I marched into Walt's and slammed my bag on the table in the office, where Nate worked on his computer. "Whoa. Take the evil queen vibes down a notch." When I scowled at him, he held up his hands. "Want to talk about it or just light some shit on fire?"

"You volunteering?"

"To light shit on fire, yes, but not to be the target." He angled his head, hitting me with his endearingly dumb grin.

Then he stood and held out his arms, and I walked into them, burying my nose in his chest. "We got a C-minus."

"You what?"

I lifted my head, leaning away slightly so he could hear me, though I loathed to leave any part of his embrace. "We got a C minus on the project."

He grunted then wove his fingers into my hair, pushing my face back to his pec. I suspected he liked me there as much as I liked being there.

"That sucks. I'm sorry. You worked really hard."

I sighed and turned, my ear against his heartbeat. "Not hard enough to cover for the other two."

"But you're done, right? Officially on spring break?"

I answered through a yawn. "Yeah."

He gripped my shoulders, holding me at arm's length. "You tired? Want to go home?"

"No. I want to work."

He bent down, eyes flicking between mine as if determining exactly how tired I was. "Okay, but if I see you flagging, I'm making you go home."

"Fine," I agreed.

"And I'm putting a stool behind the bar so you can sit while you work."

"Absolutely not." I brushed his hands off, suddenly really

energized. "I am not going to be sitting on a stool to work. No one can serve drinks that way."

"You look—"

I spun around, my finger pointed at him. "I wouldn't finish that statement if I were you."

He kissed the tip of my finger. "Yes, ma'am."

I smirked. "Good boy."

He groaned, closing the little bit of space between us, his hands sliding from my hips to my ass. "I love when you call me that."

"I know."

He gave my backside a good squeeze. "I'll be your good boy all day, as long as you let me eat you out every morning."

"Could be arranged."

With a smacking kiss to my lips, he said, "Remember, done at eight."

I nodded and hung up my coat. I was only scheduled for a few hours a night anymore. I didn't hate it. As much as I'd like to keep working full time, the bigger I became, the harder it was to be on my feet. In a few weeks, I doubted I'd want to be behind the bar at all, but I would cross that bridge when I got there.

As I turned the corner into the kitchen, he stopped me one last time. "I packed you a dinner. It's in the fridge in the kitchen. Leftovers from last night, some fruit, and—"

I attacked him.

Straight-up jumped on him.

"Hey, yo, all right." He chuckled, cupping my ass as I licked and nipped at his throat while he backed up into the office, shutting the door behind us. He set me down only after he locked the door, and I slid my hands up his T-shirt, running my fingers over his abs, the hair on his chest. I'd yet to see the guy naked, and I was suddenly desperate to get the whole picture. His arms were tattooed, but I always wondered if they extended beyond.

"Take your shirt off."

"You take your shirt off," he responded, and I didn't hesitate.

I whipped the thing right over my head. His gaze sizzled, his pupils dilating as his tongue swept over his lower lip.

He tried to reach for me, but I jerked my chin in silent instruction for him to take his shirt off too. As soon as it landed on the floor, I had my hands on him, exploring the hard planes of his torso, from the slight rise of his pecs that were clear of ink to the thick slab of muscle that made up his stomach. I skated my hands up his forearms, his left tattooed with armbands, his right with random geometric patterns. His biceps were covered in more classic designs, roses with thorns, a butterfly, a heart with a sword through it. All of them black. I'd been able to view them before, but seeing them now, with him like this—shirtless with his arms relaxed at his sides while he watched me touch each one—was different.

It was a whole new side of him.

I would need more time to properly learn each and every inch of him, but for now, it was enough to be able to look my fill. He didn't have defined lines like Hollywood celebrities or models on social media, but he was pure muscle with a fair amount of hair on his chest and small, flat nipples. I raked my fingernails over them as I dragged my fingers down his abdomen to his jeans, unbuckling his belt.

"What're you doing?" he rasped, his breath hot and fast.

I shook my head. I didn't know what I was doing, only that I wanted to show him how much I appreciated him. How grateful I was for everything he'd done for me, during the time we've known each other, but especially in the last few months.

I needed him to know that while it was difficult for me to verbally express exactly how much I loved the fact that he'd packed me a dinner, I would show him.

"Tabby," he murmured, reaching for my face, but I evaded his kiss and instead lowered to the floor, staring up at him. "Shit, Tab, your knees. Don't kneel on the floor."

"I'm fine." I popped the button of his jeans to pull down his zipper.

"You—" He cut himself off when I tugged his navy-blue boxer briefs down to reveal his cock, semi-hard. Until I wrapped my hand around it and he went fully erect, the head thick and red. I licked the tip, right over the slit, and he wrenched away. "I don't think we should do this. The baby—"

"Is fine," I told him, leaning forward to trace the length of him with the flat of my tongue, and he exhaled audibly, irritably, almost like he didn't want to agree.

"You have work to do."

"That's funny," I said, my lips brushing his balls. "*Now* you want me to work."

He squeezed his eyes shut for a moment, shaking his head with obvious frustration then flicked his lids open, irises blazing. "Fucking put it in your mouth."

I teased my tongue along the shaft.

"Tabitha." He tunneled his hands in my hair, tugging on my scalp in the way I liked. "Put it in your mouth." He thrust his hips forward, his jaw tense, abs clenched. Barely in control. Tortured. Beautiful.

When he growled my name again, I acquiesced, slipping his length into my mouth, following his directions.

Suck hard.

Use your hand.

Faster.

Normally, I didn't need him telling me what to do. Hated being micromanaged. But here on my knees with his eyes boring into mine, like he was afraid he'd lose me if he blinked, I'd do whatever he told me to.

"I'm close," he said, voice low and ragged. "Fuck, Tabby, I'm so close, but I don't want to come in your mouth. Back up."

When I didn't move fast enough for him, he nudged me back to replace my mouth with his hand. I watched with rapt attention as he worked his fist up and down his cock, already slick with my spit, the fingers of his other hand in my hair, holding me in place. He didn't say anything, merely breathed hard out of parted lips, grunting as he jacked harder, faster, eyes glazing over.

I was fascinated by his sounds. By the way he looked. The fine sheen of sweat on his skin.

Never had I wanted to watch a man come, but I couldn't take my gaze away from him if I tried.

I didn't want to.

After a few moments, ropes of hot liquid spurted out of him, landing in jagged lines across the tops of my breasts and neck. He exhaled harshly, slowing his hand until he emptied himself, smearing the glistening tip over my lips.

It was filthy.

And perfect.

Being covered in him.

With his come still warm on my skin, it occurred to me that this might have been his way of possessing me. To make up for what he hadn't really been able to do.

He left his physical mark on me in the only way he could.

"Why'd you do that?" he asked, not bothering to put his softening cock back in his pants before he helped me to stand.

"Because I owed you from this morning."

He obviously didn't believe me, and when I turned, searching for my T-shirt, he snatched it up before I could. He tried again. "Why did you do that?"

I shrugged. "Pregnancy hormones."

He squinted, mouth tense, clearly unhappy with my lies. He knew the truth, but he wanted to hear it. I got it.

And yet, I couldn't let it out.

I wasn't good with words. Never had been. I needed more time to be able to admit it all out loud.

"I just…" I dragged my hands through my hair a few times then tied it back in a ponytail. "I wanted to make you feel good like you make me feel good."

I suspected he didn't believe that was the truth, but accepted it, nonetheless. He held my T-shirt out to me. "Arms up." I raised them up, expecting him to wipe off my chest, but he didn't. Only tugged my shirt down my arms and settled the hem at my hips, a smug smile plastered on his face. "You're gonna go out there and work your shift with my come on your skin."

He pulled me to him, kissing me soundly, his tongue reminding me of what he'd done to me this morning. I started to move, aiming to circle my arms around his neck, but he stopped me, pivoting me so my back was against his torso and my chest against the door, making a mess of my T-shirt.

He scratched his beard along my temple and down my jaw. "Then tonight, when I get home, I'll clean you off with my tongue."

He didn't let me turn or glance over my shoulder, pressed so close I couldn't budge even a centimeter, a foreboding yet delicious threat. He bent to kiss my throat sweetly then unlocked the door. "Don't forget to eat your dinner. I'm gonna check on you in a little bit."

With a gentle push, I headed out to the floor, where I attempted to put what we'd done in the office out of my mind. It was easy when we were so busy, a few groups of college kids here, as well as the usual happy hour crowd. Spring was in the air, and our sales were proof of that.

Nate did indeed check on me, made sure I drank enough water, and forced me to take a break so I could eat the dinner he'd packed me. Then I worked with Bran, answering any questions he had for me about managing the bar, picking my brain for tips and tricks.

Once eight o'clock rolled around, Nate was waiting in the office with my coat and purse, a knowing smile on his face.

"See you later," I said with a kiss.

"I'll be home around ten. Be ready for me."

"I will," I promised, then headed out. To *our* home.

Where I promptly crawled into bed and fell asleep to David Attenborough narrating a relaxing story about the mating of exotic birds.

FOURTEEN
TABBY

woke up to the smell of bacon and panting breaths in my face, slowly coming to until I jolted upright, barely escaping a lick from Lucy.

"Ugh." I pushed her away. "Your breath is rank."

"She could probably say the same about you."

I blinked a few times and pushed my hair out of the way, meeting Nate's impish grin. He was dressed, his green T-shirt soaked at the collar, smelling of his soap and sweat.

"What time is it?" I asked, as he offered me a plate of bacon, scrambled eggs, and toast with butter.

"Almost nine."

"In the morning?"

"In the morning," he affirmed and pushed a glass of orange juice into my hand.

I remembered what we'd done in his office last night at Walt's, what I'd promised, then how I'd come home, washed my face, brushed my teeth, took off my jeans, and got into bed, intent on watching television until he came home. "I fell asleep."

He nodded. "Sure did."

"You didn't wake me up."

He shook his head. "Sure didn't."

"Why not?"

"Because you're growing a human, and if you're tired, you need to sleep."

"Yeah, but…"

I didn't feel guilty, but I did feel a little let down. We'd been living together, sleeping in the same bed, for almost a week now, and quite frankly, he'd promised me sex. Told me he'd be taking care of it for me, yet here I was with bed head and wild hormones, while he stood there looking all deliciously sweaty after making me breakfast.

As if he understood my thoughts, he pinched my Walt's T-shirt, which I still wore from last night. It didn't feel real nice with the way it was caked to my chest.

He bit back a laugh. "You're such a fucking horndog."

"Me?" I slapped at his shoulder. "You were the one who told me to be ready for you to clean me up."

"So, hurry up and eat your breakfast so I can clean you up." He picked up a piece of bacon and held it out to me. Lucy tried to snatch it, but he caught her and set her on the floor, where she trotted to her bed in the corner. After I bit into the bacon, he did too, basically finishing off the strip. I rolled my eyes as I sipped my OJ.

"How was the rest of the night?" I asked, starting in on the eggs with the fork he handed to me along with a napkin. Like a Boy Scout, the man was always prepared.

He helped himself to some of my juice. "Something's up with the vents. They were blowing cold air."

I frowned. "What's that about?"

"No idea. Might be nothing. I'll have to wait and see if it happens again." He sounded relaxed even though he tugged at his hair, his nervous tell.

"Or it could be an expensive fix?" I guessed, and he sighed.

"Yep."

"And not at a great time," I added, knowing he had plans for the second location already in motion.

He polished off another piece of bacon, and I bit into a triangle of brown toast. "No, but maybe it was a fluke." He motioned for me to keep eating. "Hurry up. I want to shower."

"I can't shove food into my mouth like you can."

He winked. "Right. Only my dick."

"Like you can?" I arched my brow. "Tried sucking yourself off, have you?"

He batted at my mouth with my second piece of toast, mashing it against my lips until I laughed, allowing him to stuff it into my mouth. I leaned back, almost spilling my juice in the process, earning a grunt of displeasure as if this were all *my* fault.

I shook my head, settling back into my spot, my orange juice safe. "You must've been such a little shit as a kid. Always making trouble."

He lay on his side, propping his head up with his hand. "Actually, no. I was a pretty stereotypical firstborn boy. I mean… I'm sure Evie will tell you I was an asshole and pushed her around, but that was my job."

I finished off the rest of the eggs. "A pushy asshole? Yes, that sounds familiar."

He jostled my leg. "What were you like as a kid?"

I hummed in thought. "Quiet."

"Surprise, surprise."

I tore off a piece of toast and lobbed it at him. It pinged off his forehead and landed on the sheets. He tossed it into his mouth with a smile. "Will you tell me now?"

"Tell you what?" I placed my empty glass on the nightstand.

"Your whole story." When I grimaced, he motioned between us. "One for one. Yours for mine."

I supposed we had to get it all out at some point, so I agreed with a shrug. "You first."

He pointed to the last piece of toast. "Finish that. So, my dad worked all the time. When I was little, I didn't know any better, but then I got older and started seeing all my friends' dads around and hanging out with them, and I was, like, what the hell? I didn't understand why my dad wasn't throwing the football around with me. We weren't taking weekend camping trips. None of that. Whenever I asked him, he always had an excuse, he didn't know how to play football, we didn't own the equipment to go camping, he didn't have time to go to the movies, whatever, whatever. Once I got to high school, it was pretty obvious he was checked out. My parents always argued, even when we were little. They didn't hide it. My mom was a yeller, but my dad never said anything. Me and Evie could probably reenact their arguments word for word."

He sat up and pitched his voice higher, "*I don't get you, Tim. Why do you even come home if you're not going to do anything around here? Your kids don't even know what you look like.*"

Then he dipped his chin, lowering his face. "*Goddamn it, Shannon. I'm leaving.*"

I winced. "Is that what happened? He said he was leaving one day?"

Nate huffed a derisive laugh. "He said that *every* day. My dad wasn't happy. Nothing made him happy—not work, and definitely not us—and I took it personally. Like *I* wasn't making him happy. It had to be me. I know that's not true now, but back then, I didn't know what I was doing wrong. I blamed myself."

I understood. Though it wasn't at all the same, I often blamed myself for things that happened in my life over which I had no control. Sometimes we were our own worst enemy. I reached for Nate's hand, lacing our fingers together. "So, what happened?"

"He did eventually leave for good and married Summer, who I told you about. They have two kids, and he apparently has time for them. He takes them on vacations, he takes time off work. He's even planning on retiring soon to, you know…be with his family."

My hackles rose, irate on Nate's behalf. I knew what it felt like to be left behind, and I hated that for him. For the boy he had been and the man he was now.

"So," he went on, idly picking at my nail polish, my food long finished, "my mom tried to overcompensate. She did everything for us, was at every game, recital, everything, which was nice, but she also used me and Evie as pawns. Especially me. Before Dad left, I remember her saying shit like *Look, look at how you're making Nathan cry.* And no twelve-year-old boy wants it pointed out how much he's crying, you know?"

I moved closer to him, almost in his lap, combing my fingers through his beard. "Yeah. Instead of helping you, she made the situation worse."

His hands found my waist, fingers restless against my skin. "Yeah, and after he left, she'd shove it in our faces about how much she did for us and how little Dad did. If there was one good thing my father did, he never made it a competition. There was never one between my sister and me or him and my mom. So, I guess there are perks to caring so little."

Sitting directly in Nate's lap, I wrapped my arms around his neck and tucked my face into his throat. "And yet you care so much. You're not your dad. I know you're afraid you're like him, but you're not. You won't be like him."

He smoothed his hand down my hair and spine, over and over, until he eventually caught my chin in his fingers, kissing my mouth sweetly, a silent sign of gratitude. It wasn't a chore to listen. I liked learning about him.

As much as he liked learning about me. And I wasn't getting out of it, because he reminded me, "Your turn."

I ducked my head down and whined into his shoulder. "Do I have to?"

"Do you want an orgasm?"

I jerked back, jaw dropped. "You would withhold orgasms from a pregnant woman?"

He tipped his head. "Try me."

I flopped back against the pillows, scowling at him. "Fine."

He cuddled up next to me, sneaking his hand under my T-shirt to span my belly. Frogger, of course, poked at him, and I rubbed at where I thought the head was.

"I'm not sure where to start," I mused, and Nate teased his fingertips in circles on my skin.

"You left off at how you ended up here. You were in Virginia and…"

"Right." I readjusted my pillow for no other reason than to waste time. Nate waited me out, and when there was nothing else left to do, I started, "My dad was transferred to Virginia, and we were there for a long time, until I was in fourth grade. We moved up here because he met Beth."

"Guess we don't like Beth, huh? You said it in your dragon voice." He imitated my apparent dragon voice by making his all throaty. "Beeeeeeth."

"Beth was… Well, she was a bitch. *Is* a bitch."

He motioned for me to keep going, mouth trembling with amusement.

"When I first met her, she was nice and showed me pictures of her kids, and they were about my age, so I was really excited. For context, I used to watch a lot of TV Land, and I might have set my expectations a little high for what family life was like, okay? I thought, *This is it*. We were gonna be one big, happy family, and I'm going to have a brother and a sister. It was going to be awesome."

Frowning, Nate guessed, "It wasn't awesome?"

"We moved up here into a big house, and I went from being really close with my dad and seeing him all the time to him and Beth being together all the time. And her idea of parenting was giving us all ten bucks each and saying see ya later. I didn't know anyone, I didn't have any friends, and her kids basically bullied me. Veronica was one year older than me and just as bitchy as her mom. Joel was three years older and constantly picked on me, made fun of what I looked like, would steal my allowance, and eat all of my favorite snacks. He was an asshole."

"What did your dad say?"

"At first, he told me it would get better, that we'd figure out how to be a family, siblings tease each other, and all that kind of stuff. But he saw Joel push me into the wall one day and yelled at him, which made Joel go crying to his mommy that the big bad stepdad had yelled at him. I don't know what went down between Beth and my dad after that, but they didn't speak to each other for a few days, and then she basically started ignoring me, which only made me feel like shit. I thought we were gonna be like *Happy Days* or *The Brady Bunch* or something, but instead, we were…"

"Like a Lifetime movie," Nate supplied, and I gave in to a pathetic laugh.

"Yes. We were a Lifetime movie. When I got to high school, it got worse with Veronica because my boobs were bigger than hers, and you can guess what the boys were like—"

"Talking all kinds of gross shit about you?"

I nodded. "Veronica was jealous, as if I wanted that attention, and spread all kinds of rumors about me. The usual kind of mean-girl stuff—I was a slut, I once gave head to three guys in one night…"

Nate slanted his head, eyes wide. "Girls really say that about each other?"

"Sometimes, yeah. The easiest way to bring a girl low is to label her as a slut. Works every time."

He grimaced. "That's awful."

I took a deep breath, continuing, "And then my dad died. A few days before I was supposed to take my driver's ed test."

"Jesus, Tab. I'm so sorry."

I blinked away the sting in my eyes. "From that point on, I was basically a pariah in the house, but Beth couldn't throw me out because *what would people say?*"

"It was the very least she could do," he said, and I nodded.

"I knew Danny from a few of my classes in school, and we started dating pretty soon after my dad died. I was looking for…"

Nate handed me a tissue when I sniffed. "I get it."

"Danny's family was really nice. They were religious and went to church on Sundays, but they also had family game nights and invited me for dinner all the time, and I loved being with them. I loved being a part of that, so when Danny said we should get married and go to college together, I thought it was a great idea." I dabbed at my eyes. "We had a little ceremony and moved in to a tiny apartment over his family's garage. It was... Well, you know the rest."

Nate scooted up to take me in his arms, and I played at being annoyed at his sweat-soaked shirt. He only held me closer, tighter.

"We're going to have to change the sheets," I said into his throat.

"Oh, definitely. Especially after what I'm gonna do to you."

I refused to laugh, even as his breathy chuckle tickled my ear.

We were both quiet for a minute, digesting all this new information we'd shared, our mutual desires for family. I understood why Nate would be turned off from being a parent, but he slid so easily into the role of provider and protector, it amazed me he never saw that in himself. But now that I had the full picture, I assumed it was more about the echo of not feeling good enough than it was about his fear.

Because he'd conquered that quite soundly and knew almost more about this baby and pregnancy than I did.

"You know," he said eventually, catching my gaze, "I had it wrong."

"Had what wrong?"

"I always thought you had Maleficent vibes, but you're actually the princess."

I scoffed. "What?"

"You're Cinderella with the evil stepmom."

I wrinkled my nose. "I like Maleficent better. She can turn into a dragon and light her enemies on fire."

He nodded sagely. "I'll light your enemies on fire for you, princess."

I bit my cheeks, but a smile snuck through, and his eyes lit up in delight that he'd gotten me again. "Now, come on. Let Prince Charming show you how good he can fuck you."

He scooped me up and carried me to the bathroom, Lucy happily following us. He set me down, and I promptly brushed my teeth while he turned the shower on and shoved Lucy back out the door, muttering, "Go lie down, Luce. I'm about to defile your mother."

I bent over to spit into the sink, and Nate immediately pressed the position advantage, thrusting his half-hard cock against my ass, his hands curling around my hips. "I'm not finished yet," I mumbled with suds in my mouth, but he didn't care, sinking his hands below my underwear to spread my pussy open, delving his fingers inside without any warm-up.

He smiled at my reflection. "Gotta love those morning spikes in your hormones, huh?"

I finished brushing, and he pushed the cotton down my legs and helped me to step out of them before tossing them into the laundry basket, my work shirt following, leaving me completely naked.

He stared, his gaze slowly trekking over me, pausing at my breasts, my stomach, and my legs, then finally returning to my eyes. "You're so beautiful."

I'd been complimented my whole life. A generic white girl face with big boobs and a naturally small waist will do that, make come-ons and catcalls commonplace. But Nate's honest words landed different, a direct hit to the soft spot I'd just exposed to him. He knew everything about me now, and he still thought I was beautiful. Even with my melodramatic past and growing stretch marks.

Maybe *because* of them.

With how he tenderly held my face between his hands to kiss me, it certainly felt that way.

He helped me step into the shower, leaving the curtain open as he stripped naked, permitting me a view of his sculpted backside as he placed his clothes in the laundry. I knew he attended a seven a.m. class every morning, and the idea of flirty Nate laughing and joking with women as he got all hot and bothered, doing whatever it was CrossFit people did—throw tires or something—made my dragon side want to light things on fire.

He stepped into the shower, turning so the spray hit his back, and tugged me to him, his feet on either side of mine, his erection nestled between us. "What's the mean mug for?"

"You have women in your workout class?"

"Usually a few. One of the coaches is a woman. Why?"

"You ever take your shirt off there?"

His brow furrowed, that lock of hair curling in the humidity. "If I ever get really hot. Why? I don't—Oh! You're jealous. Tabitha Jean Reynolds, you jealous little shrew." His fingertips dug into my sides, his features utterly pleased. "You gonna fight for my honor? Power up with the baby and start swinging. Karate chops and roundhouse kicks all over the place."

"No." I rolled my eyes. But… We hadn't discussed exclusivity. I'd assumed, but *we* were still very new, no matter how long coming it had been.

"Fuck, princess." He bent to suck at my throat. "The idea of you kicking somebody's ass because you're jealous is so hot."

I pushed him, my hands on his chest. "Please don't make me play the role of jealous girlfriend."

He shook his head seriously, the twinkle of glee in his eyes gone. "Never. It's you and me now."

I chewed on my cheek, this time not to cry.

"I'm not going anywhere," he promised, and I couldn't contain my tears anymore. He wiped them away, though it didn't matter with the shower spray. "I'm always going to be here. That's one thing you never need to worry about." He stuck his tongue out, swiping it over the tip of my nose. "I've licked you, so you're mine."

FIFTEEN
NATE

Surprising the shit out of me, Tabby licked me right back. Marked her territory. Mine. *Hers.*

Sure, my love language was words of affirmation, but this playful little exchange was good enough for now.

Still reveling in one of her rare smiles, I removed the shower-head from the mount and made sure the water was a good temperature before soaking her body. Using her shampoo and conditioner from her gigantic bottles, I took care of her hair, making sure to work my fingers over her scalp and comb out the tangles, and then—because it smelled better than my own stuff—I washed and conditioned my hair with it too. Why would I want to smell like a pine forest when I could smell like Tabitha?

Next, I moved on to her body wash that was deep moisturizing, according to the label, and I could attest to that truth. I squirted some onto her loofah and scrubbed her from top to bottom, front and back, with a few added tugs on her nipples. I traced the dark pink lines on the sides of her breasts. They were growing bigger, and I'd witnessed her wincing a time or two when she didn't think anyone would notice, so I knew their size was starting to bother her.

But I fucking loved them.

I weighed them in my hands, lowering my head to drag my tongue over the dark areolas. She groaned and curled her fingers into my hair, holding me to her. I gently leaned her back, pressing her against the wall, all the while gliding my hands up and down her sides, sucking on her nipples.

She moaned my name, and hearing that made my dick weep. It was already straining up, heavy and hard and almost in pain. I was tempted to carry her out of here, but I stuck with my original plan.

I nipped her ear. "Now, turn around. Hands on the wall."

She arched her brow as if she wouldn't follow my order, but she eventually gave in, spinning around to offer me all her naked splendor. I palmed the globes of her ass before trailing my hands up her back to massage her shoulders and upper arms, making sure she flattened her hands to the wall. I had no-slip strips on the floor, but I didn't want her falling over. I knew she wouldn't like me pointing it out, but homegirl wasn't as agile as she used to be with her growing belly, and she sometimes lost her balance at work.

I couldn't risk an episode of her falling for what I had planned. The shower wasn't big enough for sex, but it was plenty big for some fun. I placed my hand on her lower belly, cupping the bump, silently apologizing to Frogger for how hard I was about to fuck their mother, then slid my palm down, pushing her hips back against mine, my cock cradled in the seam of her ass.

So fucking perfect.

Keeping her in that position, I reached behind me for the showerhead and changed the spray setting to pulse then let it rain down over her neck and chest, aiming it at both of her nipples until she squirmed. Only then did I lower it between her legs, making sure it hit her clit as I sucked on her shoulder, holding her steady.

"Feel good?" I asked, scraping her wet skin with my teeth, and she nodded, but I wanted her words. Keeping the showerhead in position, I skated my other hand backward, dragging my fingers around her hip and thigh to sink into her pussy from between her legs. She was tight and hot—and already close to coming, according to her gasped breaths and stuttered words.

"S-s-so good," she panted, rolling her hips back into me, and I had to clench my ass tight to keep from giving in to my need to let go and thrust up into her like an animal.

"God, yes," she moaned, her voice reverberating in the small stall. "Nate, yes."

"Come on, princess," I murmured, feeling her inner walls clamp around my fingers, pulling me in, and thank fuck it wasn't long until she fell over the edge.

Giving in to the temptation to taste her sticky sweetness, I stuck them in my mouth while she caught her breath, still rocking her hips into the shower spray. "Mmm, you ready, Tab?" I sank my fingers back into her, and she trembled. "Yeah, you are."

Still needing to know what she liked, I slid my hand back, my middle finger coated in her juices, and circled her asshole. "What about here? You ready?"

She turned over her shoulder, hands remaining in place on the wall. Such a good princess. "Only fingers."

I nodded and squeezed her hip. "I'll get a towel for you."

After turning off the water and putting the showerhead back in its place, I stepped out to grab a new towel from the small linen closet and wrapped it around my waist, then took another to wrap around her shoulders before lifting her up. She screeched in surprise, flailing her feet, hands scrabbling to my neck.

"I'm carrying you ten feet to the bed. Calm down, woman."

"You could have warned me."

"Warning," I droned then dropped her on the bed. She bounced on her butt, her glare slipping to a sultry smile as her gaze dipped below my face, settling somewhere around my waist.

"You can't wait, can you?" I untucked the towel and tossed it to the floor then tugged on the end of the comforter, pulling it off the corner of the bed. "Towel off and scoot over here."

When she moved over, I pulled the blanket the rest of the way off, leaving only the fitted sheet. Tabby lay on her back, propped up on her elbows, the towel open, her feet up on the edge of the mattress. Her pose wanton, her eyes on fire.

I bent to kiss and lick my way down her throat, cupping her tits in my hands. She arched into me so shamelessly, I couldn't help but sink to my knees. My princess wanted to be worshiped. Who was I to deny her?

I wrapped my hand around her hips and buried my face in her sweet pussy. Her skin was still damp from the shower, but the pink flesh between her legs was *soaked*, and I lapped up all her deliciousness as I ran my fingers over her legs and belly. She writhed around, already so keyed up, her clit practically a live wire. Anytime I sucked on it, her back bowed as she let out a high-pitched keening sound. Like she was being tortured.

I fucking loved it.

"Oh, please, please," she begged, her fingers fisted in the sheet, yanking it off the corner of the bed, and Tabitha *unleashed* was the most beautiful thing I'd ever seen. "Oh, fuck me, fuck, fuck…"

I refused to close my eyes to her thrashing, but I couldn't hold on to her anymore. Not with how much my cock throbbed. I gripped it roughly, squeezing the hell out of it for some kind of relief as I slipped two fingers inside her. She was scorching hot and dripping wet, and I couldn't wait to get inside her.

I found her swollen spot, relentless in my pursuit of her orgasm, until finally, she crashed with broken, mewling sounds. I stood, watching as she licked her lips over and over, her chest rising and falling with each of her rapid breaths. But I wasn't near done with her yet.

"Flip over," I said, tapping her hip, but she didn't move. Only shook her head.

"I'm too tired."

I grunted a laugh and not so delicately rolled her to her side, smacked her ass, then pushed her the rest of the way, positioning her knees where I wanted them, wide enough to accommodate her stomach in between her thighs as I softly curled my hand around her neck, holding her down. She laid her cheek on the mattress, her face flushed, bottom lip between her teeth, spent but still so needy.

"I had a physical a few months ago and was tested," I told her. I'd never had sex without a condom, very carefully avoiding accidental pregnancy and maintaining my health, but I didn't have to worry about that since Tabby was healthy and already pregnant. I was going to fuck her bare.

As long as she permitted it.

"I have condoms," I said, "but if it's okay with you—"

"It's okay with me," she interjected, stretching her arms up, rocking her hips side to side like a cat getting comfortable.

I drew my forearm across my face, wiping off my beard, wet from the shower and her orgasm, before speaking right against her ear. "Then I'm gonna fuck you now, Tabby cat. You don't have to do anything besides take it."

I kneeled on the bed behind her and smoothed my hands up and down her ass, spreading her cheeks, showing me every-thing. With my hand on the base of my cock, I lined up at her entrance and plunged inside, hissing at the immediate clench.

Heaven.

Tabby lifted her head and arched her hips up even higher, moaning in pleasure.

Trying to kill me.

Murder by her perfect pussy.

I ground my molars, heat rising in my veins, vision going hazy, overwhelmed by the smell of her shampoo and soap mingling with her natural musk.

"I'm close," she groaned, her muscles tense under my fingers. "Oh, fuck me, I'm close."

Fuck her, I did, my balls so heavy they hit her clit with every thrust. "Take it," I grated, jaw tight, every exhale growing louder and louder, my heartbeat pounding in my ears. "Wreck you."

I licked my thumb and rubbed it over the tight hole of her ass, sinking the tip in, and she tossed her head back, crying out. Yeah, I wanted to wreck her.

Because she'd already wrecked me.

Ruined me completely.

She began to chant her nonsense words, and I drove into her again and again, not letting up with my cock or my thumb, riding her through her orgasm and straight into mine.

I rocked into her one last time, pouring myself into her until I was empty and slumping. Tabby's eyes were closed, her wet hair a mess, though she kept her ass in the air, and I kissed her shoulder as I pulled out, tenderly skimming my hands up and down her back. "You okay?"

She nodded. "You killed me, I think."

"You're still talking."

"That's my ghost."

I rested my hands on my hips, breathing deeply. Congratulating my inner beast.

I stepped away from the bed, bending to snatch up my towel from the floor, but with Tab still in that same position, I had a clear view of my come leaking out of her.

And the beast roared to life.

I skated my fingers up her inner thigh, ignoring her shudder, and gathered the cream—mostly mine, but probably a bit of hers too—and shoved it back into her. It overflowed around my fingers, exiting back out, but I couldn't stop, some animal instinct alive and well inside me.

Requiring my seed in my woman.

Demanding to claim her.

In the oldest, most basic way possible.

She peered over her shoulder at me, her eyes soft, mouth parted like she wanted to say something but never did.

She let me continue for another few seconds, feeding my come back into her before I finally stopped and forced myself to back away. I cleaned off my hand with my towel then ran it over my face and wiped Tabby down as well. I let her have it as she stood, pushing up on her toes so our noses touched.

A reminder that she was mine.

"I—"

I cut myself off, barely refraining from confessing that I loved her, realizing almost too late that it would freak her out.

I couldn't tell her yet. I'd just gotten her, and for as much as I pushed her limits, I feared that one.

She had already given so much to me this morning, letting me in on her past; I didn't want to force her into something she wasn't ready for. To receive or give.

"I'm going to change the sheets. If you want to leave all the towels in the bathroom, I'll take them down to do laundry."

She nodded and kissed me tenderly before heading to the bathroom to clean up and dress, leaving me to sink down to the bed and take stock of my life.

Tabby had knocked me out and built me back up in a matter of weeks. I was ruined.

Because I didn't live for what I wanted anymore. It was all about what she wanted.

I lived for her and this baby.

SIXTEEN
NATE

It was safe to say I kept Tabby in a sex coma for the entirety of her spring break, which made hard conversations a lot easier when she was sluggish from orgasms, curled in my arms, yawning against my chest.

Yesterday, when I'd brought up what exactly we were telling people about our relationship, she didn't have an answer. "I don't have a lot of people to tell," she'd said, and I would have rather taken a punch to the face than hear those words delivered in her absent-minded sleepy voice.

It broke my heart.

She wanted people to tell about the baby, and it kept me up most of the night, thinking about how I could provide that for her. It was around 3:20 in the morning when it hit me. I had already provided it for her.

Walt's wasn't her scene, and yet she'd been working with me for a decade. She didn't have a lot of girlfriends, yet she gladly accepted Genevieve's friendship. She didn't have a family of her own, but she was allowing me to help her build one.

So, this morning, after I ate her out and fed her breakfast, I asked if I could tell people we were together. And, *oh yeah*, she was pregnant.

After a minute of thought, she agreed then slung her bag over her shoulder, and off she went to school. Then I texted Evie.

> I'm going to tell Mom about Tabby today.

EVIE
You are? Because I was planning on talking to her today.

> Okay?

EVIE
No, like

EVIE
TALK TO HER

> Okay?

> Are we not allowed to do that on the same day?

EVIE
I'm pregnant, and I have to tell Mom.

> WHAT THE FUCK

> YOU ARE PREGNANT WITH MY BEST FRIEND'S BABY?

> WHY DIDNT YOU TELL ME?

> IM GOING TO BE AN UNCLE?!?!

> IM EMOTIONAL

EVIE
I can tell.

EVIE
You need a moment?

> I'm fine.

> Just crying into my coffee.

EVIE

So should we do it together? Drop the bombs?

Yeah, why not?

Come over and we'll FaceTime her.

EVIE

See you in an hour.

Then I texted Tabby screenshots of that text convo. Her reply?

TABITHA

The nerve.

I called her immediately, and she picked up, saying, "Class starts in five minutes."

"Did you know? That Evie's pregnant?"

"Yeah. She told me a few weeks ago."

"How come you didn't tell me?"

"Because she and Dylan wanted to wait until after the first trimester."

I trapped an argument on the tip of my tongue about how we didn't have secrets anymore. Now that Tabby and I were an *us* now, the cone of silence disintegrated.

But I swallowed it down real quick. After learning about Tabby's first pregnancy, I understood the desire to keep it quiet. Pain of loss was hard enough without others knowing about it.

"Well, she's coming over so we can call my mom," I explained. When I was met with silence, I asked, "That's okay, right?"

"Yeah. Yeah. It's fine."

I got up to put my dish in the washer. "Why's your voice all weird?"

"My voice isn't weird."

"Yes, it is. Should I not tell my parents about us?"

The background noise on her end faded like she'd stepped somewhere quiet, but she didn't respond.

"Tab. What is it?"

Entire months passed before she finally spat it out. "Is she going to be upset? I don't want her to hate me."

This girl. All she wanted was to be loved. So much so that she feared my mother would hate her.

Goddamn.

I leaned my elbows on the counter, dropping my head in my hands, pretending I didn't want to fight anyone and everyone who had ever hurt her. "No, Tabby, she's not going to hate you."

"I'm pregnant with somebody else's baby."

Lighting myself on fire would have been less painful than that reminder, but this wasn't about me right now. It was about reassuring her. "I don't know how she'll react, but I can guarantee it will not be with anything close to hatred. For all of my mom's faults, she would never judge you. Plus,"—*I love you*—"she's always wanted me to find a nice girl and settle down."

Tabby snorted.

"You're not exactly nice, but you have settled me down, so one out of two ain't bad." I laughed. "I heard your eye roll."

"I have to go."

"Okay. I'm making this potpie recipe from Pioneer Woman for dinner."

"All right," she said, but I knew she was smiling. My woman liked when I played homemaker.

To annoy her, I made smooching sounds into the phone, and after she hung up, I unplugged my laptop from where I had it charging and made myself at home in the living room to wait for Evie.

She arrived with a frozen drink from Wawa, nudging Lucy out of the way when she sat down next to me. "Come on, Luce, knock it off." She held up her drink as my dog licked at her face. "Oof. Brush your teeth."

I grabbed my dog and sniffed at her mouth. "Tabby said the

same thing. I don't think her breath smells extraordinarily bad. I give her those bones to clean her teeth."

My sister shrugged, kicking her feet up on the ottoman as she sipped her drink. It was pink with whipped cream on top. "I don't know. I guess it's not bad. Just *a lot*."

"Pregnancy give you superpowers or something?" I joked, setting Lucy on the floor. She immediately trudged over to Evie, waiting for something to drop from her drink.

"Actually, yeah. Now that you say that, my sense of smell has been stronger. I think that's what's been making me so nauseous."

I hummed, considering that information, and it certainly made sense. Tabby hadn't been able to stand the scent of meat earlier in her pregnancy. I nodded to her drink. "What's that about?"

"Goes down easy," she said, patting her still-flat stomach. My sister had been a dancer her whole life, and I suspected she might not display any outward signs of pregnancy for a while. Not like Tabby, who'd been growing rounder by the day since she'd first popped. Even her face was changing, the harsh lines of her jaw softening, her hips not as narrow, and while I didn't think of her as a particularly vain person, I also didn't think she'd enjoy me telling her how much I liked her like this, all plump and cute and complaining about her bras not fitting.

Shaking all thoughts of naked Tabby from my head, I texted Dylan as Evie talked about their wedding in June, worrying about her dress and the baby bump she'd have by that point, as well as if she was going to keep it a secret until then.

DYLAN

"Mom's not too good at keeping secrets," I noted putting my phone down, and Gen flopped her head back to the cushion.

"I know. No wonder where you get it from."

I lightly knocked her in the arm. "Hey. I *can* keep a secret, if it's worth it." I motioned to her stomach. "Worth it."

She grinned. I did too.

Then I slid my computer closer to us on the coffee table. "You ready?"

She tugged on her earring. "Might as well get it over with."

I clicked on our mother's contact to video call her, making sure Evie and I were both in the picture.

Mom worked from home as a medical coder, which always gave her lots of time to text and call us whenever she pleased. She picked up after a few rings, her brows high in surprise as she smiled, equal parts confused and happy. "What a surprise! My two children calling me together." After a second, her face paled. "What's wrong? Why are you both calling me? Are you sick? Who is sick? Why didn't you take me to the appointment with you? I—"

"Hi, Mom," Evie muttered flatly.

"Everything's good," I said. "Stop spiraling. No one is sick."

She leaned closer to her screen, inspecting us. Satisfied with whatever she saw, she backed away and smiled again. Evie looked a lot like her; both of them had dark brown hair, the same nose, and matching blue eyes, big and bright. Mine were like our father's, more gray than blue.

"So, you're just calling to say hi?" Mom clasped her hands, elated at the idea, and I hated to burst her bubble. We were not those types of kids. We didn't have that kind of relationship with our parents, no matter how Mom tried.

And I did feel bad about that. Mom constantly tried, while Dad never did. But I was a grown man, and I didn't need to call my mother simply to chat. We weren't buddies.

"We both have some news," I said, and I could see the wheels turning in Mom's head as her eyes ping-ponged between us.

"Well?" she prompted impatiently, sitting forward.

Next to me, Evie took a deep breath. "I'm pregnant."

"You're pregnant?" When my sister nodded, my mother proceeded to lose her shit, clapping and dancing and crying. "You know, I used to worry about you getting pregnant in high school, always with…" She rolled her hand in the air. "What was his name?"

"Brent," Evie supplied, and I crossed my arms with a huff.

"That fucking guy."

Evie covered her laugh with her hand, her engagement ring evidence of how long-forgotten that fucking guy was, as Mom went off on some tangent about how she'd caught them fooling around in the basement and how she'd been so worried Evie would get pregnant and never follow her dreams.

"It never happened, so I don't know why you're bringing it up," Evie said, once our mother finished her diatribe.

"Because I was so afraid and then you did go off and follow your dreams, and I was afraid you'd never get married and have kids and…"

My sister hid her face with her hand, glowering at me. Yes, my mother could be a little dramatic, but Genevieve also had very little patience.

I mean, I could see Mom's connection. She was happy that her fears weren't realized. Did she need to say it out loud? Definitely not.

"I can't believe you're getting married and having a baby. I can't believe I'm going to be a grandma," she said, circling back around. "How far along are you? Do you know if it's a boy or a girl? We need to start thinking names!"

My sister held her hands up. "*We* do not need to start thinking about names. Calm down. I'm almost three months."

"Ah." Mom started to cry. "This is so amazing. I'm so happy. I can't wait to help you."

My sister slapped at my shoulder. "Actually, I think you'll need to help him more."

I didn't mind her throwing me under the bus. I had a better handle on our mother. Besides, I would need help once the baby came. She lived in Toms River, New Jersey, with her husband, but I half expected her to sprout wings and fly here immediately.

"What do you need help with, sweetie?"

"Well…" I combed my fingers through my hair a few times. "I know you remember Tabitha."

"Of course. The girl who wears all black and never smiles. I don't know why, she's so pretty. If she wore something with color, it would brighten her up a bit."

Evie plopped her face in her hands, muttering something I couldn't hear.

I ignored my mother's advice and went on, "Yeah, her. The one who's been managing the bar and doing my books and basically—"

"Yeah, I know who you're talking about. Is she okay?"

I nodded. "We started dating."

Mom lit up. "Really? That's wonderful. You know, I always thought you two had a little something going on. Whenever I came to see you at work, you were always watching her and, of course, always talking about her whenever I asked about the bar."

"See?" Evie shot me a victorious look. "I told you."

Mom tossed her hands in the air. "I'm so happy for both of you. Oh my gosh, I'm about to burst. I need to tell Nick. He's going to—"

"She's pregnant."

Mom froze at my words, mid-text to, I assumed, our stepdad. It took her a while to raise her gaze. "I'm going to be a grandma double?"

Before she could start off in another spiral, I stopped her. "I need you to chill out about this, okay? Because it's complicated. So before you start making plans, I need you to listen to me."

She set her phone down. I didn't often—almost never—use a stern voice with my mother, but she had to understand she could unintentionally fuck up the best thing to ever happen to me. I didn't want Tabby to be smothered, and my mother knew exactly how to do that.

"The last thing I want is Tabby to feel overwhelmed," I said, more gently. "It's complicated."

"What's complicated?"

"We just got together?"

I could see Mom doing the math in her head. "What do you mean? Did you—is this a…a thing where you didn't… Was it a one-night stand or something? Don't tell me that, Nathan."

"We are together," I stated, needing to fill in the blanks. "But it's only been a few weeks, and she is pregnant, but the baby is… not mine…biologically."

On-screen, Mom slanted her head, clearly thrown for a loop.

My sister slid her hand around my arm, squeezing it in support.

"Okay. Well…" Mom nodded to herself a few times, what she did when she gathered her thoughts. "I…I am happy if you're happy. Are you happy?"

"I'm happy," I murmured, feeling oddly emotional. The last few months had been like the first big hill on a roller coaster, a weightless plunge, and now, we were starting to straighten out, but I still didn't know what to expect. But this, right here, felt like a big step forward, telling my mother.

Who shocked me when she asked, "Are you sure?"

I wrenched back. "Am I sure I'm happy? Yes, Mom, I'm sure."

Next to me, Evie made a disgruntled sound.

Mom held her hands over her heart. "I didn't say that to upset you. I can see you're getting upset. I don't want that, okay? I asked because you said your relationship is new, and this isn't *your* baby, and I don't want… I'm afraid you'll get your heart broken. Raising kids is hard, and if there's nothing tying you to her or the baby, I don't…" She squeezed her eyes shut and shook her head as I gripped my sister's hand, heat crawling over my skin. "It will be very hard, is all."

I wasn't going to yell at my mother.

I wasn't going to yell at my mother.

I was *not* going to yell at my mother.

But I would burn shit down for Tabitha.

"I wouldn't care if she gave birth to an alien," I said carefully, overenunciating so there would be no mistaking my meaning. "I am going to take care of Tabby and the baby, no matter what. Do not ask me if I am happy about it. Do not tell me how hard it is going to be. Do not give me advice about *my* relationship."

I didn't want to shove her own failed marriage in her face, but I also didn't like to be tested. "Tabby's not had an easy go of it, and I'm going to do everything in my power to make sure the rest of her life is smooth."

I hoped she understood my meaning. My relationship with my father was shit, but I would gladly toss the one I had with my mother into the ocean if she did or said anything to disrupt what Tabby and I had.

"And I'm going to tell you this in complete confidence, Mom, but Tabby was really worried about me talking to you. She, of course, would never say this out loud to anyone, would absolutely kill me if she knew I was telling you this…"

Without even knowing what I was going to say, my sister agreed with a quiet laugh and a "Yep."

"But she doesn't have any family, and I know she is desperate for one. She wants and needs people around her for support, and she was nervous that you were going to be upset when I told you, because she wants to be included. She wants to be loved, and she was afraid you wouldn't accept her."

Both Evie and our mother sniffled, undoubtedly troubled by my words, but I didn't care. Tabby lived this every day, and if it took them—specifically, my mother—getting a little upset for the point to be made, so be it.

I continued after a deep breath. "I'm telling you that I will always choose her, so please don't ask me if I'm happy or think you're going to make me second-guess my decisions because I'm not going to. There was never a choice. It was always her. It will always be her."

Mom nodded as Evie patted my back, whispering a quiet, "Well said."

"I understand," my mother said, blinking her eyes a few times to clear them of their glassiness. "I'm just so surprised, but I'm also very, very proud of you, Nathan."

"Thank you."

Then she smiled, mood shifted. "Now, what do you need me to do? I can—"

"Nothing right now."

"What about you, Evie?" Mom lifted her cell phone again. "With the wedding and the baby coming this year, we will have so much to do. Two showers! Oh my gosh, what is—"

"I'll let you know, Mom," she said. "We don't really need a wedding shower because we don't need anything for the house, so let me talk about it with Dylan. We haven't even told anyone else I'm pregnant, so—"

Mom perked up even more. "You didn't tell your father?"

"Not yet."

She was the cat who caught the canary. "Well, I am here whenever you need me. You know it's nothing for me to drive over there. If there's no traffic, I can get there in an hour and a half."

I huffed a laugh. "If you're going ninety."

Mom shrugged. "You know I have a lead foot."

When she started on a tangent about onesies and burp cloths, Evie and I exchanged a look, both of us giving our excuses.

"I gotta get to work," I said at the same time she said, "I've got to get new tires on my car."

New tires on your car? I mouthed.

My sister was a terrible liar.

She shrugged, waving at our mother. "We'll talk later, okay? I'll call you."

"Promise?"

Evie sighed. "I promise. I will call you after I've talked to Dylan about everything, all right? Don't get any ideas about driving here or sending me anything."

Mom squirmed like that was exactly what she planned on doing.

"Same goes for me," I said. "I'll send you some ultrasound pictures, though."

That's when she started crying, and I ended the call before we got stuck with her while she sobbed. "Okay, Mom. We love you. Bye!"

Evie threw herself against the back of the couch, and I snapped my laptop shut. "I need a drink."

My sister blew out a breath. "Me too. Damn it. The one time I need one, and I can't have one."

I tossed my arm around her neck, towing her roughly into me, proceeding to wrestle for a few seconds. When she settled against me, free of my hold, she tipped her head back, smiling up at me. "Don't worry too much. Tabby's too tough to be scared away from the likes of Mom, but you handled her nicely."

I accepted her compliment with a whack on her knee. "Thanks for having my back."

"Of course."

I tugged at the ends of my hair. "So, we're really doing this, huh? The blind leading the blind into the world of parenting."

"Dylan's already done it before, so I'm good."

I crossed my arms, wagging my head side to side. "Guess *I* gotta eat shit and ask them for advice after all these years of giving *them* shit."

She grinned. "Guess so."

SEVENTEEN
NATE

In the weeks since I'd delivered the news to my mother, she'd remained chill. Mostly. She still called weekly to check in and added links to stores with baby items, including notes about what she thought we would need or what would be better. I was actually quite impressed with her level of restraint. Though I feared it would be like Mount Vesuvius one day, and she'd explode, randomly showing up at our door with bags of baby wipes, throwing bottles at me, demanding I let her move in so she could babysit.

On the opposite end of the spectrum, I texted my dad to let him know I needed to talk to him. When he finally responded the next day, he said I could call him around noon, and when I did explain the situation, he reacted exactly how I expected. "That's good. I hope you're taking care of yourself and her."

And that was about it. No follow-up questions. Mostly some muttered nonsense about being happy for me and to let him know if I needed anything.

Sure, my mom was all drama, but goddamn, would it kill him to act like he had any love for me? More than some acquaintance?

That's what it felt like.

I would rather have my mother be over the top than have my father give me less than the bare minimum.

Sometimes a person just needed to hear "I love you."

But things between Tabby and me were remarkably wonderful. She was still "working" but mostly to make herself feel better about Bran taking over for her. She had a few more weeks left in the semester, and we had started discussing painting the nursery, although we had yet to open the envelope stuck to the fridge with the sex of the baby in it. Little did she know, I had two online carts full of stuff, waiting for me to pull the trigger, one for a girl and one for a boy. Sure, it was all stereotypical and meant absolutely nothing, but how could I not buy the ginormous bows for a girl or the tiny blue bow tie for a boy. I mean, *come on*.

Pushing those thoughts aside, I focused on the task at hand. I was set to meet Collin at the restaurant. He'd been in town since yesterday, staying at Liam's house, and after we'd met in person at Walt's, we hit it off immediately. I knew we would. We'd been corresponding via texts and emails, and it was all but a done deal. He'd told me how he was tired of moving and taking orders, though I suspected it was a little more than that.

Sometimes a guy exhausted himself by pretending he didn't want to put down some roots. It got tiresome, the meaningless sex and avoidance.

I would know.

We'd made plans to meet downtown at the space, and as I pulled up to the building, I saw Collin already waiting outside, his tall frame leaning against the brick wall.

He straightened up as I approached, a grin spreading across his face. He had the look of a chef, lean and scraggly with tattoos and a cigarette in his hand. He stubbed it out to shake my hand.

"Perfect location," he said by way of greeting.

I agreed, tilting my head back to take in the corner lot on Aster Street. All the buildings were connected here, the architecture from the nineteenth century with cobblestone sidewalks and wide streets sometimes closed down for festivals or street fairs. It was both quaint and kitschy, a small-town vibe in the middle of a suburb outside of Philly. We'd make *bank*.

Especially being next to these small businesses. Right next door to an art gallery. Across the street from a bakery. We'd fit right in.

Exactly what Tabby wanted.

"You ready to check out our future empire?" I asked, unlocking the door. Collin merely smirked, following me inside, our footsteps echoing off the bare walls. The potential was palpable.

I brought him over to a folding table, where I laid out the construction plans. I had the contractor lined up. All I needed was for Collin to sign on the dotted line with me. Co-owners.

"So," Collin began, his eyes scanning the room, "talk me through it. Where's the bar? The kitchen?"

I pointed toward the far end. "We'll put the bar along that wall. It'll be the first thing people see when they walk in. We can do some low lighting, maybe some hanging plants to give it a cozy vibe."

Collin nodded, stroking his chin. "Mm-hmm. You said you almost want it to feel like someone's living room, right? You need the right seating, especially at the bar. Some stools with cushions. You want people hanging out for a long time, ordering a bottle. At the tables, it'll be easy, but since the customers sitting at the bar will be the first thing people see, you want to set the precedent. Upscale yet still approachable. Walt's, but make it their rich cousin."

"*Exactly.*" My stomach flipped. We were of one mind, and I could already feel this would go well.

Collin turned. "And the kitchen?"

"Back there." I gestured to the right. "We'll need to do some major renovations, get all the proper ventilation and equipment installed. But I think we've got enough space to create an efficient workflow."

Collin paced the area, checking out every nook and cranny. "We'll need to factor in storage space too. Both dry goods and refrigeration."

I pulled out my phone, making notes, biting back a smile at his use of *we*. "Definitely. Whatever you want to make sure we're maximizing the space."

He glanced over his shoulder to me. "What about licenses? For the bar and the health department approvals."

"Already on it," I assured him. "I've got a meeting with the city next week to start the paperwork. It'll take some time, but we should have everything in order before we're ready to open."

He nodded approvingly, casting his gaze out the big front windows, to the view across the street. "And staffing? I know you've got experience with that from Walt's, but this is a different ball game."

"I figured you would want a hand in the hiring. Front of house won't be a problem. There are always people around looking for hospitality jobs."

We continued to discuss logistics and plans for the next hour or so, solidifying our combined vision. We made a good team, and I felt in my bones that this was the right move. I could already imagine opening night, the success that would come. We talked about possible menu options, décor, and how soon he'd be able to make it official here.

"I honestly don't have much," he said as I locked up. "I've basically been living out of a suitcase since culinary school."

"Real estate is tight around here, but they put up new condos a year or two ago." I pointed to the building a few blocks away, the top visible among the low-rise of the other structures. "Heard they're pretty nice. Also, pretty pricey."

He nodded absently, sweeping his gaze up and down the street from the coffeehouse and record store to the lingerie boutique and pet shop then settled his attention on the store-fronts directly across from us, Sweet Cheeks, the bright-pink bakery known for its cinnamon rolls, the tattoo parlor where I'd gotten all my ink done, and the bookstore with twinkle lights in the window.

"Got a small-town feel, you know?" I said, working the angle. "It's a nice place to live. Start a family."

He scoffed at the idea but stuck his hand out anyway, shaking on it.

EIGHTEEN
TABBY

sank into the couch cushions, letting out a long sigh as I rubbed my swollen belly. I was at the end of the second trimester and really starting to show now, getting bigger by the day.

I had a few weeks until finals and then a few weeks until the due date at the end of July.

It had been an exhausting couple of months. I hated to admit Nate was right, but juggling classes, work, *and* growing a human inside me was exhausting. Pregnancy brain kicked my ass hardcore, and I was ready to be done with school. About ready to be done with Walt's too.

Although, I was definitely *not* ready for the baby to come.

I still had so much to do. I signed up for the prenatal classes at the hospital that my OB-GYN recommended, which were every Saturday morning and sort of helpful. It was nice to get a tour of the maternity wing and to set our expectations for when the time came, but some of the postnatal information was downright anxiety-inducing. Nate, of course, attended them with me, all the while grumbling about how he "knew this stuff already."

I appreciated how much research he'd done, but he wasn't

the one who had to think about putting a pad doused with water and witch hazel in the freezer for his fucked-up vagina.

Women had been giving birth for centuries, and yet we hadn't been able to come up with any better medical remedies for birth injuries except for ice packs and ibuprofen? Atrocious.

Though, Nate did get *very* excited about possibly rubbing olive oil on my perineum.

The woman leading the class was great, but her hippie-dippie manifestation and olive oil tricks weren't going to save me from being torn in two. Because I did the thing I wasn't supposed to and watched videos.

But I had Nate through all of it. The man bent over backward to take care of me and made sure I didn't overexert myself. Whether it was cooking my new weird pregnancy-craving foods —onion rings with spicy mayo—at two a.m. or giving me foot rubs after long days, he was always there.

And now he threw himself into nesting. Even on days when he pulled double duty between Walt's and his new space, he spent all his free time converting the spare room upstairs into a nursery. I told him he didn't have to go to so much trouble, that the baby would be sleeping in our room at first anyway. But he insisted on getting everything all set up. He had even gone so far as to buy all the things we wouldn't need until the baby could start moving: outlet covers, gates, cabinet locks, and those little cushions for hard edges.

This baby would want for nothing.

Between Nate's late-night online shopping habits and his mother, we already had a million boxes and packages lining the office. Shannon—whom I still couldn't call "Mom," even though she insisted—had very kindly offered to host a baby shower for me, which I declined. I didn't have close friends or anyone I wanted to invite, so Genevieve had the idea that we have a girls' night with her friends, Kennedy and Brooke, who were with Liam and Jude, and they could bring a few small things for the baby. That seemed much more reasonable to me and something I would actually enjoy.

While this pregnancy was unplanned and a complete surprise, it was not unwelcome, and even though I still held a lot of anxiety about carrying to term, I didn't worry about not having enough support.

I had more than enough in Nate.

My wish had come true.

I had more than I needed.

I could be a glutton.

Greedy.

Hoard him all to myself. Keep all his soft, whispered words to myself. Each time he called me princess. Every evening when he kissed my shoulder and said, "Good night, beautiful." Every morning when he made me breakfast and then made me come.

He was truly written by a woman.

And he was all mine.

Especially when he trudged down the stairs with paint smeared on his jeans, forearms, and shoulder, his T-shirt nowhere in sight. He smiled at me, still in the same position he'd left me in—sprawled out on the couch with my textbook and laptop open, supposedly studying.

"How we doing down here?" he asked, crouching in front of me to lift my shirt, kissing the curve of my belly. "Frogger."

I brushed my fingers over his hair, pushing it away from his forehead. "We're good. Though someone has been extra active this morning."

"Yeah?" Nate kept one hand resting on my bump, idly stroking his thumb back and forth. "Maybe they're bored. Wanna come out and play?"

"Not yet. We're not ready."

He hummed quietly. "Room's almost finished."

"Yeah?" I pushed myself up from my reclining position.

"I just came down for a drink. I should be finished up in about an hour or so."

"Guess that means we'll have to make a decision on the furniture."

"Speaking of…" He took a breath. "I got a text from Summer."

"As in, your dad's wife?"

He nodded. "They want to buy us something."

"That's nice."

He didn't reply, and I didn't ever want to discount his feelings, because everyone had their own shit to work through. Nate had every right to be hurt and angry, but he was always so suspicious. And not to say anyone's trauma was better or worse than anyone else's, but it seemed like he didn't want to accept or believe anything positive about his father.

I'd never met his dad, yet I didn't think he *meant* to hurt Nate. In my very uneducated opinion, it appeared as if there was simply a major lack of communication.

Funny, I knew, coming from me, the girl completely inept at verbalizing any kind of emotion.

"I'm sure it was all Summer's idea," Nate said eventually, and I shrugged.

"Maybe. But it's still really nice of them."

Again, he stayed quiet. Only bent to kiss my forehead. "I'll let you know when I'm finished." Then he stood, drifting his fingertips over my shoulder. "Need anything from the kitchen?"

I shook my head, but he took my water bottle anyway, returning a few minutes later with it full and a cheese stick. I murmured my thanks as he made his way upstairs, his back to me, arm up as he chugged down water, the muscles of his back on display, marks from my fingernails still there. I bit into my bottom lip, remembering yesterday morning, how he'd edged me so hard I completely lost it when he finally let me come.

The bastard deserved those marks.

But he loved them. Joked about getting them tattooed on.

Smiling to myself, I attempted to focus on my schoolwork, but I barely lasted twenty minutes before I set my textbook aside. My mind kept wandering to what Nate had said about his dad and Summer wanting to buy something for the baby.

I picked up my phone and texted Genevieve.

> Nate told me your dad and stepmom want to buy something for the baby. Not sure how I feel about it since Nate is so weird. What do you think we should do?

A few minutes later, she replied.

GEN

> Of course he's weird about it, and of course they want to get something. Or at least, Summer does.

> That's what Nate said. That it was probably her idea.

GEN

> Oh, it definitely was. Summer is really sweet and keeps my dad from being a complete robot.

GEN

> Just because Nate feels weird about it, you shouldn't. The very least our father can do is buy something. And they have the money to get you something nice, so I think you should let them buy you the biggest item on your list.

GEN

> Look at this.

I clicked on the link she sent me for an expensive luxury stroller, all-terrain and fully loaded with features. Definitely not something I would have picked out or could afford, but Gen had a point. Their dad had the means, and if they were offering, there was no reason we shouldn't accept a gift from them. It would be their grandchild, after all.

I found a much more affordable stroller, one without all the bells and whistles but that could easily fold up with one hand, according to the description, and all the reviews were great. I sent Gen the link for that one instead, and she replied with a thumbs-up and another message.

GEN

FYI, Summer will most likely try to win you over with hugs and other little gifts. You don't have anything to worry about with her. The tension comes from how awkward our dad is and how very clearly our childhood differed from how our half-siblings' childhoods are currently. Don't overthink it. Ask for whatever you want. Summer is more than happy to provide it for you.

Feeling better about the situation, I set my phone aside and worked for another fifteen minutes before I heard Nate's footsteps plodding back down the stairs.

"Hey," he said. "You wanna come check it out?"

"Sure." I let him help pull me up from the couch, given that my stomach muscles were on their way to becoming completely nonexistent since all the pregnancy workouts I followed were about strengthening the pelvic floor. He held my hand to usher me upstairs to the nursery.

I gasped when I saw it, the walls painted a pale green with the cutest little woodland creature decals scattered around. The molding was bright white and apparently still wet since he made sure I didn't touch it as I slid my fingers along the wall.

"It's beautiful," I said, my voice thick with emotion. "You did an amazing job."

He smiled, clearly proud of his work. "Yeah, I thought it would make a nice little room for Frogger. And you were right, this color is perfect. Better than the darker one I wanted." He pulled my back to his front, banding one arm across my shoulders as he gestured to different places around the room. "I figure the crib will go along this wall, and we can put the glider over there. I'm not sure where the changing table should go, though, and I was thinking maybe we should get two since Frog'll be sleeping in the bassinet. Do we really want to be carrying them down here at three a.m.? So, maybe we should just get two."

I shook my head in amusement. When in doubt, Nate's first instinct was to overestimate.

Spinning to face him, I placed my hands over his chest. "I think we'll be okay with one."

"Are you sure? 'Cause—"

"One, Nate." I pressed my finger to his lips when he tried to argue again. "We'll be okay with one."

He sighed, pulling me closer so I would rest my head against his heart, and I'd grown accustomed to the tickle of his chest hair. "Sometimes I lie awake at night imagining you in here, rocking the baby to sleep, singing with that pretty voice of yours." He cradled my head with one hand, the other sneaking under my T-shirt to slide his fingers up and down my back. "You're going to be an incredible mom."

My heart swelled at his words. I never imagined I'd be embarking on motherhood with a man like Nate by my side. Someone who loved and supported me so completely.

"I can't wait to see it for real," he said softly. "Our little family."

I didn't do a very good job of surreptitiously wiping at my tears—never-ending with these hormones!—and he kissed the top of my head, dragging his knuckles over my cheek.

Family.

Nate was my family now.

And in a few more weeks, we would become three.

I couldn't wait.

NINETEEN
NATE

pulled open the heavy wooden door, letting the fresh spring air rush inside. Though the restaurant space was still very much a work in progress, I wanted to bring Tabby here this evening for a private celebration dinner. She had finished her final exams and completed her spring semester today. She was in the homestretch of school and the pregnancy. After the baby was born, she'd return for one single class and her capstone project before graduation. Growing a human and acing her classes, my woman was a superstar.

While the menu wouldn't be finalized for a while, I'd asked Collin to see what he could whip up for us, especially since I wanted to make sure the menu had items that Tabby loved, and I figured this would be an easy way to make that happen. Collin agreed and said he'd create a few tasting dishes for us.

Tabby stepped through the doorway, glancing around to take in the bare-bones interior. The drywall was all up and waiting to be painted "dark sienna," a deep red, almost brown color that Collin and I finally agreed on yesterday. The floors would get done after that, and then we'd install all the seating. Although, the kitchen was the first thing completed on the list because they needed to rework some wiring. I'd also asked them to take a look at the HVAC system at Walt's and was told I'd need to invest in another one sooner rather than later, which kept me up for a few nights until Tabby was scheduled for her third ultrasound. Then I let it go.

She was my priority, with this new venture coming in second. I could worry about the heating and cooling of Walt's later, once I had the first two babies settled.

Collin poked his head out from the kitchen, offering me a nod before he made his way to us in a white chef's jacket, his hair pulled back in a little ponytail and a dish towel thrown over his shoulder. "Tabby, how are you?"

"Good." She absently cupped her hand around the bottom of her belly, something she'd started doing recently, and every single time, it made me smile. "Something smells delicious."

He gestured to the small table I'd set up with padded folding chairs. "Have a seat. I'll bring out the first dish in a few minutes."

"First dish?" she murmured.

Putting her favorites on the menu was my little surprise.

"What do you think so far?" I asked after we were both seated, and I poured us water.

She coasted her gaze around again. "I think it'll be great."

"Someplace where a person could drink a glass of wine and have a nice meal?"

She slanted her head, brows narrowed. "What?"

"That's what you said."

"When?"

"When I asked what kind of place you'd go to. You said a quiet place where you could have a glass of wine and a nice meal."

It took a moment, but then she understood. "You..." She looked around again, searching for something—I didn't know what—and pointed to the floor, jaw hanging loose as she stared at me for a few seconds. "You...are doing this because of something I said?"

I nodded. "Walt's isn't your scene. I want you to have somewhere to go that's quiet with some good wine, tasty food, and you can read your books." I laughed. "Which I still can't believe you read."

Tabitha Reynolds, evil queen, liked historical romances with men in kilts.

"First of all," she started, "my books are swoony and fluffy and perfect when I need a break from the real world."

"Hey." I held my hands up. "You do you."

"And I can't believe you're opening a whole new restaurant because of something I said."

I leaned my elbows on the table. "Why?"

"Because…" She shook her head. "That's a terrible reason to start a new business."

"It's not. You should know by now I'll give you whatever you want."

Obviously flustered, she opened and closed her mouth yet formed no words. I couldn't help but smile. "Even before I realized how I felt about you, I still wanted to make you happy. That's all I want to do, Tab."

She dipped her chin slightly, still so uncomfortable with hearing the truth, and I reached for her hand, prepared to make her real uncomfortable with what I actually wanted to say. But before I could, Collin appeared at our sides with a few dishes.

He set three small plates down in front of us, gesturing to each one. "For your appetizers tonight, we have a fresh spring salad with pears, candied pecans, and a bit of goat cheese, which I already looked up," he said, turning to me, "and she can have it, so don't start your shit."

Tabby hid her soft laugh behind her hand. I didn't.

Collin went on. "It's dressed with a fig balsamic vinaigrette. The next is seared dates wrapped in bacon with aged balsamic, and last are the mushroom caps with lump crabmeat and herbs, served with a lemon-butter drizzle."

Tabby lifted her gaze to Collin, clearly impressed. "This all looks so good. Thank you."

"I'll be back to check on you in a few minutes," he said, leaving Tabby and me to try the dishes. She seemed to enjoy each one, but when I asked which one she liked best, she pointed to the dates. Collin took note and cleared our plates, returning with another three plates. "I would like to use all locally sourced produce for specials and sides, but these three dishes are pretty standard fare. We've got braised short ribs cooked in a rich Bordeaux wine sauce served on top of polenta with roasted baby carrots and a sprinkling of gremolata. The middle is a pan-seared duck breast with a tart cherry reduction, parsnip puree, and sautéed wild mushrooms. The last one is a classic. Panko-crusted chicken breast topped with house-made marinara and melted mozzarella, over al dente spaghetti with fresh basil and shaved Parmesan."

"Wow." She pointed her fork at me. "Did he tell you chicken parm is my favorite?"

Collin shrugged, not caring to hide his growing smile. "Enjoy."

Tabby dug in enthusiastically, starting with the chicken parm. "You know I love Tony's, but—" she nodded toward the kitchen "—that man is magic."

Satisfied with her reaction, I helped myself to a bite of the duck. I'd never had duck before, but I would hunt Donald and Daffy myself if they tasted this good. The short ribs were just as good. This time, I knew what her favorite would be but asked anyway.

"They're all so delicious," she told Collin. "The chicken parm is my favorite because it always is, but the other two are just as good."

"No notes?" he asked, earning a laugh.

And I could admit a tiny claw of jealousy picked at the soft space between my ribs that *I* didn't make her laugh. Someone else did. That was *my* job.

"No notes," she affirmed.

"So easy to please," Collin joked, lascivious grin in place.

"All right. Enough hitting on my woman." I handed him the plates. "Go get our desserts."

He leaned down to stage-whisper to her, "He's always so pushy."

"You're telling me."

Once Collin was back in the kitchen, I curled my hand around Tabby's chair, pulling it right up against mine. "You better watch it, princess. I'll fuck that attitude right out of you."

She deliberately licked her bottom lip. "Promise?"

I huffed, draping my arm around the back of her chair, before calling out toward the kitchen. "What's taking so long? We gotta wrap this up."

"It's literally been thirty seconds." She giggled.

Mission accomplished.

By the time Collin returned, I'd already decided which position I wanted to try. Actual penetration was getting more difficult with her bump, but Reddit was my friend, and I found a lot of good info on there. Unfortunately, Tabby wasn't up for it every morning anymore, but I was ready and willing whenever she needed me. And if the placement of her hand on my thigh meant what I thought it did, I was ready to get the fuck out of here.

"All right," Collin said, marching back out with three ramekins. "We've got crème brûlée with fresh berries and a shortbread cookie. Chocolate lava cake accompanied by salted caramel ice cream and candied hazelnuts, and an upside-down caramelized apple tart served warm with a scoop of vanilla bean ice cream and a drizzle of balsamic reduction."

The responding moan Tabby let out had my dick going rock hard, and I really, truly could not care less about dessert, but I shoved it down my throat so we could get out of here quicker. Collin joined us, asking Tabby all kinds of questions about school, just to torture me like the son of a bitch he was.

After twenty minutes, I couldn't take it anymore. I tossed my thank-you over my shoulder and practically dragged Tabby out of there. I needed to get home. Needed to feel her skin against mine and hear those soft moans escape her lips.

At home, I quickly let Lucy out then tugged my lady upstairs, not bothering with the lights. The moonlight streaming in through the windows was enough. I pulled her into my arms, my mouth finding hers in a hungry kiss. She tasted like chocolate and caramel, and I couldn't get enough.

I roamed my hands over all the curves and swells I loved, especially her breasts. God, they were so big and sensitive, and I spent a lot of time worshipping them after lifting her dress off her. She'd never been much for dresses, but she'd said she wasn't comfortable in anything else lately.

I didn't mind. Made for easy access.

Tabby tangled her fingers in my hair, pulling me closer, deeper into the kiss, and I knew I wouldn't be able to have her on her feet much longer, so I sank my fingers beneath her underwear, sliding two fingers over her clit. That first breathy gasp made my skin prick with goose bumps.

This woman was *mine*.

Every laugh, every gasp, every smile, every damn flutter of her lashes was mine, and I would show her exactly why.

I traced my tongue down the line of her neck, curling my fingers into her until she groaned and trembled, her fingernails digging into my arms. "Oh, please," she whined, already losing it, and I eased her back to the bed, sitting her down but never removing my hands from her. "Nate."

"Yeah, princess?"

"I want to come."

I sucked on her nipple. "So, come. Come all over my fingers. I'm not stopping you."

She splayed back on a mound of pillows, and I took advantage of the new position, peeling her underwear down her legs with my free hand. Naked and beautiful, she shone like a goddess in the moonlight.

"Let go," I rasped over her other nipple. "Let me hear you. Feel you. Come on."

A few more strokes of my fingers inside her, and she finally fell, her inner muscles gripping my fingers tightly, and I didn't waste time shedding my jeans and T-shirt. She reached for me, tracing the lines of my tattoos as I kicked off my boxer briefs to hover over her.

As much as I loved to admire and adore her body, she liked to take her time with me too. Something I wasn't about to stop. So, I held myself up above her, steady and patient as she tickled and teased me with her fingers and tongue, sucking on a spot below my shoulder while playfully scratching at my nipples.

When I couldn't stand it anymore, I urged her to her side, her ass at the edge of the bed, then lifted her top leg, opening her up but still keeping her comfortable. A real pillow princess now.

With one hand holding her leg up and the other twisting at her nipple, I slowly entered her. She was tight, wet, and warm, and I had to fight the urge to thrust into her hard and fast. I wanted to savor this, enjoy these fleeting moments when it was still only the two of us.

I moved lazily, my hips rocking against hers, listening for every hiccuped breath, making sure she could feel every inch of me because I could certainly feel every ripple and contraction of hers.

She gripped the sheets, her eyes closed, and I shifted forward slightly, skating my hand up from her breast to below her throat. "You okay, princess?"

She nodded. "Fe-feels so go-good."

"Yeah, it does." Well worth the little bit of research it had taken to find a good position. "You know how fucking good you feel? Every time with you. It's always so good. If I didn't have to go to work, I'd do this all day. Fuck this sweet little pussy until you screamed my name. Over and over, all day long. Hm? What do you think of that?"

She nodded, mumbling something.

"Didn't quite catch that." I brought my hand down to where we were connected, circling her clit. "You need to speak up."

She sucked in a sharp breath. "Make me come. Make me come hard."

I increased the pressure, the speed, the tingling and heat in my spine building until I was there too. She panted my name, her muscles convulsing around my cock, milking it for all it was worth. Greedy little thing.

I emptied myself into her, continuing to move slowly in and out of her, not wanting to release her yet. Enjoying this hazy middle-of-nowhere bliss too much, but she didn't seem in any big rush to move either. With her leg still wrapped around my middle and my fingers still trailing all over her, we stared at each other, our chests rising and falling at the same rate, our breaths synced.

When I finally did pull out of her, I cupped my hand over her pussy, because it was mine and I liked the idea of keeping my come inside her.

From her irritated yet amused puff of air, she liked it too.

She was mine, I was hers, and I loved anything that proved it.

After a few moments, she shifted, telling me, "I have to pee."

I helped her up and then chuckled as she waddled to the bathroom, knowing she didn't like the cleanup. But she'd have to get used to it.

I'd be coming in and on her for the rest of our lives.

Couldn't put the beast back in his cage now.

TWENTY
TABBY

I smoothed my hands over the curve of my belly, taking a deep breath as I checked myself out in the mirror. I owned exactly one cocktail dress that was neither appropriate for a June wedding nor able to fit over my gigantic belly. So, I'd ordered this pleated black chiffon dress online.

I wrinkled my nose, turning side to side.

"What's wrong?"

I glanced up from the mirror in the bedroom to find Nate leaning against the doorjamb, handsome in his black suit and tie, beard and hair freshly trimmed.

"You look really good," I said, gesturing between us. "And I look like I'm wearing a garbage bag."

He crossed the room, wrapping his arms around me, Lucy dancing at our feet. "You look beautiful."

"I look huge."

He skated his hands down to palm my belly. "I think you look like an eight-months-pregnant woman."

"Very swollen." I poked at my face. I'd never thought of myself as particularly worried about my appearance, but lately, I couldn't stop obsessing. My face was broken out, my feet didn't fit into my shoes, and I couldn't stop sweating. Physically, this pregnancy was relatively easy, but I still didn't like how different I felt in my body. Like it wasn't my own.

I had no control over it.

Nate kissed my jaw, his beard soft against my skin. He used this beard oil that smelled delicious, and sometimes I found myself dragging his face down to mine just to get a whiff, let it soak into my skin so I still smelled him when he left for work.

"Did you drink enough water today?" he asked, and I pointedly ignored him. "Tabitha," he chided, steering me out of the bedroom.

"I don't want to have to pee every five minutes."

He took my hand to lead me downstairs. "I think you'll have to pee every five minutes, regardless of how much you drink."

In the kitchen, he filled up my Maleficent water bottle to hand to me.

"I can't take this with me."

"Why not?

"It'll be weird, me carrying this around the whole time."

So then he shrugged and tucked it under his arm. "Let's go."

I didn't bother with a bag since I had my own personal man-sized purse, and I let him usher me out to the car, parked in the back. Gen and Dylan's wedding was at the historical society's building downtown, only two blocks from where Nate's new wine bar and bistro was located.

After we parked, he laced his fingers with mine and waved to another couple, Liam and his fiancée Kennedy, making their way inside. They slowed so we could catch up, a little boy antsy between them.

Kennedy greeted me with a hug. "How are you feeling?"

"Terrible," I said, only half joking.

As promised, Gen had put together a little girls' night with Kennedy and Brooke a few weeks ago. It was fun. We ate junk food and watched a few rom-coms and talked about our guys. I'd never had very close girlfriends, and while I hadn't known Kennedy or Brooke that long, we all got along. We would have to anyway since all four of our men were best friends. Where one went, they all followed, and if they had their own little club, Gen said we'd need one too.

Brooke had suggested Tits and Tater Tots, and we all agreed, so our group text thread now had a name and a little graphic Kennedy had put together of a tater tot with red lipstick and big boobs.

Now, Kennedy gently squeezed my arm. "Not much longer until Frogger's here."

I nodded in agreement as Liam scooped up his son to introduce him to me. I'd heard about Finn, the hyperactive little boy and the reason Liam and Kennedy had met, when she was hired to be his nanny.

"Finn, this is Tabby," he said. "Can you say hi?"

"Hi!" he shouted, while waving a dinosaur in my face. "This is Rex!"

"Hi, Finn," I laughed as Nate held out his hand to him for a high five.

"Volume down, buddy," Liam said. "Everybody can hear you fine in your normal voice."

Finn merely kicked to get down and then tugged on Kennedy's hand so she'd lower her big purse. The little boy plucked out a snack-size bag of cheese crackers. He tore it open, the crackers spilling everywhere. Kennedy bent in her dress to pick them all up as Finn proceeded to put his mouth on the ground and literally hoover them up.

"Jesus fucking Christ," Liam muttered as Nate tossed his head back to laugh before kneeling down to help with the crackers.

"Don't worry," Kennedy told me cheerfully as she stood, about half the crackers in her hand. "They're not all like Finn."

Thank god for that. He was adorable with his glasses and messy hair, like his dad, but that kid was *a lot*.

"Yeah." Liam slapped Nate's back. "I'm sure yours is gonna be an angel."

I shook my head in amusement and accepted a cracker when Kennedy held her hand out to me. Why not?

By the time we found the room, Finn and I had polished off the crackers, and we all ducked into a row of open seats. A few minutes later, Jude showed up with Brooke, his two kids in tow. Sebastian was somewhere between eight and sixteen—I couldn't remember if they paid me—while Amelia, the little girl, was in kindergarten. They filled out the rest of the row, Finn playing on the floor in front of us.

Gen had told us this would be a kid-friendly wedding. They wanted to include Dylan's kids, so they decided to let everyone bring their kids. But according to some of my quick math, there were still only about eighty people here, even with the few young ones included.

Dylan appeared at the end of the aisle, his four-year-old son Tucker next to him, both of them in navy suits and pink ties. Dylan jutted his chin in our direction as his attention skirted over the guests. When it landed on a few people in the front—his family, I assumed—he smiled at them then took a visible breath, his shoulders rising.

I settled back in my seat as the music started, signaling the beginning of the ceremony. All heads turned to watch as Scarlett, Dylan's seven-year-old daughter, trotted down the aisle first. A huge smile graced her face as she carried a small bouquet of light-pink roses, clearly relishing her role as maid of honor.

Then we all rose as the bride emerged on the arm of her father. I had yet to meet Mr. Kozlowski and studied him with interest. He had salt-and-pepper hair and a somber face, carrying himself stiffly in his suit. Though, he looked at his daughter with clear affection.

Genevieve was a vision in her gown, with lace and crystal embellishments that made it look like something out of the 1920s while still displaying her small bump. She wore her short hair pulled back with two tiny diamond clips, her mouth curved with the biggest smile I'd ever seen. Of course, she wore her red lipstick. It was a staple, after all.

Dylan fidgeted ever so slightly with every step, as if he couldn't wait for her to get to him, and when they finally held hands, he bent to whisper something in her ear that made her blush and laugh.

The officiant began speaking, his voice carrying through the microphone, but I found myself only half listening, studying Nate's profile instead. He looked so much like his father—same jaw, intense gaze, tall frame. Yet Nate's eyes were warmer, his smile easier, his presence more open and approachable.

My heart fluttered as he turned to meet my eyes. The corner of his mouth quirked up before he reached over to give my hand a quick squeeze. I laced my fingers through his, leaning into him. His body was solid and reassuring against mine.

Nate had become my rock, my safe place, and with him, I'd found a family again. Being here, surrounded by his loved ones, I felt that sense of belonging even more strongly.

Maybe one day, it would be me walking down the aisle toward Nate. But for the moment, I treasured the journey we were on together. I rested my head on his shoulder, listening to his steady breathing, as we watched his sister pledge her love.

And when Dylan and Gen were pronounced husband and wife, Nate let out a loud whoop, tears in his eyes.

This man. Such a softy.

The rest of us stood, clapping and cheering for the couple as they walked down the aisle. Finn tried to make a run for it, but Nate caught him and hung him over his shoulder, the little boy kicking and giggling.

All the guests were led out to a terrace, and Nate immediately found me a chair to sit in, even while everyone else stood around high-top tables. It was gorgeous outside, the sun just starting to set with a light breeze. Small appetizers were laid out buffet-style at one end, with a bar at the other.

Nate brought me a plate with one of everything, and he

stayed by my side as friends and family stopped by to talk to him. He introduced me to each of them, but every single name immediately left my brain, though they were all kind and welcoming.

After about an hour, we were brought back inside to the same room as the ceremony, transformed for the reception. Nate plucked our seating cards from a small side table, next to the gifts, and we made our way to our seats, next to Liam, Jude, and company.

When the DJ announced the newlyweds for their first dance, Nate stood and pulled me up too, keeping me close as we watched Dylan and Gen sway together, foreheads touching. The pure love surrounding this little wedding was overwhelming. I felt tears prick my eyes and leaned into Nate's side.

"You okay?" he murmured, noticing my tears.

I smiled and nodded, wiping at my eyes. "Just happy."

Nate's eyes softened. "Me too."

As more couples joined the newlyweds on the dance floor, Nate tugged me out as well. He held me as close as my belly would allow, slowly rocking us back and forth, Frogger making themselves known with a few kicks.

Nate laughed against my ear, his hand moving to find the movement.

"Careful, Frog. Mom's got to last a few more hours."

I grinned, loving each and every time Nate acknowledged me as Mom or Mama.

Though I hadn't called him Frogger's dad, he was in every way that counted. I still needed to gather my courage and take that step. Tell him how much I loved him and let him know that he was Frogger's father. That I wanted him to be a permanent person in not only my life but the baby's life too.

But then we were asked to be seated for dinner, and I was given a reprieve. I would tell him. Eventually.

Not tonight.

TWENTY-ONE
NATE

With the reception in full swing, everyone hit the dance floor, and Tabby lasted about twenty minutes before she required a chair. We sat and chatted with a rotating roster of people, Dylan and Gen, Jude and Liam, all the kids wanting to show us what they were coloring at the kids table set up with lots of crayons and paper.

But eventually, everyone faded away, and we needed a refill on our drinks. At the bar, I watched Tabby from across the room, unable to keep the smile from my face. I knew she didn't like the dress she wore, but I thought the ruffles were cute. Plus, it showed off her belly and hit her mid-thigh. Easier for me to sneak my hand up her skirt during dinner. Each time, she smacked my arm, shooting me her sternest eyebrow arch.

As if *that* would dissuade me.

She was so tired I doubted we had much more than an hour left before I would take her home. And maybe, possibly, hopefully, wear her thighs as earmuffs.

After receiving my order of ginger ale for me and sparkling water for Tabby, I turned to find my dad in line right behind me.

We'd barely spoken all night, one single short conversation with Summer and my half-siblings, Addy and Carter, about their summer plans. The kids appeared suitably bored for young teenagers, and Summer tried to get my dad to say a few more words besides "Yes" and "No" and "That's good."

Now, we stood a mere two feet apart, him appraising me with the same gray-blue eyes as mine.

"Hey," I murmured, stepping to the side. The same awkward tension filled my gut. The same anxiety I'd always felt, waiting for him to acknowledge me. *Pick* me.

I motioned to my table with our drinks. "I gotta get back."

"Is she doing okay?"

I froze.

My father was asking me a question? About Tabitha?

Is she doing okay?

I nodded. "Yeah. She's okay."

"Good." He cleared his throat, head bobbing. "That's good."

We stood silent again. His hands in his pockets. Mine still holding these fucking drinks.

Why couldn't we ever have a normal goddamn conversation?

I doubted he knew how to have one. He didn't know enough about me to say more than a few stilted words.

When I tried to move around him again, he cut me off. "I, uh, wanted—"

"Excuse me."

Dad and I both turned to another guest, waiting for the bar, and my father gestured for her to go ahead of him then stepped toward me, forcing me to step back so the two of us stood in a quiet corner.

With his focus on the floor, he still didn't say anything, and I couldn't keep my temper out of my voice. "What, Dad? What do you want?"

He opened his mouth, a cracked sort of sound releasing instead of any actual words, and I leaned back reflexively.

Was he going to puke?

Maybe that was how it felt for him. Standing here with me.

Like he could vomit.

The ridiculous yet plausible idea pulled a smile out of me, and I found myself laughing derisively up at the ceiling. "Why are you doing this?"

Then my father said the last thing I expected. "I'm sorry."

I wrenched my gaze to his, though his eyes flitted away almost immediately. "You're what?"

"I'm sorry," he repeated, so quietly I almost couldn't hear him over the music.

Stunned, I had no retort.

"I guess…" He lifted one shoulder. "Everyone has times in their life they look back and…reflect. I've been doing a lot of that lately. I want you to know I'm sorry."

I blinked a few times, still unsure what was happening here. I'd never heard my father apologize. Not to my mother and certainly not to me. He was not a cruel man, simply…cold. Indifferent.

I searched out Tabby, and when I spotted her at the table, her eyes were already on me. She slanted her head in silent question, a knowing arch of her brow. She had her hand on the back of her chair, as if she might get up and come to my rescue at my signal.

I did kind of want to signal her.

And yet, I didn't.

I also kind of wanted to hear what my father had to say. If anything at all.

Call it masochism. Constantly seeking out my father's attention, only to be disappointed. Why not do it again?

Dad took a deep breath. "It was hard being the son of an immigrant. We felt a lot of pressure to excel. My father's trauma…" Dad dragged the tip of his index finger across his upper lip, something he did a lot when in thought. "He had high expectations of us, and I had even higher ones of myself. The man survived Nazi Poland—it's not like I could ever bring home a bad grade. *Sorry for all your troubles, Dad, but I got a C in chemistry.* I couldn't do it."

I set the drink glasses down, needing to have my hands free to… I didn't know. Cross them over my chest.

I felt like I needed to do jumping jacks or something. Release this growing strain in my chest. I'd taken off my suit jacket during dinner and loosened my tie, but I was sweating now.

I knew close to nothing about my father's past. He so rarely spoke. About anything. But especially his childhood.

Dad went on. "My father worked very hard for the life he provided for my brother and me, and I had no other… I didn't know what else to do besides work hard and provide for you and your sister. That's…" He rubbed his finger over his lip again, his eyes resting on some place over my shoulder, a place in his mind. "I know it wasn't enough for you, but it was all I knew how to do, and I'm sorry I wasn't enough."

His words felt like a punch in the throat, and I had trouble swallowing past the rock there. I pulled at my collar, the puzzle pieces coming together in my mind, and I didn't like what I saw.

"You thought you weren't good enough?" I asked, my voice too high-pitched. "I thought *I* wasn't good enough. Not what you wanted or expected."

My father's eyes shot toward mine, his brows deeply furrowed, the wrinkles there overpronounced. He looked angry, and my instinctual reaction was fear. Not that he would hit me, but that I would be ignored or pushed aside once again.

"No." He shook his head. "That's not true. That was never true." He took a step toward me. "Nathan, I never, not once, believed that."

He set his hand on my shoulder, and I horrified myself when my eyes welled up with tears so badly I couldn't see clearly. I'd stopped crying over my father long ago.

Or so I'd thought.

I couldn't get any words out, but I didn't need to, because he kept right on going.

The dam had broken.

"I knew what you wanted and needed. I heard you, but I…I

didn't know how to give that to you, and I was afraid to try and fail, so I didn't. I know now that was wrong, and you deserved better from me. You and your sister both deserved better from me, and I'm sorry. I'm truly sorry."

His fingers squeezed the muscle of my shoulder, though he didn't move to hug me. I couldn't remember the last time he had, but I didn't want him to either.

I wouldn't know how to react, and I didn't know if I would want to accept it or not. Especially with my mind reeling from his confession.

"I see the man you've become," he said after removing his hand, settling it back in his pocket. "I see how you run your business and how you take care of those around you, and that is all I could have asked of you. To be happy and be a good person."

I nodded, rubbing my thumb and index fingers along my eyes, grating out a ragged, "Thank you."

"And I think you'll be a great dad. A hell of a lot better than I was to you and Evie."

When I finally lifted my head, meeting his gaze, he offered me an uptick of his lips. His version of a smile. "I'm proud of you, Nathan."

I cleared my throat, but my voice still sounded like it had been through the garbage disposal as I answered, "Thanks, Dad."

He leaned away, glancing over his shoulder, clearly wanting an out, so I gave him one. Picking up the drinks I'd ordered, I pointed to Tabby. "I've got to get back."

He nodded, I nodded, and then we parted ways.

From the strangest and most enlightening conversation I'd ever had with my father. One that broke open old scabs and offered some resolution.

"Everything okay?" Tabby asked as soon as I reached her.

"Yeah. No. I don't know."

She pulled me right up next to her, ignoring the water I placed in front of her. "Are you going to throw up?"

"No. I don't know. Maybe."

"What happened?"

"My dad talked to me. Like, *talked*."

"Are you okay?"

I hauled her into my lap, sitting her sideways, her legs draped over mine. She turned to mold her hands to my jaw, her thumbs smoothing over my beard, her fingertips stretching up to the hair at my temples and behind my ears. I closed my eyes, taking a few breaths through my nose, and she pressed her forehead to mine.

And this—*this*—was what I needed. All I'd ever need.

"I want to be good to you," I rasped, my emotions still so high I didn't know how much more I could say without exploding.

"You are. You're so good to me. You always have been, and it fucking wrecks me to know you've felt like you haven't. As if you bending over backward for me hasn't been enough." She gripped my hair at my scalp, urging me to look at her. When I did, her eyes were glassy too. "I don't know what happened just now, but I suspect you finally learned the truth about your dad."

I nodded, holding on to her wrists to release her hands from my hair and bring them to my mouth, kissing each of her palms.

She licked her lips, breathing hard. "I understand why you've never felt good enough, but I want you to know that I have not ever and will not ever feel that way about you. You've been really patient with me, and I know you need words. I know."

I smiled against her fingertips, enjoying her nervous babbling. Yes, I did need the words, but I also knew she needed time. I felt everything I needed from her. She wouldn't be here, at my sister's wedding, if she didn't love me. She wouldn't have let me be so demanding and all but kidnap her to live in my house. She wouldn't have kept coming back to Walt's year after year if there had not been a spark inside her.

The same one that kept burning inside me, urging me to keep her around, keep cracking the hard shell, fitting her puzzle pieces together.

"I'm trying," she said, drawing me to her for a kiss, and I knew that too.

That's why I loved her, I thought.

"That's why I love you," I said, not expecting to hear it back, so it didn't hurt when she responded by pressing her face against my neck, making my skin damp with tears.

After a minute, I sat her up, dabbed at her face with a napkin, and then took her hand in mine. "Come on. Let's go home."

TWENTY-TWO
TABBY

"What are you doing?"

"Nothing," I muttered, struggling to bend over, my foot on the edge of the bathtub.

It was the day before my due date. With the nursery finished, bags packed, and Genevieve lined up to take care of Lucy, I was beyond ready to have this baby come out of me. At my last appointment, the doctor told me I was a few centimeters dilated, but I could stay that way for a while.

So I had to find ways to keep myself busy while wondering if any little pain or hiccup was a contraction.

I had exactly zero patience for it.

Nate had all of it. Of fucking course.

"What are you doing?" he asked again.

When I kept on going, he caught my wrist, stealing my razor from my hand.

I heaved a sigh. "I'm shaving. Obviously."

"Obviously," he repeated flatly. "Why?"

"I haven't in a while because it's really hard, but I'm about to have multiple people all up in my business, and I don't want to have hair everywhere."

He smiled an annoyingly irritating smile. "Why? I don't mind it."

"We haven't had sex in weeks. Not since your sister's wedding."

"Yeah. When are you going to let me touch you again?"

I rolled my eyes. Never. I felt like a water balloon about to pop. A cranky, sweaty, hairy balloon.

I didn't want him touching me. Let alone even looking at me. Securing my towel firmly under my arms, I grumped, "You are the worst."

He hummed in agreement, sitting down next to where I still had my foot propped up. "I know. The absolute worst." He picked up the shaving cream can and shook it a few times. "Buying a kiddie pool so you could stay cool."

He did do that. After I'd complained about how hot I'd been, he put up a plastic pool in the backyard for me and filled it with ice-cold water. I sat in that thing for hours every day.

"Giving you back rubs all the time."

His hands were magic; I had to give that to him.

"And now, shaving your legs."

I blew out a loud breath, acquiescing. "Fine."

"Well, don't sound so put out about it. I'm doing you a favor, princess. Take the towel off."

I made a face. "No."

"I can't see." He'd started rubbing the cream up and down my leg and motioned to my thigh as if he couldn't possibly reach it with me wearing a towel.

"I don't want you looking at me."

He widened his eyes, *looking* at me. The smartass.

"I'm huge and uncomfortable."

"Yeah, so stop making this difficult. Drop the towel, and let me do this. It'll take a few minutes. Come on."

I mumbled a few curses and let go of the towel, only to cross my arms over my chest and hinge forward, so he couldn't get an up-close view of the jungle between my legs.

In a matter of minutes, he had my entire right leg clean-shaven then moved to my left and asked, "You want anything else done while I'm down here?"

"No," I snapped because I knew what he referred to. My *jungle*.

"You sure?"

"Yes, I'm sure. I'm not having you shave my vagina."

He had the audacity to actually appear put out. "Why not?"

"Because!"

"Because why?"

"Because this is already embarrassing enough. I'm completely helpless. I can't bend over, can't put on underwear, can't fucking get up from the toilet. I have to literally roll out of bed every morning. You don't know what it feels like to be so completely out of your own body. I hate it."

He nodded, calm and understanding. "Makes sense."

I hated him for that, too.

While I silently seethed, he finished my left leg then snatched my towel from the floor and walked to the bed. "Come on."

I spun around. "What?"

He merely waved his arm after spreading it out on the mattress. "Come here. I'm gonna finish shaving you. You want to feel *in your body*? Let me do it for you."

"Ugh!" I stomped over to him and shoved him in the chest hard enough that he took two steps back. "Do you have to be so goddamn perfect all the time? You know how frustrating that is? You're all...just...so...ugh!"

He muffled his laugh behind his fist, his eyes alight with mirth while I lost my mind. This baby was making me lose my mind.

"I can't stand you," I pouted, reclining on the bed, on top of the towel. He stuffed a few pillows behind me so I wasn't completely flat then disappeared into the bathroom for another few minutes, returning with the razor, a warm, wet towel, and the shaving cream.

He settled between my legs, placing the towel over me as he made idle chitchat about how he had to pop over to check on the bistro and then planned on going to the grocery store.

I loved him, but I literally could not care less and stopped listening, trying to ignore how his thick yet nimble fingers pushed and pulled my sensitive skin taut so he could drag my razor down in easy, even strokes like he did this every day.

Like he was some professional barber who shaved vulvas all day.

Zoning out, I hadn't realized I'd started singing until Nate sat up, grinning ear to ear.

I frowned at him. "What?"

"Are you taking requests?"

"What are you talking about?"

"You're singing. First, it was 'Fast Car,' then it was that song from… Was it *Dawson's Creek*?" He mangled a few bars of the song.

I shook my head. "It was 'Torn' by Natalie Imbruglia, and it was definitely not the *Dawson's Creek* song."

"Sorry," he said with a charming quirk to his lips, "I was too busy having a life as a kid to remember."

I kicked at him, though he ducked out of the way, taking all his supplies with him. He'd finished already. I heaved myself up, struggling to peer down, over my stomach. When I couldn't get a good look, I stuck my hand down there, drawing my fingers over the smooth skin. He'd done a good job, even around the creases and at the bottom by my butt.

Nate rounded the door of the bathroom, stopping when he saw me touching myself.

"Tabitha," he droned in a pleasant singsong. "What are you doing now?"

"I wanted to see how you did, but I couldn't. So I used my hand."

He slowly closed the distance between us, wagging his head

side to side. "You know the rule, don't you, princess? That pussy's mine. You need someone to touch it, I will."

"Stay away from me." I held my hand up. "Don't even think about putting your dick anywhere near me."

He smirked. "Good. Because it's gonna be my face."

He launched himself onto the bed, and I shrieked in laughter because even when I couldn't stand him, I couldn't help it. The man was a giant golden retriever, doing anything he could to make me smile.

I yelped as he buried his head against my thigh, rubbing his beard over my skin, but a familiar kind of pain hit my uterus. I gasped. "Wait, no. Stop."

Nate froze. "What?"

I grimaced, smoothing my hand over the top of my stomach to the lower curve. "I think… It feels like I'm having a cramp."

He placed his hand over mine, as if he could feel it too. "You think it's a contraction?"

"I don't know. I don't know what contractions are supposed to feel like."

He dropped a line of kisses on the bottom of my stomach, murmuring words to Frogger about being gentle as he fished his cell phone out of his pocket. He pulled up one of his many apps and proceeded to rattle off information about contractions and reminders about time between and breathing.

"Since you're so anxious to get him out," he said, raising his brow in question, "we could give that old wives' tale a shot and see how many orgasms it would take to induce it."

I played back the last five seconds in my head. "What did you say?"

"I could give you a couple'a orgasms. Help the process along."

I struggled to sit up, waving my hand. "No. No. Before that. What did you say?"

He eyed me. "You're anxious to give birth and asking about contractions…?"

I pointed at him. "That. Then. You said I was anxious to get *him* out."

He shot up. "No, I didn't."

I sucked in a breath, my hand on my racing heart. "You said him!"

"No, I didn't. I didn't."

"And you look totally guilty." My nose started to burn, throat clogged. "You said him. I'm having…" I cupped my hands on my bare stomach. "Frogger's a boy?"

Nate shook his head as the guilt fled his eyes, his gaze going soft. And then he nodded, whispering, "I didn't mean to look, but the envelope wasn't sealed and I accidentally knocked it down last week and the edge of the paper poked out and I—I'm sorry, Tab. I know you wanted to wait, but I—"

I struggled to push off the bed, and when Nate bent to help me up, I threw my arms around his neck. "Frogger's a boy."

He breathed out a laugh against my cheek. "Yeah. Frogger's a boy." He kissed my temple. "Are you happy?"

"I'm so happy," I sniffed. "I'm having a boy." I placed my hands on either side of Nate's face, holding his gaze. "We're having a boy."

That was when his eyes went glassy. "We're having a boy."

We held each other, reveling in the knowledge that soon we would have a baby boy. Frog was real, and he'd be here.

"So," Nate started after a few minutes, his hands journeying down my still-naked back to my ass then around to my hips and thighs. "Where did we land on the orgasms?"

I laughed, shaking my head. "No, thank you."

"Fine," he whined good-naturedly then helped me to put on clothes. All the while I couldn't stop thinking about the boy in my belly.

After dressing me in underwear, shorts, and one of his T-shirts, forgoing a bra, he sat me down in the living room with Lucy. He gave me my water bottle, along with a suggestion. "We could play a game."

It's a boy. "What kind of game?"

"I've got one or two buried somewhere in the basement. Probably Clue or checkers."

I shook my head. *What color will his eyes be?*

"A movie?"

I sighed and put a pillow between my knees as I turned on my side, pushing against the lump in my belly. His butt. *Come out already.*

As if he heard me, I felt another cramp. This time, it was a tiny bit stronger and in my back too.

Nate noticed my wince. "Is it a contraction?"

"I honestly don't know. It could be or not. It's not much different from other things I've felt. And it could be Braxton-Hicks."

He tugged at his hair, playing on his phone. "Well, it's been like ten minutes. You weren't feeling anything this morning or last night?"

"Yeah, but I've kinda been feeling little things here and there for the last couple of days."

He gaped at me. "Why didn't you tell me?"

"Why should I?"

"Because they were probably contractions."

"How would you know?"

He wiggled the phone in my face, as if it and therefore he knew everything about pregnancy.

I hope he is thoughtful and funny like Nate. "Listen, every single thing I feel could be a contraction. Okay?"

Nate harrumphed as if *I* was being stubborn about this. I wanted them to be contractions. If I could fast-forward, I would.

"I thought you were going to check in downtown," I said, and he shrugged.

"I already texted Collin that I won't be in today."

"What about the groceries?"

"Meh."

"Meh?" I dug my toe into his side until he set his phone down and met my gaze. "*Meh?*"

"Meh, meaning I don't want to buy food and then take you to the hospital in a few hours and have it all go bad."

"But what if it's not labor and we starve?"

"We're not going to starve. We have food, just no fresh produce."

I needled him. "Oh, so you want to feed me frozen chicken fingers and french fries right before I give birth?"

He pinched my big toe. "No, actually. I was going to force you to eat the multigrain Cheerios."

I gasped. "You wouldn't dare."

He nodded seriously. "I dare."

Turned out, we still had a few pieces of watermelon left, along with some frozen burgers he put on the grill, and we spent the night buying tiny little graphic T-shirts and planning family Halloween costumes, because why not?

This was what we did now.

Oohed and aahed over baby onesies that read *Don't Touch My Rolls* with a picture of sushi and argued over whether we would be Mario, Luigi, and Frog as a mushroom—my pick—or Snow White, the prince, and Frog as Dopey—Nate's pick.

And when the pains didn't increase through the night, I told him to go to work in the morning.

Only so I could call him three hours later. It was time.

TWENTY-THREE
TABBY

I cradled my newborn son in my arms, overwhelmed by a love deeper than any I'd known before. His tiny fingers curled around mine as he nursed, his eyelids fluttered open and closed, sleepy and comfortable with me. The past nine months of worry and anticipation had led to this perfect moment, this precious child who was wholly and completely mine.

After days of what I hadn't realized were mild contractions, I'd waited as long as I could before I called Nate. He would have stayed home again with me, but I, quite frankly, didn't want him around. He pecked and prodded at me, mother-henning me to utter exasperation.

And almost as if Frogger had been waiting for that exact moment, the *Oh shit, these are real* contractions came on immediately. Without Nate fawning over me, I made myself a peanut butter and jelly sandwich, took a bath, and tried to relax as much as I could since all the online advice said I wouldn't be getting any rest once I went to the hospital.

When I finally did call Nate, he went off on such a long-winded tangent, he arrived home still shouting at me through his cell phone even though I was in the next room. Then he texted Gen and put me in the car.

The check-in was easy, along with the labor. Once the pain really started to kick in, Nurse Veronica told me not to be a hero and to get the epidural if I wanted to, so I did. Nate stood by the bed, petting my hair as we decided we would name the baby after my father, and then he snuggled up next to me as I took a catnap, on more good advice from Nurse Veronica.

When it finally came time to push—with all 30,000 students, interns, nurses, and residents in the room, so I was right, and there were a lot of people up in my business—it wasn't too bad. For all the horror stories I'd read and watched and listened to, my pregnancy and labor were smooth. I felt pressure and a bit of pain, but nothing unmanageable.

Especially when the doctor placed the wiggling and wailing boy on my chest.

Born at 10:13 p.m. on July 16, George weighed in at a hefty eight pounds, eleven ounces, and was twenty-one inches long.

I hadn't been able to really see him at first because I was crying so much, but Nate kept muttering about how perfect and beautiful he was. It took no time at all to clean up and for everyone to exit the room—at least, that was how it felt. Like I'd waited so long for my rainbow baby, nothing else mattered.

Now, the three of us sat in the quiet, learning everything about one another.

Like how George was insatiable and took to nursing like a fish to water.

"A boob man," Nate whispered as he dragged his fingertip over George's forehead. "Like me."

I gave in to a quiet laugh. "I hope he takes after you for more than just that."

Nate stilled, the meaning of my absently delivered words settling between us. He'd been leaning over the railings on the bed, but he shifted to gently sit on the mattress by my knees, facing me. He placed his hand on my thigh over the blankets. "You want him to be like me?"

"Of course I do." I shook my head in faux annoyance. "Who else is going to teach him how to be so considerate and understanding? Who else will show him how to treat others with generosity and to love with his whole heart?"

Nate's face flushed as his Adam's apple bobbed, his eyes glassy.

My own voice cracked. "Of course I want him to be like you. You're the best person I know."

He licked his lips then bent to kiss my forehead, curving his hand over the side of my face. He swept at my tears with his thumb and pressed his mouth to mine. "I love you." Then he brushed his lips over mine again. "I love you so much."

Only after a third kiss did he back away, allowing me enough space to gather the courage. "I love you too."

The words had been there on my tongue for a long time, but they might as well have been glued together, locked in a box, and buried six feet under the ground for how difficult it was for me to get them out.

Nate rested his forehead on mine, his hands dragging over my head and shoulders. "Jesus, Tab, you're everything to me. I can't believe I'm here with you. I can't believe we're here *together* after all those years working with each other. And you…" He shifted back, his eyes red-rimmed as he took in George. "I can't promise I'll never let you down, but I promise I'll try so goddamn hard not to." He placed a reverent hand on the top of George's head, promising him too. "I won't let you down."

And the next part came out much easier. "I want you on the birth certificate. As his father."

Nate's eyes widened slightly before a slow smile spread across his face. He reached out to curl his hand around the back of my neck, nodding. I knew how much it meant to him to be recognized as George's dad. I also knew he wouldn't let either of us down.

"It's my honor and privilege," he said eventually. "Thank you for giving it to me."

We sat like that for a long time, long after George had finished eating and drifted off to sleep, his tiny body lax in my arms.

It was after one in the morning by the time I could take a shower and change into the pajamas I'd packed. Nate texted everyone to check in, sending pictures and the stats. With George sleeping soundly in the little cart they'd brought in for him, we turned the lights down low and tried to get some sleep. Between the diaper changes and occasional check-ins by nurses, the first night was okay. By no means a breeze, but it was okay.

But the second night in the hospital was an absolute nightmare. George cried a lot, and neither Nate nor I could calm him. I barely got a wink of sleep, and by the time the sun came up, I was ready to get the hell out of there.

After filling out forms and receiving the sign-off from the doctor, we strapped George into the car seat and left the hospital.

It was sort of surreal. That we went in as two adults and came out as a family of three.

And we were allowed to just leave.

With all the supposed knowledge and confidence to be a parent.

The drive home from the hospital was painfully slow. I sat in the back, next to the car seat, my hand on George's socked feet beneath the blanket we'd tucked around him. Every bump and turn made me wince.

Nate kept glancing in the rearview mirror, his brows pinched together in concern. "We're almost there. A few more minutes."

I nodded, biting my lip against the discomfort. I felt like I'd been hit by a truck after the sleepless night. The euphoria of meeting my son had worn off, replaced now by bone-deep exhaustion and pain. My milk had come in, and it felt like I had two very large, very tender watermelons strapped to my chest.

Nate parked the car in the driveway and rushed around to

help me out. He held the car seat in one hand while settling the other on my lower back to guide me into the house. Genevieve said they were going to keep Lucy for another night or two to give us some time without her peeing all over the floor in excitement, so we didn't have to worry about taking care of her too. Especially since Nate had planned ahead and bought doggie CBD to help with the separation anxiety.

But Gen had obviously been over to the house. Multiple bouquets of flowers lined the dining room table, along with a basket of snacks. I read each of the cards with the flowers to see they were from Shannon and Nick, Nate's mom and stepdad, Tim and Summer, Nate's dad and stepmom. Dylan, Gen, Liam, Kennedy, Jude, and Brooke all chipped in for the third bouquet and the huge basket of foods. It was very thoughtful.

But neither one of us dug through it for anything. Instead, we went right upstairs to the nursery, where I sank into the rocking chair. Nate unbuckled George from the car seat, murmuring a quiet, "Come on, Frog. Time to see your new digs."

He held our son in the crook of his arm like it was the most natural thing in the world and walked him around his nursery, pointing out the animals on the walls, the mobile, and the small bookcase with cardboard books. "What do you think? Hm? You like it. You do. I can tell."

George fussed, and Nate turned to me. "Want to try to feed him?"

I opened my arms for him and unlatched the strap of my tank top, positioning George's mouth at my nipple. He didn't hesitate. Nate sank down to the floor, lounging at my feet, quiet yet attentive as he kept vigil over us.

I hummed softly, every once in a while singing a few words to one of my favorite songs, "You and I" by Lady Gaga. And by the time Frogger fell back to sleep, I was ready to pass out as well.

Nate scooped him up, telling me to lie down. I didn't.

I stayed by the door, smiling to myself as Nate rocked

George. After a minute, I crossed the hall to our bedroom, where I showered and changed and swallowed a few ibuprofens. And *then* I lay down.

Our first night home went about as well as last night at the hospital, with George crying a lot. I fed him about every two hours, with Nate taking charge of all the diaper changes. He did end up moving the changing table into our room to make it easier, and I didn't know if it was hormones or anxiety or an overwhelming love so big for my baby that I couldn't breathe, but I had a hard time functioning. I kept crying yet couldn't pinpoint why.

Nate was beside himself, offering water and food and back rubs, but I didn't want anything. Only to hold George.

So I did.

The days and nights blurred together. Our friends and family stopped by to visit in shifts, and right when I thought I had a handle on things, George would have a diaper explosion or I'd leak breast milk all over the bed. I'd start to panic, but Nate was there, his calm and collected self, reassuring me with his usual line. "Don't worry, princess. I got it. No big deal."

But it was a big deal. Every gesture of care and support. The way he kissed my forehead and told me I was beautiful, even as I felt the exact opposite, needing help to change my pad. He was there, kneeled on the floor, holding the gigantic postpartum underwear out for me to step into, tenderly sliding them up my legs with the cooling pads he'd prepared during that first day home. He would smile at me and kiss my still-full belly before settling the elastic at my waist then helping me back into bed. He took care of all my needs before his own, drawing me baths and bringing me tea and snacks, forgoing sleep and taking on all the responsibilities in the house.

But it was his love for George that awed me most of all. The way his eyes lit up when our son grasped his finger. How he always bent to trail his nose over Frogger's head, inhaling that sweet baby scent like it was the most precious thing in the world.

I'd quickly given up on the bassinet. It was easier to co-sleep, and Nate said we could tell everyone to fuck off about it. And with Frog between us one night as he slept, Nate stroked his finger over the baby's belly. "I never thought I could love someone this much." Then he peered over at me. "It feels like sometimes I can't do anything else because it's so huge, the love I feel for him."

I nodded in agreement. That was *exactly* what it felt like.

"But I do," he went on. "I love him so damn much." He reached out and skated his knuckles across my wet cheeks. "You too. I love you more than life itself."

But that wasn't right. Because these two boys, they were my life now. And nothing was bigger than they were.

TWENTY-FOUR
NATE

'd officially been a dad for three weeks.

Felt like three years.

Every day was 120 hours long.

I didn't have anything to compare it to, but I supposed Frog was an easy baby. He was mostly content, and with Tabby breastfeeding, there wasn't a whole lot for me to do besides stick around to make sure she had everything she needed.

Because, goddamn, could my kid eat.

We'd been to visit with a lactation consultation a few days ago because Tab was overproducing. Something that mortified her at first when it sprayed all over. But I'd done some research and purchased these cups she could wear to catch excess milk. We already had a bunch of bags stored in the freezer because my woman was a machine.

A beautiful yet exhausted machine.

My mom had come over three times, staying from morning until night each day, so Tabby could sleep and I could go to work. Those days, I made sure to stop at the store for groceries and two bouquets of flowers. One for Tabitha for baking and birthing the most perfect baby on the face of the planet and one for my mother because moms were superheroes. Pushed bowling balls out of their bodies and then got up and continued about their business like it was nothing.

Incredible.

The very least I could do was bring some flowers and do loads of laundry.

And get out of the house. Tabitha had spent the first two weeks pretty much horizontal, save for the appointments to the pediatrician and the lactation consultant. Between bouts of crying and feeding George, she hadn't moved much from the bed. But the last few days, she'd been up and about. While I didn't mind waiting on her hand and foot, it was good to see color in her cheeks and have her rolling her eyes at my dumb jokes.

We'd tested out the stroller Summer and my dad gifted us with some short walks around the neighborhood, and last night, Gen, Kennedy, and Brooke had come over to coo at the baby while giving one another manicures and pedicures. I stayed out of their way, knowing Tabby needed time alone with them, and it had been while I cleaned up the kitchen that I'd received my texts.

JUDE

Meet us at Imagination tomorrow at 10.

LIAM

Welcome to the club.

The dads club??

DYLAN

don't be weird about it

Do I get a badge or something?

DYLAN

thats being weird

So, this morning, I packed the diaper bag with everything I

might need and probably a dozen things I didn't then carefully loaded Frogger into the car to spend a few hours with my bros while Tabby got to relax in the quiet at home.

After parking, I slid the diaper bag over my shoulder and carried the car seat in one hand, careful not to jostle my boy too much. He was asleep, and I didn't want to accidentally wake him up.

I was the last to arrive, finding my best friends already seated on the bench in front of the doctor's office. They'd all popped over to the house to meet George, but the three of them watched me with interested gazes as I set the car seat down at my feet and slid onto the end of the bench next to Liam.

He kept his focus on the baby as he asked, "How's it going?"

"Okay, I guess."

Dylan bent forward to meet my gaze. "How's Tabby?"

"She's good. She's feeling a lot better the past few days."

Jude grinned at me. "And how are you?"

I shrugged, rubbing my hand over my beard, thinking about the last three weeks. The last nine months. "Tired. Overwhelmed." I looked at each of my friends in turn. "Really fucking happy."

They all nodded as if it made perfect sense.

I stared down at George, his eyes closed, hands in fists on top of the muslin blanket with Winnie the Pooh all over it. So peaceful. I inhaled deeply, admitting to my friends what I kept from Tabby. "I have no idea what the hell I'm doing." Lowering my voice, I met their gazes. "I'm afraid I'm gonna fuck it all up."

Jude waved his hand. "None of us know what we're doing."

Liam agreed. "We're all figuring it out as we go along."

Dylan crossed his arms. "And don't listen to anybody's advice. Nobody knows your kid better than you do."

"But also remember that nothing lasts forever, and as soon as you have it figured out, things will change again," Jude amended.

"And vice versa," Liam added. "It might be terrible, but it will eventually get better."

I huffed. "So what you're saying is none of you have anything helpful to say?"

Dylan removed his baseball hat to drag his hand over his head a few times. "We didn't say that. We've got tons of helpful shit to say."

I circled my hands, waiting for this sage advice. "Like…?"

He shrugged and thought for a few moments. "Like don't watch Blippi. It'll make you want to break things."

"And try to avoid YouTube as long as possible. Pretend it doesn't even exist," Jude told me.

"Miss Rachel is good, though," Liam said.

Jude tipped his head in acknowledgment. "For cartoons, Bluey's the best. Brooke says it's the most feminist show on TV."

Liam pointed at him. "Agreed. I could write a thesis on the excellence of Bluey."

I made mental notes. "Okay. What else you got?"

Dylan sliced his hand through the air. "No slime, no play dough, no glitter."

"But watch out, because other parents will send bags of crap home with your kid because it was their kid's birthday, and if they see the slime, play dough, or glitter in those bags, it's a fight to the death," Liam warned.

Jude shook his head as if imagining it. "There's also a fight to the death about food. Everything they liked as a baby, they'll hate as a toddler, and everything they ate as a toddler, they'll throw away when they're older."

"You said you wanted chicken nuggets for dinner. Here's your chicken nuggets," Dylan said, pretending to hand his hat over as a plate of food before pitching his voice to a squeak. "No! I wanted pizza!" He rolled his eyes, leveling me with a glower as if I were the one demanding pizza over nuggets. "Sends me through the roof every time."

"It's the absolute worst," Liam muttered.

Jude eyed me seriously. "And don't be fooled by the well-behaved first child. The next one will be a savage."

"Got that right," Dylan grunted.

Liam lifted a careless shoulder. "Unless the first one is Finn. Then you're fucked."

I stared at my friends for a second, letting all that soak in before I dropped my head back, laughing.

The answer was there was no answer. I'd mess up. I'd get mad. I would definitely make mistakes, so I guessed all there was left to do was love my boy.

I'd do everything I could to protect him and help him and teach him everything I knew, and hopefully, thirty years from now, he'd think I did the best I could.

I leaned back against the wall. "I get it. Kids are hard. Buy a helmet."

"Take it one day at a time," Liam said, his attention focused on Finn, playing with some random child in the grocery store.

Jude leaned forward to slap my knee. "The only thing you really need to worry about right now is Tabby. Postpartum is tough."

I nodded, thinking of the long nights when Tabby could barely sleep, plagued by worry and doubt. "Yeah."

Dylan finally replaced his cap on his head. "In all seriousness, you're doing great. You're a good dad."

"He's right." Jude grinned. "You were made for this. Like I always said."

I felt a swell of gratitude for their faith in me, and I rubbed at the knot in my chest, where all my love for George resided. "Thanks, guys."

It was at that moment Scarlett noticed me, and she screeched in joy. Dylan and Gen had brought Scarlett and Tucker over to meet their new cousin, and it had been practically impossible to pry her away from him. She raced right over to me, accidentally knocking into the car seat. All the other kids followed her, so George fluttered his eyes open to not only Scarlett but Sebastian,

Amelia, Tucker, and Finn. All of them talking over one another and asking their dads questions about holding him and how old he was and what babies liked to eat and when they got teeth.

"Hey, all right." Liam pulled Finn away, his finger dangerously close to George's face. "Give the baby some room."

"I wanna hold him. Can I hold him?" Scarlett folded her hands, pleading at me with her big brown eyes. "Please?"

"How about I hold him, and you can each take a turn holding his hand?" I suggested, starting to undo his straps.

He fussed a bit but settled when I had him in the crook of my arm, holding him away from me a little so each kid could get up close and personal.

"He's so cute," Scarlett cooed. Even Sebastian—too cool for school—seemed taken with the little guy.

"Here!" Finn thrust a cookie—a real cookie that I suspected came from somewhere on the floor—at George's mouth, making him squirm and whine.

"Buddy, don't do that," I said, nudging Finn's hand away.

Liam scooped up his son. "Where did you find this cookie? It's garbage."

Finn stuck it in his mouth, and Liam rolled his eyes up to the ceiling, his mouth forming words I couldn't hear but understood clearly, nonetheless.

I smothered a laugh as I brought Frog up to my shoulder, telling the kids, "Go on and play. You'll have lots of time to hang out with him later."

They scattered, and my friends all nodded at me.

I smiled. This dad thing was totally easy.

TWENTY-FIVE
NATE

This dad thing was totally fucked.

George was over a month old, and Tabby's last semester of school was about to start. It was only a few hours a week on campus, and it was easy to work my schedule around her classes.

I'd taken care of Frogger on my own before and never had a problem, especially since he was more solid now. He went from being tiny and entirely too breakable to a stone. My little man was a brick.

Since he loved to be held, the sling we'd bought got a lot of use. Anytime Tabby wasn't feeding or cuddling with him, I usually had him in that thing. He did the house chores with me and even came to Walt's one time when I had to meet the HVAC people there. I got so much done as long as he was strapped to my chest.

Which was why I didn't think anything about Tabitha leaving today to meet with her adviser at school. A couple hours away? No big deal.

Until a summer storm hit.

It came on without warning. Or maybe a little bit of warning since Tab did ask me to find her an umbrella since her weather app called for rain.

With lightning and thunder hitting every other minute, Lucy was losing her goddamn mind, and the more she barked, the more George cried.

I didn't know who to help first.

I put Frog in his crib in his bedroom with the sound machine and fan on, hoping I would calm him down so I could get Lucy's thunder jacket, which did shit all because she wouldn't calm down enough to let me put her in it.

My attempts to swaddle George tightly were futile, his little face scrunched up in distress, and I struggled to juggle both him and Lucy, swaying back and forth with George pressed against my chest as I tried to wrangle a trembling Lucy. She squirmed in my grasp, letting out sharp yelps with each rumble of thunder. George's cries rose in pitch, tiny fists waving.

I tried to give George a bottle, but he wasn't interested in anything besides wailing, which didn't help Lucy's anxiety. They fed off each other. The more Luce barked, the more George cried, and the more he cried, the more she barked.

An endless fucking circle that slowly crushed my soul.

At the end of my rope, I tossed the sling on and put Lucy in it, bouncing up and down, and she quieted. Then I picked up George, kissing his cheek. "It's okay, Frog. It's okay." I held him against my shoulder, cradling his butt in one hand and his downy head in the other. "I got you. Shh. I got you."

After a few laps around the house, I had them both settled, though Lucy still panted against my chest, and George whimpered into my neck. As I completed yet another loop around the dining room table, the front door opened.

"Nate?"

"Oh, thank god." I'd never felt such relief in my life.

Tabby stepped out of her shoes as I bounce-walked toward the front door. She froze mid-stride, eyes trailing over the scene in front of her, a slight frown marring her lips. "What's going on?"

I shook my head, at a loss for words.

"Rough day?"

I nodded.

Without a word, she came to me, wrapping her hand around my neck, tugging me down for a kiss. She smelled of rain and coffee and everything I loved most in the world. Then she took George from me, cradling him against her chest, whispering words that soothed him. Soothed me too.

She petted Lucy's head, not at all fazed that I had her in the baby sling, and I swear to God, now that she was home, the thunderstorm stopped.

I breathed out an exhausted laugh, earning a wry smile, and took off the sling to put Lucy on the floor before hugging Tabitha from behind, my hands on her hips, my lips on her neck. "I love you."

She hummed. Since the day in the hospital, she hadn't said it again, and while I knew she loved me, I sort of loathed her reluctance to say the words out loud.

"Let's go upstairs," she suggested, and that sounded like such a good idea, I didn't need to be told twice.

Lucy followed us, still recovering from her panicked state, and curled up in her bed, as I collapsed on our bed. Tabby crawled to the middle of the mattress and propped up pillows in position to feed George. I rolled to my side, my head in my hand, watching as she eased our baby to the crook of her elbow then tugged the collar of her loose T-shirt down, revealing her nursing bra. With a snap of her fingers, the material fell to reveal her swollen breast, her nipple already erect. The baby didn't hesitate. He latched on, one arm slipping down to her side while he lifted his other, opening his tiny fingers to splay over her skin and grab at her necklace. The one she wore in honor of his sister who'd never made it earthside.

Tabby stared down at him with so much love and tenderness

it made my chest ache. Every time. I loved to watch her feed our son. It was such an intimate and special experience for the two of them, it almost felt like an invasion of privacy for me to be here, yet I couldn't ever force myself away.

I slid the tip of my finger over the delicate shell of George's ear and down to his cheek, feeling the movement as he sucked. Then I trailed my fingers up to Tabby's breast, dragging them back and forth across the top swell. It wasn't a sexual caress, more admiration and appreciation for what she was doing.

Made me love her even more.

She shifted her gaze to me, half lidded and a little sleepy. Nursing always made her drowsy.

"How was your meeting?" I asked, moving my hand to her neck, brushing away strands of hair.

"Good. I'm on track for graduation. She wanted to make sure I'll have enough time and support to finish my capstone project."

I nodded. "You don't have to worry about that."

She bit into her lip a little shyly as she smiled, her eyes closed, head tipped back. "That's what I told her. That I have a house husband at home."

"House husband?" I scooted up to kiss her neck. "I like the sound of that."

She hummed. "Me too."

I'd make an honest woman out of her one of these days, but we had the next few months to get through. The bistro was slated to open in a few weeks, and then we had the holidays and Tabby's graduation. It was a lot, but we'd be okay.

"Will you sing?" I whispered, and she barely opened her eyes to me.

"What song?"

"Anything."

After a few moments, her chest rose on an inhale, and then she started singing a song that took me a few seconds to realize was Green Day's "Last Night on Earth."

I dropped my head to a pillow, nestled into Tabby's side with my hand on George's back, the three of us physically connected as she sang about love making it through a fire.

In no time at all, I fell asleep, only to wake up a little while later to find Tabby and George still sound asleep. His little body was completely lax, mouth open right next to Tabby's nipple. Her head was tilted back on the pillow, eyes closed and breathing deep and even.

Smiling, I slowly slipped off the bed, careful not to disturb them, then snapped a picture on my phone. I had hundreds of these candids of Tabby and the baby. I supposed one day I'd clue her in. Until then, I hoarded them all to myself. Shuffling through them during quiet moments, from the first photo of Tabitha sitting on the edge of the hospital bed, her profile in view as she stared out at the window, her hand on the top of her belly, to this latest one.

Padding softly downstairs to the kitchen, I texted Collin. We had interviews scheduled for tomorrow to hire staff for the new restaurant. I wanted to confirm the time and go over the list of candidates one more time.

Collin responded right away, eager as always. We exchanged a few messages, hammering out the details, and by the time I tucked my phone away, we had a plan for tomorrow.

Riffling through the fridge and pantry, I gathered ingredients for dinner—salmon with asparagus and potatoes. I put on a sports podcast and got to work, not hearing Tabby until she was right next to me.

"Smells good."

I jumped out of my skin, letting out a very undignified shriek, before recognizing it was her. "Goddamn, Tab." When she bit back a smile, I aimed a glare at her. "Not funny."

"A little."

I waved my hand to George. "You're embarrassing me in front of our son."

She repositioned him on her shoulder, tilting her cheek to his head. "Are you embarrassed of your father?" she asked him.

"Hmm?" Then she bent as if listening to his answer. "He says your scream was not at all embarrassing and very manly."

I huffed, wrapping my hand around her hips to grab hold of her ass, squeezing. "I'm ordering that bell tonight."

She shook her head. "You're not going to collar me."

"No?" I pulled her against me. "What if I promise you'll like it?"

She rolled her eyes, hip checking me away from her so she could head out of the kitchen. "Maybe I should collar you."

"Promise?"

At the doorframe, she glanced back, her evil smirk in place. "If you're a good boy."

If she didn't already own my heart, I'd have thrown it at her then.

"Oh, princess, I'll be a very good boy for you."

TWENTY-SIX
TABBY

I woke to the familiar sound of Nate's cell phone alarm, followed shortly by his groan as he slapped at it. Beside me, he shuffled around before flopping onto his back with a huff.

"Morning," I mumbled, scooting closer to rest my head on his chest.

He grunted in reply, not quite ready for words, though his fingers did find my hair. I let him take his time waking up, tracing idle patterns across his bare stomach, enjoying the warmth of his skin.

The last few nights, George had been sleeping in his crib for a few hours. When we came to bed, I nursed him then put him next to me in the bassinet until he woke in the middle of the night. Nate would change his diaper, and I'd feed him a little before walking him down the hall to his crib, where he'd sleep for a good stretch of time. It was a nice way to ease us into moving him out of our room. Plus, I thought Nate and I were both sleeping better. *Everyone* was sleeping better.

But I especially loved the mornings before the baby woke up that I could spend with Nate. Sometimes we'd cuddle or just sleep, but this morning was different.

It was Nate's thirty-fifth birthday.

And I had plans.

After a few minutes, he craned his neck to peer at the clock. "Shit, I gotta get up."

I didn't move. "You sure?" Stretching my arm across his torso, I set my chin on the back of my hand to watch as he dipped his chin, blinking at me. "You should sleep in. It's your birthday."

"I can't miss my workout," he said, even as he toyed with pieces of my hair, rubbing them between his thumb and forefinger. "Got a million things to do before the opening."

The soft opening of his wine bar and bistro was only two days away, and he'd been stressing about every detail.

"But you deserve to relax a little bit today." I skated my hand down his side to the elastic of his underwear and slipped my fingers inside. He inhaled sharply when I wrapped them around his cock. "Enjoy your present."

His rumbling groan reverberated through his chest. "You're my present."

I shook my head and sat up, keeping my hand on his hardening length as I nipped and sucked on his throat, across his Adam's apple to his ear. When I bit the lobe, Nate hissed, his back arching slightly.

"You know what I was thinking about? How I'd gotten spoiled. It was so nice waking up to an orgasm every day for months." I drew my thumb along the tip of his cock, right over the slit. "I love being your princess, but I think it's about time I remind you that you're my prince."

He tried to catch my mouth for a kiss, but I ducked away, crawling backward. Dragging my hands over his stomach, I pulled down his boxer briefs on the way, his shaft stiff and thick and straining toward me. I didn't even take his underwear off, too impatient to put my mouth on him.

It had been weeks, *months*, and I missed this. Missed *him*.

I curled one hand around the base and the other around his balls, lightly tugging at them as I licked the drop of salty precome from the head before tracing the underside with the tip of my tongue. I stared up at him, making sure to keep eye contact when I took him fully in my mouth, only to pull back and swirl around the tip again.

He groaned, tunneling his fingers into my hair. "Fuck, princess, you know just what to do, don't you?" He tightened his grip. "Make me come."

I hummed around him, earning a spasm of his muscles, and he breathed out a laugh. "Yeah, you'll make me come hard. Down your throat, hm? That my birthday present?"

He stroked my cheek and jaw, his eyes alight with lust and admiration, praising me with his hands and words. Mumbling curses and directions. Telling me how he'd missed fucking me. How he'd been desperate to touch me.

"I love you so much," he said. "Being your partner and watching you become an amazing mom has made me fall in love with you so much more. Every day, I love you more and more, and you wake me up like this? You are everything."

He fisted my hair, holding my head in place as he began to lift his hips, taking over the movement for me, his teeth gritted, and yet, he still went on. "Fuck, princess. I love you. I love you. Look at you. You're so pretty like this. Your eyes all big and sleepy and glassy. Your mouth taking my cock. You were made for me. Fuck yeah." He breathed harder, repeating it over and over. "Fuck yeah…"

And then he orgasmed with a moan, his head relaxing back to his pillow, his skin flushed, the vein along his throat throbbing. I swallowed, gagging a little, as he released shots of warm liquid at the back of my mouth, his cock jerking between my lips and against my tongue.

When he finished, I slowly dragged my mouth back up his softening length, following with my fist, until he was clean.

Crawling back up his body, I found Nate utterly blissed out, a dopey smile on his face.

"Best birthday ever," he declared and reached for me, his intent obvious when he slipped his hand up the tank top I wore. But before he could do anything else, George's cry echoed down the hall and on the monitor.

"Frogger," Nate whined. "You couldn't give me fifteen more minutes?"

I stifled a laugh at his pitiful pout and hopped out of bed. By the time I fed and changed George, Nate had showered and dressed, so he took the baby downstairs, allowing me time to get ready for the day. We ate breakfast together and chatted, mostly about Genevieve, who was due soon, and what still had to be done at the bistro.

I'd always marveled at Nate's ability to stay positive and be productive, but these last few weeks, he'd really exceeded anything I thought possible. I had a hard time getting anything accomplished some days, still so tired, but he was up every morning at six to work out and then out the door around nine to do whatever he needed to at Walt's and the bistro before returning so I could go to campus and complete whatever schoolwork I had. Then after dinner, he was back out again after he helped with Frogger's bath time. The man was incredible.

A juggler doing it all. Never letting any one of his responsibilities hit the floor.

But I could see it taking a toll on him.

Before he stood to leave, I hopped onto his lap, which signaled Lucy to leap up from her place in front of the back door. She assumed it was family hug time and pawed at my leg to pick her up, but she was definitely not invited in this embrace, and I shook her off before hooking my arms around Nate's shoulders. "You sure you don't want to play hooky with me and Frog?"

His hands rounded my ass. "I can't."

"But it's your birthday." I bumped the tip of his nose with mine. "And I want to relax with you. Play more."

He started to shake his head, but George gurgled quietly in his bouncer as Lucy sat in front of him, the two good buddies.

"See?" I smiled at my little guy waving his arms. "Frogger wants you home too."

Nate heaved a sigh at our son. "You're supposed to be on my side, dude."

"He wants to hang out with his daddy."

I could see the war waging behind Nate's eyes as he gazed at me, his lips pursed. I scratched at his beard, because that always got him. Like finding the spot that made a dog kick.

He tilted his head, catching my fingers in his mouth, playfully biting at them as he growled.

"Hey!" I giggled, and he let go, only to kiss me.

"I love your laugh."

"So stay and make me laugh more."

"I can't. I really can't. We have the final inspection this morning."

I nodded, knowing I couldn't keep him from that, so I gave him a lingering kiss that would hopefully bring him home early tonight before I stood up to clear the table. After Nate said his goodbye to George, he patted my butt and headed out.

I worked a bit on my graduation project while George spent some tummy time on the play mat, and we both napped after lunch. Even though I had returned to school, it wasn't a full schedule, so I sometimes felt like I should be doing more, but both Shannon and Summer liked to remind me to enjoy my time with the baby because it would pass fast. In a few months, I'd be working full time, and I wouldn't be able to sleep with him in my arms whenever I felt like it, so I took the advice of both of my mothers-in-law and didn't worry about what I *should* be doing because it was right here. With George, being his mom.

Nate returned in time for me to pass off the baby, instruct him not to make dinner, and then drive to campus for my three o'clock class. On my way home, I picked up a couple orders of fish tacos, his favorite—apparently the Kozlowski siblings both had a thing for tacos—and a small cake.

I walked into the house to find Nate standing close to the television, Frog strapped to his chest as he explained the ins and outs of football.

"See? You see that? That's called a blitz. That's when the defense rushes the offense. That's what I used to do. And that guy right there? He's the best cornerback in the league." He raised George's hands, chanting. "E-A-G-L-E-S, Eagles!"

I cleared my throat, and Nate swung around in surprise. "Tabby cat."

I held up the bag. "I got your favorite. Extra guac for the chips."

He came straight to me, his hands on my face, kissing me. "You're the best."

"Picking up dinner is hardly a chore." I leaned in to kiss George's head. "I'll get the plates. I would ask if you wanted a birthday beer, but since you're going out—"

"I'm not. Well, I mean, I am going out, but not to work." When I quirked a brow, he said, "I'll take that beer. And after dinner, I want to take you out. Show you something."

Intrigued, I set the bag on the dining room table. "Where?"

"You'll see."

I shot him a look.

"Patience."

"Funny *you're* telling *me* to be patient."

He winked in that annoyingly charming way of his and then turned back to the television in time to see something that made him clap a few times. I spread the food out on the dining room table and called him to sit down, taking George to place him in his bouncer.

After we finished the tacos, I lit the number candles on the small vanilla cake with sprinkles then sang "Happy Birthday," punctuating it with a kiss. "Make a wish."

He paused, gazing at the flickering candles for a moment before blowing them out. "What'd you wish for?"

"Can't tell you that. It won't come true," he teased, but as I sliced into the cake, he placed his hand on my hip, finger hooking under the belt loop, admitting, "It was anal."

I gasped, refusing to give in to a laugh, and walloped his shoulder. He caught my wrist, pulling me into him, his mouth smiling against my neck. "What else can I wish for? Everything I want, I have."

I melted into him, angling my head so he had better access to my throat. "I guess we can talk about it."

He perked up. "Really?"

I shrugged. "We won't be doing it tonight, obviously. We haven't even had regular P in V sex yet."

He left an openmouthed kiss on the slope of my shoulder. "Mm-hmm. I'm ready when you are."

He ground me down on his dick to emphasize his point.

Technically, I'd gotten the go-ahead two weeks ago, but I hadn't felt very sexy, and I especially didn't want to get naked in front of Nate. Then again, I'd really enjoyed this morning and would like to do more of that.

I placed the slice of cake on a plate, but Nate kept me in his lap, splitting it between us, feeding a piece to me and then to himself until we finished. He didn't even give me time to clean up before he instructed me to put shoes on so we could go out. "Come on," he said, pushing me out the door, with George in his car seat. "Quick trip."

I played along, curious about where he could possibly be taking us on a random weeknight, but we didn't end up going far. Only downtown, where he parked in the back of his bistro.

"What are you—"

"You'll see," he said, smiling as he pocketed his keys to remove George's car seat. He escorted me around the side of the building. "Close your eyes."

When I did, he tucked my hand into the crook of his elbow, ushering me farther along. "Don't open them," he warned. "Here. Turn a little. Yeah. Like that. Now, don't move." I heard him step away from me, a door unlock and open, and then more footsteps after half a minute or so. "Did you open your eyes?"

"No."

His breath fanned over my face. "Are you sure?"

"I swear." I laughed. "I didn't."

"Okay." He shifted behind me, his hands on my hips. "Now you can look."

I opened my eyes to the sign above the thick green door, illuminating the night sky. There, in elegant script, were the words *Tabby Cat*. Though understated and subtle, the metal logo curved around to make what appeared to be the top outline of a cat, and the meaning of the gesture stole my breath. "You… That's… You named it after me?"

He nodded, his beard rubbing against my temple. "Who else?"

My eyes and nose stung with emotion, but he didn't let me stand there too long, taking my hand once again as he picked up the car seat from the sidewalk, escorting us inside.

The interior was even more stunning than I'd imagined from Nate's enthusiastic descriptions. The ambiance was warm and inviting, with soft lighting that cast a golden glow over the polished wooden bar and the cozy bistro tables. The open kitchen gleamed with stainless-steel appliances, and the wine cellar, visible through a glass door, promised an impressive selection.

"Nate, it's beautiful," I whispered, feeling a surge of pride for the man who had worked so hard to make his dream a reality.

He watched me closely as I took it all in. "You're my muse. Every bit of this place, it's all for you."

I spun in his arms, my eyes watering with unshed tears. "I don't know what to say."

He took a step closer, his hand gently cupping my cheek.

"You don't have to say anything. Just know that every part of my life, every piece of my heart, is yours."

The intensity in his gaze made my breath hitch. He loved me, and it was written all over his face. I wanted to say it back, to give him the words he deserved, but deep-rooted fear held my tongue. Before, in the hospital, it was spur-of-the-moment. I was exhausted and overly emotional, allowing the words to come easily, but I was back to myself now. Back to fearing the loss of what I loved most. I knew it wasn't true, but some part of me believed that if I told him how I felt, it would be taken away.

He would be taken away from me.

So I kept quiet and leaned into his touch, hoping he could feel the depth of my love for him.

We walked around the bistro with George's car seat tucked under my arm, Nate pointing out all the little details he had painstakingly chosen—from the local artwork adorning the walls to the greenery that added a touch of life to the space.

By the time we settled back in the car, I was brimming with a mix of admiration and hunger for the man beside me. He had built that for *me*. He had taken my offhanded comment and made it real.

The drive home didn't take long, but with the energy shift between us, it might as well have taken years. Dinner had been full of smiles and laughter, but the time for amusement was over. If there had been any question about if my body was ready before, there wasn't now.

Already, I felt overcome with need, my skin warm, pulse hammering.

We settled George into his crib, and after ensuring he was sound asleep, we retreated to our room, the air thick with anticipation. Nate didn't spare a moment, spinning me against the wall, his hands on my face and throat as he kissed me with as much vigor as the very first time.

Like he couldn't get enough.

Like he'd never get enough.

He stopped only to lift my shirt over my head and then his own. I traced the lines of his tattoos and muscles, the pieces of the man I'd come to know as well as I knew myself.

He stood still, letting me explore and kiss for a few minutes, until he had enough. He picked me up easily, his lips back on mine as he deposited me on the bed to tug my leggings off, leaving me in my ugly nursing bra and cotton underwear. He stood at the foot of the mattress, his eyes roving over me. I tried not to squirm, knowing what he saw: stretch marks and squishy skin. But he didn't care. In fact, he rubbed his hand over the bulge in his jeans.

"Don't think I don't want you," he said, as if he could see into my brain. "I want you even more now. You know how amazing it's been for me to watch you physically grow our baby. I knew you were strong, but seeing you give birth and recover from everything you went through, what you're still going through. I have no words for how much I love you."

He bent to unhook my bra and rid me of my panties, then stood back once again, admiring me for long moments. "Tabby," he murmured, his voice a thick rumble. "You're beautiful."

He placed a reverent hand on my stomach, holding himself above me with his other arm, then slid his fingers down between my legs, where I was throbbing and already wet. He parted me with one finger, groaning.

"It's been too long." He brushed his lips over my jaw and neck as he pushed two fingers into me. I gasped, my hands curling around his forearm. "I'll be gentle," he rasped. "Don't worry. I know what you need."

Then he scooted back, baring my clit with his other hand, holding me open to the steady pleasure of his tongue as his fingers worked inside me. I writhed, not caring about what I looked like anymore, only focused on what he made me feel.

Beautiful.

Wanton.

Wild.

Heat built low in my belly and spread through my body, my nipples taut and painful. I reflexively gripped my breasts, full and heavy in my hands, needing to rid them of the pressure. And suddenly, I was coming, panting and moaning, liquid bliss oozing over me.

It wasn't until Nate hissed a low curse, dragging his tongue over my nipple, that I realized I was leaking.

"Oh my god!"

"No, no," he rushed, pushing my shoulders back down, his hands cupping my breasts. "Let me." He licked the milk off my skin then sucked at each of my nipples in turn.

"Oh my god," I moaned, this time less embarrassed and more turned on, which made me feel… I didn't know how it made me feel. A little bit of shame.

Although the way Nate stared at me with hunger blazing in his eyes, I couldn't feel *that* ashamed.

He loved it.

I knew because he kept muttering it. "I fucking love you. Fucking love this. Anything your body does or wants, I love." He pushed my breasts together, licking down the valley he created, squeezing out even more milk. "I'll worship these tits."

And he did. For I didn't know how long.

Until he made me come again, my hips lifting off the bed.

"Please, Nate," I begged, desperate and needy, nails digging into his shoulders. "Fuck me, please. *Please.*"

"Okay, princess, okay," he said with a taunting laugh. "You don't need to beg."

"You love to hear me beg."

He licked his tongue into my mouth, positioning himself at my entrance. "That's right. I love to hear you say my name."

With one swift movement, he was inside me. I inhaled sharply at the sudden fullness, the exquisite sensation of being joined with him in the most intimate way possible. He rolled us over so that I was on top, straddling him, allowing me to set the pace and rhythm. Giving me time to become familiar to him again.

"Ride me," he ordered, clamping his hands on my ass cheeks, urging me to move. I swiveled my hips, each movement hitting exactly where I needed, stoking the fire rapidly growing within me, and he nodded, spurring me on with soft words. *Yes* and *that's it* and *look at you*. His hands roamed my body, cupping my breasts, teasing my nipples, tracing the curve of my hips. His eyes never left mine, and in their depths, I saw a reflection of my own desire, my own vulnerability.

Tension coiled in my core, the promise of a climax within reach. Nate sensed it too. He reached between us, his fingers finding my clit, circling it, applying the exact right amount of pressure. "Come for me, princess," he said, voice ragged. "Let go."

I did. The orgasm hit me like a wave, crashing over me, through me, leaving me shattered and whole all at once. Nate followed soon after, his body tensing beneath mine as he found his own release, his arms holding me tight against him.

As we lay there in the aftermath, our bodies still connected, I hoped he felt my love for him. I hoped he knew my heart belonged to him just as much as his belonged to me.

"Hey." He jostled me, so I'd meet his gaze. When I did, his eyes searched my face, his lips parting like he was about to speak but never did.

I quirked my brow. "You okay?"

He closed his mouth, cleared his throat, and then kissed my head. "Yeah. I'm fine."

I didn't believe him, and I had a good guess at what he might have wanted, so I tried my best. "You're the best thing to ever happen to me, you know that?"

He traced his fingertips over my forehead and down my cheek to my lips like he was trying to learn the shape of my words as I said them. "You and George, you're all I've ever wanted."

That eased some of the tension in his face, and he offered me a satisfied smile, sinking his fingers into my hair, exhaling a noisy, sleepy breath. He closed his eyes, and I placed my fingers over his pulse, feeling the beat of his heart matching my own.

With Nate, I had found my home. And that was worth more than any words could express. I closed my eyes, inhaling the scent of his skin, falling into an easy sleep.

TWENTY-SEVEN
TABBY

The opening of Tabby Cat was as stressful as any other leap off a tall building. Nate had been spending a lot of nights there, making sure everything ran as smoothly as possible.

Unlike the day Genevieve gave birth, which did not go as planned, between her water breaking in the car and Dylan getting pulled over for speeding. Though the officer had let him go when he realized what was happening, it had, according to Gen, put Dylan in a foul enough mood that he shouted at everyone to help Gen anytime she whimpered in pain. It was a long labor, but their baby finally made his appearance at the end of September. They named him Bennet, but apparently, Gen had to be talked down from naming him after some character in a fantasy romance novel she loved. Though he was a Matthews, the little guy looked like a Kozlowski through and through, with big blue eyes and a full head of wavy chocolate-brown hair.

The day we went to meet him, George in tow, Dylan playfully complained about how much his son looked like Nate, but the love and support between the two men was obvious. Especially when they both held their babies in their arms, talking by themselves in the corner, so Gen and I could swoon over them.

But as September slipped into October, I could tell something was bothering Nate. He had been quieter than usual, lost in his own thoughts even when we were together. At first, I figured it was just stress from the restaurant opening, but even as Tabby Cat thrived, he remained distracted.

There were moments of levity, like when we finally settled on our Halloween costumes, George as a cow with Nate and me as farmers, but his smile didn't reach his eyes as it normally did.

After we finished our pumpkin carving, I took George up to feed him and put him to bed while Nate cleaned up the kitchen, and I spent that hour contemplating what I would say to him. Contrary to my sarcasm and quick comebacks, I was actually terrible with confrontation. I had trouble expressing my emotions and telling people how they might have been hurting me. It was why I had hated living in the house with my dad and Beth, and why it had gotten even worse after he died. I couldn't properly get my points across. I couldn't verbally defend myself to her. I cracked way too easily. And then later with Danny, we were terrible at communication, neither of us capable of talking about our grief with each other. There was never going to be a happy ending for us after our baby died. It just wasn't possible when we were so inept.

But I wanted to do better now.

I had to in order to keep our family healthy and whole.

Nate and George were my happy ending, and I was determined to keep it that way.

I found Nate sitting at the kitchen table, Lucy in his lap as he typed something on his phone. I walked over, making my entrance obvious with noise. I didn't want to scare him like I sometimes did by accident, and I wanted to let him know that I had a purpose.

He glanced over as I pulled out a chair, the legs scraping on the floor, mumbling a "Hey."

I set my chin in my palm. "Thanks for cleaning up."

"Yeah, of course," he said, attention on his phone. "You don't need to thank me."

I watched him for a few seconds, tension crawling up my spine. "It feels like I do need to."

He set his phone facedown on the table and paid me his full attention. "Need to what?"

"Thank you."

He leaned back, crossing his arms over his chest, eyes narrowed. "What are you talking about?"

I bit my lip, still unsure how to start, afraid to stumble. "I feel the need to thank you for everything you're doing."

He shook his head, obviously confused.

"You know…how you take care of the house and me and Frog. I… Thank you."

He threw his attention out to the window, the dark night sky illuminated by a few stars. It was after ten, and by now, I was usually in bed with my pajamas on, but I couldn't do it anymore. I couldn't pretend like I didn't know something was wrong.

I set both of my hands on the table, picking at my chipped purple nail polish. "Is everything okay? I know the restaurant has kept you busy, but you seem…off lately."

Still keeping his gaze outside, he combed his fingers through his hair a few times then scratched at his beard. Any other time, I would follow with my fingers since I loved the sounds the short bristles made, how it felt against my fingertips, but I didn't dare right now. Merely waited.

He eventually exhaled audibly and brought his eyes to mine once again. "I guess… You know it really bothers me when you say thank you. I cleaned up the kitchen because our kitchen needed to be cleaned up, not because it's some gift to you."

I swallowed thickly, a foreboding feeling clawing at my throat, smothering my words. When I didn't reply, he shook his head, sighing quietly. "It's not…" He dug into his hair again. "Listen, I love you. I love you, and I know sometimes stuff is hard for you. I get it. I really do, but…"

"But what?" I asked so softly I almost didn't hear it myself.

"You never talk to me."

I furrowed my brow in confusion. "What do you mean? We talk all the time."

"No, I mean really open up. Share what you're thinking and feeling."

My unease began to curdle into defensiveness. "I do. I try."

He leaned forward, his elbows thumping on the table as if tired. "I tell you I love you all the time, but you never say it back. You never initiate it. So you thanking me for cleaning the kitchen makes me feel like shit."

My jaw dropped. "How does it make you feel like shit? I'm trying to show my appreciation."

"Because, Tab." He huffed and nudged Lucy off his lap, strain filling his body. My golden retriever turning Doberman. "It's not enough. That's not what I want."

"What do you want?" I searched the kitchen as if I could find the answer among the appliances. "I don't understand."

"I want you to tell me you love me," he said, his voice raised slightly like he'd been *waiting* to tell me that. "It's really starting to bother me. I tell you all the time. I try to show you. I know you need people to be there for you. You need people to be physically around you. I understand that, and I love it." He pressed his hands to his chest. "I love giving you what you need, but it feels like you aren't even trying to give me what I need."

My jaw flapped up and down. "I…"

"Even now, you can't do it," he went on, waving his hand in my direction. "I've been so patient because I love you, and I've told you over and over and showed you. I know it's hard for you, and I know it's taken so much for you to open up the way you have with me already, but goddamn, I love you. I need to hear it. I need to hear those words. *I love you.*"

His shoulders curled as if it had taken everything out of him to get all that out in one breath, and maybe it had, yet I couldn't help the trace of resentment that coiled in my belly. How long had he been feeling like this? How long had he been "patient" with me? I knew he didn't mean it to come off like condescension, but that was what it felt like. Like he was the perfect one, and I wasn't. He'd been doing everything right, and I'd been taking advantage of him.

That was why I thanked him for doing the dishes. Because some people didn't feel the need to be so supportive. Some men let their wives and girlfriends do everything. Some fathers took no responsibility. But Nate did, and, yes, I appreciated and loved him, and I tried to show him. Maybe not with words but with time we spent together, in the nights I stayed awake until he returned home, in the texts I sent him checking in, the ways I touched him, cuddled him. Still, he made me feel like I wasn't doing enough when I'd had a baby three months ago, no matter that we weren't even talking about George.

"I'm sorry," I said, not sounding at all apologetic. "I didn't realize you were so needy."

As soon as the words were out, I wanted to suck them back in. I hadn't even thought of them; they'd just tumbled out, my mind all over the place. The fear I'd long since hoped to overcome still clung onto my heart, never letting me fully give myself to the one person I should.

"I'm needy?" Nate spat. "The guy you said you appreciated so much not even five minutes ago? *He's* the needy one? Not *you*?"

I hung my head, my words and thoughts all jumbled together, so much that I couldn't reply.

"I might be the needy one, but at least I'm not so fucking frigid all the time."

I winced, reeling back in my chair like he'd slapped me.

Of course, he hadn't, but I teared up, nonetheless.

Nate frowned, shaking his head. "I'm sorry. I didn't mean that."

I nodded and pulled the sleeves of my sweatshirt over my hands to dab at my eyes. After everything, I still didn't want to seem weak. Even if he was the one who made me feel that way.

"I just wanted to talk," I murmured, voice cracking.

Next to me, he took a few deep breaths, stretching his hand out to curl around my neck. "I know. I think... I'm really stressed, and I don't want to keep having this conversation right now. I don't want us to keep saying things we don't mean. I need to go to Walt's, and we can talk later tonight or tomorrow. Okay?"

It wasn't okay, but I nodded anyway.

Then he stood, gathered his cell phone, keys, and wallet, and headed out the door without so much as a backward glance.

TWENTY-EIGHT
NATE

"Hey, boss, I'm heading out unless you need anything else."

I spun in my chair at the desk in the back office of Walt's. I'd been here for a couple hours, trying to catch up on everything I'd let slip through the cracks the last few weeks. Between the baby and Tabby Cat opening, I'd been neglecting this place. But what better time to work than now since I'd already fucked up at home?

"Nah, Bran, I'm good."

"All right. See ya—"

"Hey." When he stopped mid-pivot, I leaned back, raising my chin so we had each other's gaze. "I wanted to let you know I'm happy you've stepped up, and I appreciate all your hard work."

Bran grinned. "Thanks, man."

We clapped hands as a goodbye, and I swung back around to my computer once he left. Although, I didn't feel any more motivated than before. I stared at the screen, the columns of words and numbers blurred together into a meaningless mess. I couldn't focus, not after that argument with Tabby earlier.

My heart ached as I replayed the hurt in her eyes when I had called her frigid in a moment of frustration. I didn't mean it. She had hurt me, calling me needy, which I was sure she hadn't meant either. But goddamn, that was the one thing to knock me down. Straight back to when I was a kid, crying and emotional, my parents arguing, feeling entirely inadequate all over again.

It didn't excuse anything, but I was upset, and I knew she was upset.

The irony was neither one of us wanted to argue, neither one of us wanted to hurt the other. I could tell from how she winced and curled in on herself. She would never purposely say anything to cause me harm. We were both just…learning how to be new parents with shorter tempers than usual from too little sleep and not enough time together.

Tabby had experienced so much pain already; it was a miracle she trusted me at all. Even now, after everything we had been through together, she struggled to say those three little words that I so desperately longed to hear.

Sure, she'd said them once, but I *was* needy. I was a needy bastard who didn't want to share and required all her attention. She was mine. I was hers. And that's all there was to it.

I huffed, rubbing my temples. This wasn't even that big of a deal. We would have a few conversations about this and hopefully put the issue to bed, but with how much stress we were under, it felt bigger than it really was.

It wasn't like I didn't believe she loved me.

This was only our insecurities making us assholes.

"Fuck me," I murmured, checking the time on my cell phone. After two in the morning. George would be waking up soon for his middle-of-the-night feeding. I hoped Tabby had gotten some sleep.

God, I was such a dick. I shouldn't have left her. She was probably still up, never having gone to bed. She'd told me one night she had trouble sleeping without me next to her.

I was such an asshole.

I should be at home. I should've just talked it out tonight. But here I was in my fucking office like a coward.

Crack.

I whirled around in my chair, my brooding thoughts interrupted by the loud sound. I frowned, listening closer. More popping and crackling noises, like electricity arcing. And there was an acrid, burned smell in the air too now. My hackles rose. Something was very wrong.

I hurried out from the cramped office toward the front of the bar. The smell grew stronger, and thin wisps of smoke began wafting through the air vents above. A feeling of dread settled in my gut.

A snap sounded directly above me, and I reflexively covered my head, even though nothing fell. "Shit," I muttered, realizing what was happening. "Fire."

I had been told that I needed a new HVAC system here. That this one was old and I'd probably have to replace the insulation as well. But I'd kept pushing it off and pushing it off.

It was only a minor inconvenience with the heating and cooling.

But this was no minor inconvenience anymore.

This was my livelihood literally up in flames.

Adrenaline flooded my system instantly. I had to get out of here, fast.

I sprinted for the front door, fumbling to pull my phone out of my pocket with one hand, intent on calling 9-1-1. Flames were already spreading through the ceiling. The thick smoke choked my lungs and burned my eyes.

Thank god Bran had left when he did.

As I neared the front entrance, a flaming plank crashed down in front of me, blocking my nearest escape route. The fire roared to life, consuming the wooden beams with ravenous ferocity.

Panic surged through me, and I pivoted, looking for another

way out. I scrambled toward the back exit, but with the thick smoke, I had trouble seeing and breathing. I pulled my shirt over my mouth and nose, coughing violently. The heat was unbearable.

The sharp crash of another beam collapsing came from behind me, and pain flared in my leg. I yelped, falling to the floor, bending to see a fiery piece of something lodged in my pant leg.

All those lessons in elementary school came back to me. I stopped, dropped, and rolled for my life, gasping for air through the searing pain in my leg.

I had to get the fuck out of here.

I had to get back to Tabby, to the baby.

My eyes stung, tears forming from the smoke and whatever the hell had happened with my leg.

I crawled to the back door and burst out onto the sidewalk, gasping for clean, cool night air.

The cold October wind bit at my skin as I staggered, collapsing against the back wall of the building. With trembling fingers, I dialed.

"Nine-one-one, what's your emergency?"

"My bar's on fire. Walt's, the whole—" A violent coughing fit overtook me, making it hard to speak. "The whole roof's burning up."

"What's your address?"

"It's 523 Pine," I got out between hacks.

"Is anyone in the building?"

I shook my head even as I knew the operator couldn't see me, but with the way my vision began to blur and how fuzzy I felt, I didn't know if I could string enough words together. "No. I... Me..."

In the distance, faint sirens wailed. Relief washed over me, but it was short-lived as I felt myself sinking to the ground. The last thing I saw was the flames licking higher into the night sky, painting everything in an eerie, flickering glow. The last thing I thought of was Tabitha—*my Tabby*—sitting with George—*my son*—as she fed him. His tiny hand curled around her starburst necklace and her gazing down adoringly at him.

I thought I smiled.

But I couldn't be sure.

Because everything went black.

TWENTY-NINE
TABBY

hadn't been able to sleep. I tried. I brushed my teeth, put on my comfiest pajamas and white-noise playlist, but I couldn't. I even tried a few chapters of my Scottish romance, but when that didn't help, I gave up and went downstairs, settling on the couch with a blanket and the monitor next to me as I mindlessly watched *Planet Earth* with Lucy at my feet.

I checked the time once again. Almost three a.m. and still no word from Nate.

My stomach churned with guilt and worry. Our fight earlier tonight kept replaying in my head. I hated leaving things so raw and unfinished between us. Especially after he'd confessed how much it hurt him that I wouldn't yet say "I love you" back.

I understood where he was coming from. I'd felt his love through his actions for months now. The nursery he'd meticulously decorated. The foot rubs and back massages when I could barely walk because of my gigantic belly. He never even blinked when it came to diaper changes. Or, hell, helping *me* change in those days after I delivered George.

He showed me he loved me in all the ways I needed, and he told me over and over because that's what he needed—words.

But my hesitation to say them wasn't about him. It was the

barricade around my heart, cracked but still standing from my past. I wanted to tear it down brick by brick. I was trying. But old wounds didn't heal easily or in a straight line.

I sighed, shifting positions on the couch again, too restless to get comfortable. Where was he? I needed him here so I could explain. So I could wrap my arms around his sturdy frame and whisper "I love you" into his neck. The words were there, waiting to be released. I just needed him to come home so I could set them free.

My phone lit up, buzzing on the coffee table. I grabbed it quickly, heart leaping when I saw the hospital's name on the screen.

"Hello?" I answered urgently.

"Tabitha?" a woman's voice replied. "This is Salma from Memorial Hospital. I called because you're listed as Nathan Kozlowski's emergency contact."

The phone slipped from my fingers, clattering to the floor, and I fumbled to pick it up, my hands trembling. When I put it back to my ear, the woman was mid-sentence.

"I'm sorry, could you—could you repeat that?"

"I'm calling to inform you Nathan's been brought in by an ambulance. He's in—"

My hand flew to my mouth. "Is he okay?"

"He is currently being tended to by the medical staff, but if you're able, you should make your way here to—"

"I'll be right there. As soon as I can. I'll be there." I hung up and raced upstairs, my mind reeling with possibilities and none of them good.

But the more I panicked, the more difficult it was for me to do anything. I tripped while changing, couldn't find my sneakers, and nearly flattened Lucy as I ran in circles.

"You have to get out of the way," I snapped at her, throwing the diaper bag over my shoulder. I ran down the hall, Lucy trailing at my heels, to wake up George. He wouldn't be happy, but there was nothing I could do. We had to get to the hospital.

Now.

"Come on, Frog," I rasped, voice cracking with worry. He wiggled and squirmed, nose wrinkling in the telltale way before he would let out a cry. Which he did.

I tried to soothe him, offering him the elephant WubbaNub, which he hated, but I stuck it in his mouth anyway. "We have to get in the car, and I can't feed you right now."

Downstairs, I stuffed my cell phone into the bag, buckled George into the car seat, and slammed the door behind me, leaving Lucy howling in rage. I didn't care. I had only one destination in mind.

Nothing else mattered.

With George safely stuck in the back seat, screaming his lungs out, I headed to the hospital. This time of night, there was no traffic, and I made it there within minutes, my mind consumed with worry, my eyes blurry with tears.

I burst through the emergency room doors, George wailing in my arms. I frantically scanned the room until I spotted the intake desk.

"Nathan Kozlowski," I nearly shouted to the nurse behind the counter. "He was brought in by ambulance. I'm his emergency contact."

She nodded, fingers clicking on the keyboard. "Let's see… He arrived about thirty minutes ago. It looks like he's still being evaluated and treated, but he's listed in stable condition."

My knees nearly buckled in relief. "Can I see him?"

"Not just yet, hon. As soon as the medical team finishes up, he'll be moved to a room, and then you can visit."

I blinked back tears, adjusting a screaming George on my shoulder.

The nurse gave me a sympathetic look. "Why don't you have a seat in our waiting area? I'll come grab you as soon as we get word you can see him."

I nodded numbly and made my way over to the small waiting section, collapsing into a chair. George cried, face scrunched and red. "Shh, it's okay," I murmured, tugging my shirt up to pull my bra down to feed him. I didn't care about modesty or judgmental looks, and if I couldn't feed my kid here in a hospital, where could I? "We're gonna see Daddy soon."

George gulped down the milk greedily while I held him, my nose clogged and my eyes stinging with tears. I adjusted my hold on Frogger to find a tissue in my bag. A few seconds later, the check-in nurse appeared by my side. She rested a hand gently on my shoulder and offered me a box of tissues.

The simple act made me absolutely crumble.

"Oh honey, it's all right," she said, sitting next to me. "Try not to worry too much."

I nodded, barely able to utter a thank-you through my hiccuping sobs.

She rubbed my upper back until I caught my breath then asked, "How old is your baby?"

"He's, uh…" I sniffled into a tissue. "He's thirteen weeks."

"You've got yourself a big boy."

I huffed in amusement, despite my misery. "Yes, he is."

After a few moments of us watching George eat, she told me quietly, "Your husband's injuries aren't life-threatening. He'll be fine, but he'll be moved to a room for some monitoring because of the smoke inhalation. He's awake and talking."

I let out a shaky breath, gratefulness washing over me for her giving me information I doubted she was permitted to. "Thank you."

She smiled kindly. "I'll come back for you as soon as he's settled in his room, but you let me know if you need anything, okay?"

I managed a small, watery smile in return. As she walked away, I sagged back against the chair, nestling George close in the crook of my arm, my other hand on his head, cradling him completely against me.

Nate was okay. He was here, and he was alive. I only needed to see his face. To touch him and know that he was still mine.

I traced my fingertips over the crown of George's head. "Daddy's gonna be fine," I told him, willing it to be true. "He's too stubborn not to be."

After George finished eating, and he fell asleep, I adjusted my top to cover up but continued to hold him, not wanting to put him down. When everything else felt so precarious, I needed the physical tether to my baby to keep me whole and sane. As we waited, I texted Genevieve to tell her I was here with Nate, not wanting to call her with the baby.

But I should have known she'd answer.

GEN

OMG WHAT HAPPENED

I'm not sure. I got a call that he was here and now I'm waiting in the er.

the check-in person told me he's okay

he's going to stay here though

GEN

OMG. OMG.

GEN

Are you okay? Where is George?

with me. we're both here.

GEN

I'll send Dylan.

No don't

I don't know what exactly is going on except he is going to be moved to a room for observation

please don't send Dylan

there will be nothing for him to do

GEN

Fine. But keep me updated. Every ten minutes.

you need to sleep

GEN

I haven't slept in days. I think I'm delirious. Text me. Call me. I don't care but if you don't I will send Dylan, and you don't want his grumpy ass coming down there making a scene.

I outright laughed. Leave it to her to make me *laugh* now.

as soon as I know more I'll call you.

The minutes crawled by for what felt like an eternity, but the nurse eventually waved me over.

"He's asking for you," she said, eyes crinkling with a secretive smile like maybe we weren't supposed to be doing this. "Come on back."

I followed her on shaky legs down the hall, George asleep in his car seat, my heart thudding in my ears.

She paused outside of a room and nudged the door open. "Go on in. I'm sure he'll be glad to see you both."

I stepped inside, breath catching at the sight of Nate propped up in the hospital bed. His color was good, eyes alert, and he broke into a grin when he saw us.

"There's my family," he said, voice gravelly but wonderfully familiar.

I set the car seat on the floor and rushed to his side, tears spilling over once more. This time, they were tears of joy. He smoothed his hand over my head and hair, shushing me, kissing me, murmuring, "Don't cry, princess."

It took a minute until I could pull myself together and lift my head, finding Nate's eyes red and glassy. His hair was complete chaos, his body covered in a hospital gown, with wires hooked up to him and a few machines, one of them a heart monitor, displaying the beautiful and perfect rhythm.

"How are you?" I asked, and he shrugged, vaguely motioning to his left leg.

"They got me on some pain meds. I got a pretty good gash and burn on my calf that they fixed up, and besides some smoke in my lungs that feels like I swallowed a cheese grater, I'm fine."

His voice did sound like it had been dragged over broken glass and then put in a blender. "How's Frog?"

I leaned over to tug the car seat closer, our son blissfully asleep and unaware. "He's okay. I fed him while we were in the waiting room."

I couldn't help the way my voice broke on the last syllable, but I bit the inside of my cheek to keep from crying. Perched on the edge of his bed, I laced my fingers through his, unwilling to let him go. "What happened?"

He dropped his head back to the pillow, his eyes half lidded. "Remember how I said the HVAC system was fucked?" When I widened my eyes in horror, he released a long, painful sigh. "I was by myself in the office when I heard some sounds. By the time I got out to the floor, the ceiling was already on fire."

"Oh god," I whispered, scooting as close to him as possible, reaching out my free hand to curl around his bearded jaw.

"It spread quick," he went on, though I didn't need much more of an explanation. "It's bad, the damage. I'm not sure..."

I shook my head. "It doesn't matter. None of that matters." I cupped his face with both of my hands, catching the vague scent of smoke off his skin. I assumed his clothes were trashed. "As long as you're okay, that's all I care about. You're here with me and George. That's all. That's everything."

Tears fell from my cheeks and onto Nate's face. He didn't wipe them away, merely bent forward to kiss my wet skin. "I was so scared," he said, and I could hear his own tears in his voice. "All I thought about was you and George. You two were the last thing I saw."

I dropped my head, crying and kissing him, barely breathing as I tried to get it all out. "I love you. I love you so much, and I'm so sorry about what I said to you. You're not needy. You're perfect. I love you, and I won't hold back. I—" My breath hiccuped. "I promise, no more holding back, because I love you."

He wiped his palms across my eyes and face. "I'm sorry too. You're not frigid. You're the very opposite. You're full of emotion. You just needed a fire to let it out."

I thumped his chest, snorting a laugh that caught in my throat, causing me to cry more. "I fucking hate you so much. Never do that to me again."

He pulled me toward him for a kiss on the lips that tasted salty and full of promises. "I love you," I said against his mouth. "I love you. I love you."

He smiled. "I think I like that even more than you begging."

I pushed away from him to roll my eyes. "Do you ever take anything seriously?"

"Yeah." He covered my hand with his. "Taking care of you and our baby."

I couldn't deny that.

"But until I know more about the damage to Walt's, I'm not sure about our financial situation," he said soberly until his blue-gray eyes lit with levity, his mouth curving into a teasing smile. "You might have to support us, and I'll have to be a house husband for real."

"That's okay," I agreed easily. "I kinda like the sound of that."

He raised an eyebrow. "Oh yeah? Gonna keep me barefoot and pregnant in the kitchen?"

"You'd look damn sexy vacuuming in an apron."

His laugh melded into a cough that had me reaching for the cup of water on his side table, holding it out for him to sip from. When he finished, he smiled at me. "Anything for you, princess." Then he pressed a kiss to my forehead. "I love you."

"I love you too," I said and reached down for George when

he whined. I handed him over to Nate then snuggled into his side.

Even waiting in this emergency room with the love of my life hooked up to beeping machines, I felt content.

Nate was going to be fine.

Our family was whole and happy.

And that was all that mattered.

I was theirs, and they were mine.

THIRTY
NATE

In the almost two months since Walt's had caught fire, life seemed to speed by in double time.

I had held multiple meetings with contractors and insurance agents about the future of the bar. It had sustained a lot of damage, but nothing that was completely irreparable, though it would be quite extensive to get it back to working order. Tabby and I had spent many long nights discussing the options, but we ultimately decided on selling it and brought all the staff over to Tabby Cat.

It was a difficult decision. After all, Walt's was my first baby. It was the place Tabitha and I met, the reason we even had a relationship to begin with, but having the bar and the bistro was a lot for me. Maybe splitting my attention would have been possible if I were still single, but I had Tabby and the baby now. I wanted to focus on them. I had to focus on them, and in doing so, something else had to go.

I used the insurance payout to install a new HVAC system and complete some of the aesthetic repairs. Currently, I was in the middle of getting it ready to go on the market in the new year, and since Walt's was a well-known bar with a good location, my real estate agent already had some interest.

The day we would have to officially say goodbye would be hard, but it was time to start the next chapter of my life. Today. With the woman up onstage.

I couldn't wipe the grin off my face as I watched Tabby cross the platform to accept her diploma in her black gown, purple sash, and mortarboard. She shook a few hands then turned to look out over the audience, and when she spotted me standing at the end of the aisle, she smiled, waving her fingers.

Her cheeks flushed pink as I whooped and cheered with pride, hollering and clapping louder than anyone else in the crowd. Even George gurgled and kicked his feet in the carrier strapped to my chest.

"You see your mama?" I held his hand and pointed. "You see her? Aren't you proud?"

Because I sure as shit was.

"That's your mama!" I told him, even though he was too young to understand how long and hard she had worked for this moment. Trauma and grief and new motherhood.

She was incredible, and I was so goddamn proud.

Prouder than I'd ever been of anyone.

My fierce, resilient Tabby. The woman I loved with my entire being.

My gaze followed her as she walked offstage, back to her spot, and I wiped a loose tear from my cheek. Because, yes, I was *emotional*.

Frogger and I stayed standing through the end of the ceremony because the little guy preferred motion over anything else lately. Tabby met us, and I swallowed the lump in my throat when she flung her arms around my neck, careful not to squeeze George between us.

"I'm so proud of you," I said against her hair and then once more against her mouth. Pulling back, I brushed away the moisture from her cheeks before kissing her again.

When we separated, she playfully tweaked George's tiny foot. "What did you think, baby? Did you see Mama graduate?"

He blew a few bubbles in response, and her answering laugh made my heart swell. She laughed often now. She was so much lighter than she used to be. I knew it wasn't all because of me, although my ego liked to believe so.

She was merely safe now. She felt secure enough to let go, to smile and giggle and ask for help if she needed it. She wasn't on her own anymore, and I was determined to keep it that way.

With her hand in mine, I towed her away from the crowd. I folded her hands between mine as I stared into those dark eyes of hers that were once as mysterious as the ocean but now so easy to read, like peering in through a window. "You amaze me every day with your strength and heart and willingness to show me all the parts of yourself you don't like others to see. I am honored to be the man you chose, and now…"

I reached into my pocket to present her with the simple diamond on the plain white gold band. She gasped when she realized what it was and what I was doing. I sank onto one knee, George waving his fists in the air. "Tabitha Reynolds, I want to spend the rest of my life being amazed by you. Will you do me another honor of becoming Tabitha Kozlowski?"

She nodded. "Yes! Yes, please."

I popped up, laughing into a kiss, parting only because George forced us to with his kicking. I slipped the ring on the fourth finger of her left hand to a smattering of applause, and I held her hand in front of our son. "What do you think, Frog? You ready to be a flower boy?"

He gurgled happily, and Tabby bent to kiss his head, murmuring an "I love you, Georgie" to him before rising on her toes to kiss the words into my mouth. "I love you."

"I love you too," I said. Those words still hadn't lost their glow.

I wrapped my arm around her shoulders, heading out of the gymnasium and into the parking lot, where we'd get into our car, so I could drive us to Tabby Cat to celebrate with our friends—our chosen family.

With my family.

EPILOGUE
NATE

t was a usual Saturday afternoon at Imagination Station with the packs of children shrieking and sprinting all over the damn place.

But *this* Saturday was different.

Because this Saturday, my son was *walking*.

"Look at 'im! Look at 'im!" I gestured wildly at my almost one-year-old as he toddled toward me, one unsteady step at a time. Liam, Jude, and Dylan, with Bennet in his arms, watched.

I stayed crouched down on my haunches, hands out and waiting for him. "Yeah, buddy! You got it!" He grinned at me, drool running down his chin. "That's it!"

With one last step, he threw himself at me, and I caught him, laughing. I held him up, circling around, winning delighted screeches, before facing my friends, puffing out my chest.

"You see him go?" I crowed, proud motherfucking papa. "Gonna be a track star."

Dylan smirked, his baseball cap pulled low enough that his nine-month-old could grab at it.

"What?" I asked, setting George back on his feet so he could take another few steps, this time holding on to my fingers.

"I just can't believe it," Dylan said, his eyes on his son, voice quiet.

I led Frogger toward the bench so we could sit down. "What?"

"You." Liam stretched out his long legs in front of him. "You went from literally grimacing about being here to being the first one to arrive every time we meet."

I shrugged, tapping my hand on the bench. "Somebody's gotta save our seats."

Next to me, Jude chuckled. "Yeah, you're the president of the Single Dads' Club."

I nodded, proud, but raised my hand when a thought crossed my mind. "We never did take that vote on our new name. Married Dads' Association."

"Why do we need a vote?" Dylan asked. "That's just what it is."

I frowned at him. "Says who?"

"Says all of us since that's what we are," he said, sweeping his hand out.

Technically, Jude wasn't married, but he was headed that way without question. They only wanted to wait until their new house was built.

After Dylan and my sister were married last summer, Liam and Kennedy had taken a quick weekend trip to elope, while Tabby and I had made it official this past May with a small ceremony at the town hall and a reception at Tabby Cat. Of course.

In the months since the wine bar and bistro had opened, it had earned rave reviews. Collin's food was top-notch, and he even started working with Brooke to have fresh seasonal produce delivered. A win for everyone.

Tabby had been immediately hired after her graduation, flourishing in her career and as a mother. Though she was a big-time corporate accountant, she still found time to handle my books, and I found time to eat her out for breakfast almost every morning. A win for everyone.

A small group coming through the doors of Imagination caught my eye, and I turned to see a man who I'd become familiar with after the fire. "Hey, Captain," I called out, George still wobbling on his feet beside me. "Didn't expect to see you here."

Captain Stone, the firefighter who I'd spoken with multiple times, met my hand for a shake. "Hey, uh, Nate, right?"

I lifted George up into my arms. "Yeah. Good to see you."

He swept his gaze over me and my son. "I'm glad to see you're doing well."

"Me, too. And thanks again for everything you did."

He shrugged off my appreciation, and I noticed the gift bag in his hand.

"You here for a party or something?"

He pointed out a boy and girl running around with a few others by the firetruck, ironically. "Those two belong to me. Here for some classmate's birthday."

"Nice," I said, though he obviously didn't think so. Bringing his wrist up, he checked the time on what appeared to be some kind of fancy military watch.

"I hate these kind of parties. All the…chaos."

I chuckled. "You're welcome to hang out with me and my friends."

He shook his head. "I'm not staying. Their nanny is coming to pick them up. I gotta get to work."

Nanny? Fancy. Then again, he didn't wear a wedding ring, so I assumed, with his job, a nanny was probably a necessity.

"Hey, well, have a good one," I said, and he tipped his chin at me before sticking his fingers in his mouth and whistling. It caught everyone's attention, including his two kids who immediately ran over. He bent, speaking in a low tone, giving them directions.

I didn't know much about Captain Stone, but he seemed like the type of guy who didn't stand for any shit. I watched as he patted his kids' heads then stood up straight as an arrow and marched back out of the doors.

He was a captain, all right.

"Anybody have big plans this summer?" Liam asked, when I walked back over to the guys.

Jude held out a Tupperware of chocolate chip cookies for us to help ourselves. "Not this summer. It's tough for us with Brooke's schedule. I've been trying to get her to loosen the reins on being a micromanager."

All three of my friends slanted their gazes to me.

"What? I've already done that. I'm, like, a macromanager now."

Liam muffled his laugh with a bite of cookie. "That's not a word."

"Yes, it is," I argued, knowing full well it wasn't. But I couldn't look bad in front of my kid.

Jude elbowed Liam. "What about your plans?"

"We're going to Boston for a week," he said, then craned his neck, cupping his hand around his mouth. "Hey, Finn, you gotta watch what you're doing."

A few months ago, Finn had been diagnosed with ADHD, and he'd started some different therapies to try to help. He was still hyperactive but followed directions better now. Finn had often been a topic of conversation during our meetups and on our text threads because the diagnosis process had been stressful for Liam, Kennedy, and Finn's mother. They'd all been on the same page, but it hadn't been easy.

Before, I might not have appreciated how often parents stayed up at night, anxious about the decisions they needed to make for their children on a daily basis. But I understood it now.

And I did not envy Liam and the struggles he had to endure with Finn.

The three of us then turned to Dylan, awaiting his answer on their summer plans. He switched Bennet to his other arm. "We're taking the kids to the beach for a few days. It's gonna be fucking awful."

I snickered. "You're outnumbered now."

He nodded. Scarlett and Tucker were eight and six, respectively, and Dylan was starting all over again from the beginning. Another one I didn't envy.

Sebastian slinked over to us, his hair in his eyes, a cell phone in his hand. "Dad, are we leaving soon? My friends are all going to the movies. You said we'd only be here an hour."

Jude nodded and checked the time. "Yeah, and we've been here for, like, twenty-five minutes."

"Ugh," Seb grunted. I did feel bad for him. The kid was turning thirteen in a few weeks, and he was being forced to tolerate "imaginative play." I'd hate it too.

"This is so stupid," he groaned, and Jude threw his hands out in response.

"I told you, you coulda stayed with Brooke."

"Or I could just stay home by myself."

Jude threw his son a flat look. "Last time I did that, you had a girl over."

I ducked my head, pretending to be very interested in the stain on George's onesie. Dylan and Liam found some other things to engross themselves too, as Jude lowered his voice, speaking to Seb in a strict tone. Whatever it was had Sebastian stomping back over to the corner.

It had been a *big* deal. Three weeks ago, Jude had permitted Sebastian to stay home by himself for a few hours while he worked at his store and Brooke ran errands with Amelia. Jude returned home to find Sebastian had a girl over.

They were fully clothed and apparently only sitting next to each other.

But still.

Jude had texted us to talk him off the ledge of locking Seb in his room for the rest of the year. I had shit all advice to give, joking—somewhat—about me being the uncle to buy him condoms.

Jude *did not* think that was funny.

And I certainly didn't envy his job of parenting a teenager.

They scared the shit out of me.

Besides, I had my hands full enough with my boy.

"Me and Tabs were thinking about renting a house somewhere for a weekend or something. Somewhere quiet." I jutted my chin for Frogger. "See how he does with the water."

"That would be fun," Jude said, snapping the lid back over the cookies. "If one summer we could all rent a place somewhere. Get a big house and let the kids run wild."

Dylan nodded. "I'm already not looking forward to staying in a hotel. Three kids plus a Pack 'n Play and all our shit? There won't be any room to move."

Liam scratched at his jaw. "If we ever decided to do that, Kennedy would jump at the chance to put it together."

I shrugged. "Let's do it. Maybe next summer. I'm sure we'd have to book out that far anyway."

Liam pulled out his phone, probably texting Kennedy. "On it."

"You hear that?" I lifted George, pumping his fist up and down. "Me and your uncles are gonna get everybody together at the beach. We'll eat s'mores and swim and—" I stopped when I noticed Finn *in* the mailbox.

"O'Neil," I said, snapping my fingers. "He's stuck again."

Liam rolled his head back to his shoulders, eyes closed, and I took a wild guess that he was mentally counting to ten.

Something I'd learned came in handy in those moments of overwhelm.

In the chaos.

In the screaming and crying.

And then he calmly stood up and extricated his son's head from the mailbox. Like a pro.

I slapped his back when he returned for a job well done.

Never in a million years had I ever thought I'd be here.

In a jungle of kids. With my own wiping his fingers covered in disgusting chewed-up Cheerios all over my T-shirt. Yet here I was.

And I fucking loved it.

There was nothing better than being a dad. Knowing that I was the best father I could be.

Then again, I'd found something that was just as good.

Loving my wife. Making her laugh. And hearing those words.

I love you.

———

WHAT'S NEXT?

If you want more Nate and Tabby content, use the QR code to have it delivered straight to your inbox!

Sadly, the Single Dads' Club series has come to an end, but I have much more in store, including more single dads! Use the QR code on the next page to stay in touch!

ACKNOWLEDGMENTS

Indie publishing is a wild ride. Thank you, reader, for coming along with me.

Thank you to Echo Grayce for the amazing cover, and to Libby and Lisa for editing my brain vomit into an actual book. I'd especially like to thank my ARC team for helping me spread the word about my books. I'm forever grateful.

If you'd like more information about me, you can find it at https://sophieandrewsauthor.com/

ABOUT THE AUTHOR

Sophie Andrews is a contemporary romance author who writes steamy books that will leave you smiling. As a millennial, she's obsessed with boybands, late 90s rom-coms, and will always be team Pacey. When she's not writing, she's most likely trying to wrangle her children or drinking red wine. Or both at the same time.

ALSO BY SOPHIE ANDREWS

Tangled Series

Tangled Up

Tangled Want

Tangled Hearts

Tangled Beginning

Tangled Expectations

Tangled Chances

Tangled Ambition

Single Dads' Club

The Rehearsal Fling

The Nanny Tenure

The Dating Pact

The Bartender's Baby

Stand-Alones

How to Ruin a Wedding

Love at a Funeral and Other Awkward Conversations

Hart Brothers Novellas

Made Over by Meredith

Wrapped Up in Holly

Collections

Tangled Series books 1-4